AUTHOR
BRADFORD, K.

CLASS F
C

TITLE
Footprints

M5119

FOOTPRINTS

6

FOOTPRINTS

A WomanSleuth Mystery

by KELLY BRADFORD

THE CROSSING PRESS
FREEDOM, CALIFORNIA 95019

03785119

Library of Congress
Library of Congress Cataloging-in-Publication Data

Bradford, Kelly.
   Footprints / by Kelly Bradford.
       p.   cm. -- (A WomanSleuth mystery)
    ISBN 0-89594-319-0 : ISBN 0-89594-318-2 (pbk.)
    I. Title. II. Series.
  PS3552.R217F66 1988
  813'.54--dc19

1

*J*eannie Walker was running late, literally. Every morning after leaving Christopher at the day care center she drove up to the top of Lagunitas Road in the little town of Ross, one of the many exclusive Marin County communities dotting the hills just north of San Francisco. Her goal was the small parking lot at Natalie Greene Park which gave direct access to a fine network of trails crisscrossing Mt. Tamalpais. There she would lace on her running shoes and start off on her daily runs: five miles of sprints or hill work on Mondays, Wednesdays and Fridays, ten miles of distance running on Tuesdays and Thursdays. On Saturdays, she looked for local races she could enter and occasionally win. On Sundays she rested.

Today Christopher was fussy, and Don was working on a late project, so Jeannie made his breakfast that morning in a spirit of wifely supportiveness. And now she was twenty minutes behind her regular time with a ten-mile Thursday run before her.

Running relaxed her. She enjoyed the feel of gliding along the paths at the base of Mt. Tam. The trail she took would wind through groves of madrone and redwood and then break into open stretches above the yards of houses which backed up onto the mountain's slopes. Jeannie liked the trail because of its variety. That variety made it safe. Jeannie had lived in Marin during the days of the Trailside Killer who haunted the upper slopes of Mt. Tam and other, more secluded spots. She stayed on the trails near the base behind the Lagunitas Country Club, where you could never run far without coming across other people or open stretches with a view of back yards where people lived.

Jeannie enjoyed the people. Because of her schedule, she got to know the morning habits of the locals who lived in the houses along the edge of the trail, and she returned their waves and nods of recognition. She knew by sight all the regulars on the trail and made note of all the newcomers. She gave them all nicknames and played a game in which she tried to guess what kind of people the newcomers were, and how long they would stick with their new regimen. She was usually right.

This past week's crop of newcomers included two business executive types, a young mother wheeling her newborn around on a bicycle rigged with a high-tech baby carrier, and a high school kid who was obviously trying to get in shape for football and had a great many beers left to work off. The executives were predictably out of shape as well, and one of them, who seemed to be coming early and leaving late from the upper trails, carried a little backpack and wore what Jeannie guessed must be the latest thing in executive portable stereo headsets. Only the young mother was in shape. Jeannie admired the discipline implied by the mother's relative thinness when she must be only a month or two past her delivery. Jeannie also admired how the baby seemed to have inherited that quiet discipline—unlike Christopher, who fussed.

Which today had made her late: Christopher's fussing and Don's project, whatever it was. Jeannie pushed away the irritation and tried to concentrate on today's run.

For the man partway up on the slopes of Mt. Tamalpais, the morning was going well, if not exactly according to plan. From his vantage point under a grove of trees off the main paths, he had a perfect view of the trail coming from the Lagunitas parking lot just around the shoulder of a hill, several long stretches of the jogging path in both directions, and most importantly, a particular house in the row of back yards directly below him. For several weeks he and the new girl had been scouting the houses backing up onto Mt. Tam and last week they had settled on the large house with the secluded yard and the patio open to the wooded trail and the woman who kept to a routine.

He glanced at his watch. 8:12. He picked up his powerful field glasses and scanned the trail again. To the left, the high school kid had cut short his run and was limping slowly back to the parking area. To the right, the trail was deserted. There was no sign of the young jogger who seemed to be a regular. If she did not appear for the next several minutes, there would be time.

The Watcher turned his attention back to the large house. At 8:16, right on schedule, the woman came out of the house with the baby and put it

2

in the rocker on the patio, patted it soothingly, and disappeared back into the house. Ninety seconds later, she appeared with the coffee tray and newspaper. He gave one more quick check of the trail, pulled a portable two-way radio out of his backpack and thumbed the send button.

"Go," he said.

"Check," came the response. They needed five minutes.

He pulled a portable cellular phone out of his pack and plugged it into his headset from which two powerful antennas could connect him through his car to any telephone in California. Quickly, he punched the number he knew was the private line of the house below him and raised his glasses.

The Watcher smiled grimly as the woman got up from her chair and went quickly inside, empty-handed. Getting the unlisted number had been relatively easy. The hard part had been confirming that she could not watch the patio from where she answered the phone. That had required a risky visit to the house by the girl posing as a canvassing realtor looking for future leads, timed with a "wrong number" phone call to the unlisted line. Mrs. Albertson ("You can call me Buffy") was unsuspecting and somewhat happy to find her reputation was such that she might be considered a Source of possible future references.

The ringing stopped. "Hello?" There was a note of irritation in her voice.

"Ms. Albertson, this is Tom Bates. . ." he started smoothly and started to buy as much time as he could.

Down below, Jeannie Walker had just completed her climb above the parking lot and started down the path. She passed the high school kid earlier than expected, limping back to the parking lot with a look that suggested more self-pity than real pain. Smiling to herself, she passed under a grove of trees which sheltered the next stretch of trail.

Still talking on the portable phone, the Watcher continued to observe the yard through the field glasses. The girl had reached the yard, leaning her bike against the chain link fence. For too long a moment she fiddled with the little-used padlock which he had broken open the day before, and then she was through the gate.

Suddenly the Watcher became aware that Buffy was trying to cut off the conversation. Desperately, he started pouring out phrases and excuses, gambling that she would be too polite to simply hang up on him while he was talking.

Through the stream of words he watched the scene unfold below as if in slow motion: the smooth pass of the girl's hands over the baby's mouth, and the girl half-running with her bundle back through the gate, nearly stumbling on the metal bar that was the gate's base while pulling it shut behind her. She reached into the baby carrier bolted between the handlebars and in one movement pulled out her hand and sent a small, cloth-wrapped bundle spinning up into the bushes. Too slowly, she put the baby in the carrier and fastened its straps. And then, just as she was pushing the now-heavier bicycle back up to the path, she slipped.

His stream of words faltered. He heard Buffy break through the sudden silence, triumphantly and indignantly dismissing him as the phone clicked and went dead. He threw it in the bag, ignoring the wire that still connected it to his headset, and found the girl again with his glasses.

Somehow she had gotten back up to the trail and was racing toward the parking area. The Watcher quickly scanned the trail in both directions. With a shock, he realized he had been concentrating so hard on the yard below him that he had not noticed that the young woman who was a regular had left the parking area, well behind her usual schedule, and was now only a few hundred yards from the house. He picked up the two-way and punched it.

"Rabbit coming!" He spoke into the girl's earphones, giving the code name they had given to the regular. Then more calmly, "Slow it down. Don't pass her too quickly. Wait till you pass and then go like hell." He was still talking in the girl's earphones when she nearly ran Rabbit off the path.

Jeannie had just rounded a turn in the path when she had to dodge suddenly to avoid being run over by the young mother on the bike. To Jeannie's great irritation, the mother sped by without acknowledging how she had nearly run Jeannie over, intent on her own baby who seemed to be noiselessly squirming, the only sound of her passage the crackling of a voice over her stereo earphones.

Jeannie never wore earphones. They were unsafe. She prided herself on being totally aware of her surroundings on her runs. That is why, even though she had over two hundred yards to go before she got to the second row of houses that backed up on the trail, she heard Buffy Albertson's scream.

The Watcher didn't hear the scream because of his headset. He had dropped the two-way and the glasses back into the bag and stood up while the yard of the large house was still empty. Popping off the phone cord, he took off running down the back trail toward a second access area where his own car was parked.

Down below, the young woman on the bicycle didn't hear the scream either. She was already back at the Natalie Greene parking area, unhooking the baby carrier from the bicycle and placing it on the floorboard of the passenger side of her car. Feigning calmness, she snapped the bike into place on the removable rack on the trunk of the car and got in on the driver's side. As she drove out of the parking area she saw that the high school kid was still there, sitting in the open doorway of his car, massaging his ankle with his earphones still perched on his head. The kid gave her only passing notice, and then she was gone, down Lagunitas to Sir Francis Drake and finally onto U.S. 101.

As she eased into the fast lane of northbound 101, the young woman reached down to her right and, as carefully as she could, removed the surgical tape which had held the pacifier firmly in the baby's mouth. Suddenly freed, he let loose a shriek. He was still screaming as the car turned east at Novato and headed toward Vallejo and Interstate 80. The woman stopped once, outside of Vallejo, to make a phone call.

For Buffy Albertson, Proud New Grandmother at the age of 50, the day started busily and, for a still-young divorcee who was a minor pillar of Marin society, busy was good. Busy meant you had something new to talk about with DeeDee and the others over lunch or tea. Busy meant that you could strategically excuse yourself from lunch or tea when you wanted to because you were... well, busy. Busy implied that you were in demand. Busy meant that you were needed.

For the past two weeks, Buffy had in fact been needed, but Buffy was not going to let the necessity of the situation rob her of the joy of playing the role of Proud New Grandmother to the hilt for the benefit of her mostly older companions. Buffy had made Patrick Albertson-James, three-week-old son of daughter Marguerite Albertson and son-in-law Ronald James, into a Project.

Making Patrick into a Project conveniently hid the real reason for her newly rediscovered motherly duties. Maggie and Ron had separated recently. Ron was somewhere in New York, and Maggie had insisted on returning to spend her mornings at her job as an account manager for a prestigious San Francisco public relations firm, far earlier than seemed reasonable even after an amazingly easy delivery.

Buffy didn't understand these modern young women, including her daughter, who insisted on a career even though they had perfectly well-off husbands to support them. Besides, normally when your husband left you would hurry up and have separation papers drawn up to formalize the support arrangements and take care of your baby, not rush back to work.

Buffy also didn't understand why Ronald would have decided to leave her daughter just before the birth of their first baby. Quietly she closed ranks with Marguerite and made necessity into a lark in the same spirit in which she had organized a hundred charity fundraisers. In any event the settlement would surely be coming through soon. Maggie wouldn't need to work anymore, and Patrick would be off Buffy's hands long before she could exhaust all the possibilities of her new role.

The morning began typically enough. Marguerite dropped Patrick off at 7:15 on her way to work. Buffy put him in the spare bedroom while she finished her own breakfast, heated the formula, and talked with DeeDee on the phone about today's luncheon. At 7:40 she fed Patrick and burped him. By 8:15, the coffee ready, she carried Patrick outside to the patio and put him in the little rocking cradle, which was now sitting in the morning sun next to her favorite lounge chair.

Her daily routine continued: back to the kitchen to bring out the coffee tray and the morning paper; place these on a small table opposite the rocker so she could sit and pour coffee with one hand while she dandled Patrick with the other. From her lounge chair on the patio she could sit and watch the joggers and bike riders drift along the trail that bordered the top of her yard just beyond the chain link fence. She considered this invasion of privacy a small price to pay for having an entire forest as her back yard.

This morning, she poured herself a cup of coffee and was settling down in her chair when the telephone rang. Irritated, she got up and went inside. The telephone seemed to be ringing a lot in the mornings lately with society matrons asking her to co-sponsor this or that function, appeals for donations from organizations she barely knew, and just this week at least two wrong numbers on her private line. This was her private line ringing now, and she had to go into the office to take it.

The voice on the other end was polished and male. It was a Mr. Tom Bates, representing some newly-formed neighborhood organization for the preservation of Mt. Tamalpais. She was so startled by the vague but imminent threat he outlined to the future of the forest in her back yard that it was a minute or two before something clicked in her mind. Suspicious, she interrupted him.

"Excuse me, Mr. Bates, may I ask how you got this particular number?"

The caller seemed ready for this question. "I really couldn't say for sure, Ms. Albertson. All the members of our group submitted the names of people we knew who we felt would be willing to help, and then we simply divided up the list of people to call. I believe the Martins may have given it to us." The Martins were Buffy's next-door neighbors. To name them was inept, and Buffy knew how to handle the situation.

"I doubt that, Mr. Bates. The Martins have made it clear to me in the past that they do not wish to be bothered with pleas from charitable causes. We never speak, least of all on a phone line whose number they do not have." She added coldly, "And if the person who gave you this number thinks that I would be willing to help your cause, whatever it is, then he or she can call me directly with a much clearer explanation of the danger our mountain is supposedly in and an apology for having given out this number."

Buffy smugly waited for the man to wither and hang up. Incredibly, the man persisted in a jumble of excuses, apologies and explanations. Buffy's anger grew with her incredulity. Finally, she seized on a pause to cut him off.

"Mr. Bates, I find your lack of manners unbelievable. You may tell your board of directors that I cannot support any organization which allows people like you to represent it. Good day."

Buffy hung up the phone. Still seething but satisfied with the correctness with which she had dealt with the stranger, she went back outside to the patio.

Now she stood frozen in shock and confusion.

Refusing to believe what she saw, she tried to remain calm as she walked back through the house to the spare bedroom, numbly retracing her steps that morning. Faster, she crossed to the kitchen, then hurried back to the office, and then finally raced in a blind panic through the entire house before bursting back out to the patio to stare wildly about the yard. At last, beyond hope, she stared transfixed at the rocker while the horrible reality swept over her.

The rocker was empty. Patrick was gone.

In a corner of her mind Buffy realized that she was screaming.

2

*T*he morning after the kidnapping a very unusual thing was happening in a house on the slope of Telegraph Hill in San Francisco. Torrance Adams and Monica Rubens were having breakfast together in Torrance's kitchen, looking at a single copy of the *Chronicle*. It wasn't at all unusual for Torrance and Monica to have breakfast and even to have it at the same time, but Torrance usually had hers on the second floor with her cats and Monica had hers on the first floor.

As for the *Chronicle*, two copies appeared on the doorstep each morning, and for good reason. Torrance Adams, Special Assistant Attorney General, was expected to come to the office in the morning knowing whether anything of interest to the A.G. had appeared in the paper, so she perused it with her job in mind while she enjoyed her morning coffee. Monica, on the other hand, had a mind that was in a constant state of free association and, to her, reading the paper was a lot like strolling through the zoo pretending she was in Africa. Torrance and Monica both understood this, which is why they stayed away from each other in the morning even if they happened to meet at the front door while picking up their respective papers.

Monica, after immersing herself in the paper for a while, suddenly climbed the stairs to the second floor and knocked on Torrance's door. Torrance, having worked late the night before, was about to start her breakfast an hour later than usual when she suddenly heard Monica call out dramatically, "Torrance, are you in there?" The two Burmese cats, who had been waiting for any benefits to be derived from Torrance's breakfast, became nervous because of Monica's excitement and ambled away to the upper regions of the house.

Puzzled, Torrance went out to her front door and opened it to a caftan-clad Monica, whose short grey hair had a definitely slept-in look. Clutching the *Chronicle* under her arm, Monica looked up at Torrance and exclaimed, "Thank God! I was beginning to think you were one of the people who'd been killed."

Torrance, who was quite used to the fact that Monica tended to leave out several necessary steps, put an arm around Monica's broad shoulders and steered her toward the dinette. There she pulled out a chair and put a coffee cup in front of it.

"I was just about to defrost some blueberry muffins. Do you want to share?" Monica nodded and sat quietly watching Torrance put breakfast on the table and start some more coffee dripping. She looked quite content now that she saw that Torrance was actually alive and walking around.

Torrance finally sat down, put her hands around her coffee mug, and looked at Monica with a smile warming both her mouth and her large green eyes. "Now, what is it that made you so worried about me?"

"You went to Sacramento yesterday," Monica answered as though this made perfect sense.

Torrance laughed. "I've had a few legislators put my feet to the fire, but they've never actually come close to doing me in."

Monica picked up her *Chronicle* which had been lying on the table and held the front page up to Torrance. "There was this big crash on I-80 yesterday, just outside of Sacramento. A lot of people were killed. I didn't hear you come in last night. And when I went to get the paper this morning, yours was still out there even though it was almost time for you to leave."

"Ahhh!" Torrance announced, the conversation suddenly becoming clear to her. She took the paper Monica proffered and read the article about the crash that had happened in the late morning the day before on the Interstate 80 freeway, the main traffic corridor between the San Francisco Bay area and Sacramento. Now that she thought about it, Torrance had heard there had been a crash yesterday, but her mind was focused on the juvenile court reform bill which had taken her to the capital, and by the time she headed for home she was too tired for news and listened to tapes instead of the car radio.

The crash had been caused by a freak grass fire, she now read. It happened on the Sacramento-bound side of the freeway, just short of the elevated causeway that crossed the Yolo bypass, a wide, shallow flood channel into which the Sacramento River was permitted to overflow during the winter and spring flood stages. Now in early September the channel was dry of course, with crops growing in the riverbottom dirt left by successive floods.

Torrance could picture the scene as it had looked the day before—she must have passed through just before the fire, she thought. The I-80 freeway went through Davis, past the University of California campus, and then there was a short stretch of farm country before it entered the causeway. As she recalled, both the field on the right and the shoulder of the freeway had been covered with tall dry grass right up to the bypass levee. And just at the causeway entrance Caltrans, the state highway department, was repairing the road surface, so that traffic had to squeeze from three lanes to two.

Apparently, a grass fire started on the right shoulder. It made its way across the nearest dry field and up the levee enclosing the bypass, with a tongue of fire reaching down the freeway shoulder. The gusting wind which had blown all day drove the fire east toward the bypass. Drivers ignored it. Torrance could understand that. To the extent people thought about it at all, she figured, they would expect the fire to move on until it found itself out of fuel at the far side of the levee where bare dirt and a green crop succeeded the dry grass.

But the wind suddenly shifted, and a strong gust from the south accompanied by a vicious downdraft cast a black pall of smoke across the busy highway. Squeezed into two lanes, the traffic closed up, cars and trucks with little space between them but still moving at sixty miles an hour. Instantly the dense smoke reduced visibility to virtually zero, and the first drivers automatically hit their brakes in fear and surprise. The vehicles that followed piled into them. Five people were already dead and a large number were injured, some severely. Details were still sketchy pending identification of the victims and notification of next of kin.

Torrance shuddered as she imagined the scene. She looked up at Monica, "I can see why you were worried. I really didn't know anything about it. I must have gone through just before it happened, and when I was coming back it was pitch dark—I don't recall noticing anything around that area, but it would have been on the far side of the freeway from me."

Monica, who was by now calmly munching on a buttered blueberry muffin and starting on her second cup of coffee, nodded her understanding. "If you'd been in that crash, your office wouldn't have thought to tell me," she went on. Torrance understood her point. Dramatic and colorful though she was, Monica was also very level-headed.

Torrance thought back to how Monica had come into her life four years ago. Harry was alive then, and he and Torrance bought this lovely Victorian on Telegraph Hill which had previously been divided into three apartments, one on each floor. They started the remodeling from the top down, because that's where the view was, and turned the second and third floors into a very nice home for themselves before seriously considering what to do with the first floor. They had a vague sense that they would have children some day and perhaps use the first floor apartment for a live-in nanny. Until then they left it as it was, a place for occasional visitors. They didn't need to rent it out since they were doing well enough on their two incomes.

Then one day Harry had brought Monica home. She was a very distant relative, a black sheep of his family, who had turned her back on middle-class values and started painting the colorful people of San Francisco—the homeless, the runaways, the prostitutes (straight and gay), the Vietnamese refugees, the street artists, and anyone else she found interesting. She had a way of getting close to people and winning their confidence. She signed her very compelling paintings "Monica Rubens." Torrance never had found out whether either name was one she was born with.

Harry had discovered her painting one of his patients, a Chinese patriarch suffering from lung cancer. They started talking, and he found out she was about to be tossed out of her apartment because the building was being replaced by a large office complex. Being Harry (Torrance smiled to herself as she thought this), he invited her to stay with them until she could find another place to live that she liked. He was diplomatic enough not to ask what she could afford. He knew Torrance well enough to know this invitation wouldn't bother her.

So Monica moved in, and somehow she'd stayed. Well, actually Torrance knew exactly why she stayed. The living room had just the right light for finishing her paintings, and she liked having Harry and Torrance around because they were friendly but left her alone unless she wanted company. At intervals her iconoclastic and often hilarious presence enlivened the house. When she felt like it she dispensed samples of her excellent cooking, and she took care of cats and plants when Harry and Torrance were gone. A superb arrangement for all concerned.

Now, of course, Torrance thought, I need her to be here, so I won't be alone. She put the thought aside very quickly. It wasn't one her mind dealt with easily yet. Instead, she returned her thoughts to the point Monica had made. The Office of the Attorney General would not think to call Monica Rubens if Torrance were injured or dead. This was true, and Torrance really ought to change it. She looked at Monica and smiled. "You won't have to worry in the future. I'll make sure they know that you're to be notified first."

Monica smiled back, comfortable with the thought that Torrance was more likely than most to keep a commitment she'd made. "I'd like that," she said. "Now let's forget about this accident and read the rest of the paper before you run off to the office."

Torrance might not have thought that her particular job had anything whatsoever to do with a freeway crash, but her employer, the State Department of Justice, quickly became involved. A call came for help the Monday after the I-80 crash. The freak chain reaction was one of the worst local road disasters ever and became the subject of numerous conversations. Seven people ultimately died in the massive pileup, and over a dozen others were injured including one old man who was traveling in the other direction, barely affected by the smoke but so overwhelmed by the murky scene in the far lanes that he had drifted off the freeway and crashed into the ditch next to it.

The California Highway Patrol and the Yolo County Sheriff's Office were jointly working on the mess the accident had left behind. By common consent, the chore of identifying the dead fell to the sheriff. In most cases, it had not been difficult. All but one of the cars in which someone had died had California plates, and the travelers carried identification. The out-of-state couple had taken some time, but a relative had flown in and confirmed the tentative I.D. the driver's licenses and credit cards had provided.

Ironically, it was one of the local cars which presented the greatest hitch. The car, a late-model Buick with Sacramento dealer tags, was registered to Edward and Janet Bowen, at an address in the South Land Park area. From the locked and unresponsive house on an attractive middle-class street, discreet questions led to a local computer technology firm where Mr. Bowen was said to be a mid-level executive. There the inquiring deputy had his first inkling of something unusual. Upon being told that Mr. Bowen's superior would not divulge any information about the man's relatives without knowing what this was all about, the deputy reluctantly disclosed that he was trying to identify the bodies of a man, a woman, and their infant son who had died in the I-80 crash, riding in Edward Bowen's Buick and possessing the Bowens' driver's licenses and credit cards.

After a shocked exclamation and a brief pause came the odd response, "I don't quite understand. Ned and Janet don't have a son. It can't be them."

The executive was easily convinced, however, that anyone who had been driving Ned Bowen's car and carrying his documents should have the attention of his family in death. He told the deputy that the Bowens' closest local kin, so far as he knew, was Janet Bowen's brother, Tyler Havening.

The deputy was taken aback. "You mean *Assemblyman* Havening?" Upon being told that that was precisely whom the executive meant, the deputy expressed his thanks, hung up, and walked straight down the hall to the captain's office. He knew when a job was bigger than he was. Only a short time later, Sheriff Paul Oreston himself was informed that not only was there something very strange about three of the I-80 crash victims, but someone would have to call Assemblyman Havening and ask him about it.

Sheriff Oreston could not have asked for a better local representative to the state assembly than Tyler Havening. Although Havening was a lawyer who had obtained his education in Davis (which Paul Oreston, not entirely without cause, thought of as a hotbed of liberalism), he was a law-and-order Democrat who often voted with the Republican side of the state legislature on issues dear to the sheriff's heart. He got along as well as anyone both with the Republican attorney general and with the Democratic governor and was therefore able to get his way in situations where many others could not. Paul Oreston didn't want to be the one to call him and tell him that his sister might be dead, but he knew that the call had to be made and that he had to make it personally.

Tyler Havening was at his Sacramento home when Sheriff Oreston called. Shocked by the initial questions, he readily confirmed that the Buick seemed to be his sister and brother-in-law's car. He added details to the descriptions on the Bowens' driver's licenses which suggested that they were indeed the victims in the Yolo County morgue. Asked about the infant, he confirmed that the Bowens had no son and clearly clutched at this fact as a possible reason to disbelieve his sister and brother-in-law were dead. But finally he painfully advanced a theory.

"Ned and Janet have wanted children very badly. I know they've been trying to find a child to adopt. The agencies were of no help to them, but recently they've been working with some sort of foundation that assists couples who want to adopt. They've been trying to find an independent placement—one without an agency involved. They would never talk much about it because it was so very stressful for them when things were going badly. And I think they felt very superstitious about talking about it if things were going well." Suddenly his voice broke and Paul Oreston could sense him struggling to control himself. "If they had finally found a child to adopt .... If they were coming home with a child.... My God, how could this have happened?"

Arrangements were made for Tyler Havening to go to the Yolo County morgue and view the bodies tentatively identified as Edward and Janet Bowen. In spite of the ravages of the accident, there was no doubt that the tentative identification was correct, but the distraught assemblyman was unable to say anything further about the child.

It was at this point that Sheriff Oreston decided to call Justice for help.

Under the overall administration of the attorney general, the California Department of Justice consists of two divisions which function for the most part with minimal contact with one another. Most members of the public are primarily aware of its legal services side, the Office of the Attorney

General, where over 500 deputy attorneys general handle the state's civil and criminal litigation. Law enforcement officials, however, think mostly of the other part of Justice: a large and complex law enforcement agency which includes the state's criminal records system, criminalists of every discipline that might be needed in a case, dozens of special agents including undercover narcotics officers, and any number of other specialized services local law enforcement might need.

When Sheriff Paul Oreston was faced with an infant crash victim he knew could not easily be identified, he called Ellert Morrison, the supervisor of Justice's print specialists. Since the two had worked together often, they were well acquainted.

Oreston explained the situation. He had three crash victims, two identified as Edward and Janet Bowen. "It'll break on the news tonight, I'm sure, that they're the sister and brother-in-law of Assemblyman Havening. I've also told the press that there is an unidentified infant less than a month old. I've told them not to go crazy with it—that it's just a 'technical' non-I.D. In fact, I've got information that indicates that this child may be one the Bowens were planning to adopt. I've asked Tyler Havening to look through their effects and try to get us a lead to where this kid came from. Nothing in the car gave us even the slightest clue, but I can't believe that they won't have some documents in their home that'll tell us what the hell was going on.

"Once we know who handed them the kid, we ought to know tentatively who he is, but we'll still need a positive I.D. This little boy got pretty messed up in the crash. There isn't much hope of his mother (or anyone else for that matter) recognizing him, especially since we don't know when she gave him up. So what I'm leading up to is I'll need your help. I need footprints to be able to say who the kid is."

Ellert Morrison sighed. He had tried to identify lost, kidnapped, or dead infants before, and each time he liked it less. Every child born in a hospital in California had its footprints taken immediately upon birth, and in theory those footprints could be used as a source of identification when identity was questioned or uncertain. Unfortunately, as Morrison often pointed out, the footprints were taken by nurses, not by print specialists. About half of them were either totally useless for identification or only good enough for elimination—that is, you might be able to say the child you had wasn't the same child as the one who had been printed but, if the clear portions of the prints looked similar, you wouldn't have enough detail to know whether you had a match or not. So the technical problems were trouble enough. On top of that, having to fingerprint and I.D. dead children made an unpleasant job even worse.

But, listening to Oreston's quiet drawl, Morrison knew that he had to give him the help he was asking for. With all the victims of the I-80 crash identified except one little baby, the press would quickly begin asking a lot of questions. With Tyler Havening involved, you didn't mess around whether you were the local sheriff or you worked for the A.G.

"O.K., Paul, I'll give you Tim McDonald," he said. "He's the best we've got on baby prints. But let me tell you what you're up against." And then he carefully warned Oreston what the odds were that he'd come out of this with a positive I.D. "I know you have to do it," he quickly added to cut off incipient explanations. "Just don't come after me if it doesn't work. On this sort of thing the best effort may not be enough."

3

*D*erek Thompson steered his 1966 Mustang V-8 convertible into the left lane of the northbound traffic and cruised across the Golden Gate Bridge, leaving San Francisco behind. There was a bank of fog just outside the Gate, resting against the cliffs at Land's End in San Francisco and pressing gently against the Marin headlands, waiting for the heat of the Sacramento Valley to fire the great engine that drives San Francisco's natural air-conditioning system.

Derek knew that in two to three hours, the broad valley would have baked in the late summer sun sufficiently to form a great column of hot air. Rising from the valley floor, this column would create a center of low pressure over Sacramento and, as the air over the Bay rushed through the Carquinez Strait to fill that vacuum, the fog would suddenly awaken, stretch, and reach out to cradle The City in its cold arms. It was a logical and scientific explanation for one of San Francisco's most romantic characteristics, Derek mused. But then, Derek made his living by finding the logical and objective explanation behind otherwise mysterious events.

One such event was now taking him to Marin. The three-week-old son of a young woman by the name of Marguerite Albertson-James had apparently been kidnapped from his socialite grandmother's back yard in the exclusive community of Ross. Derek had gotten from Marguerite's phone call the details of the kidnapping which he hadn't already seen in the local press.

The interesting thing about this case was that the mother was just as convinced that the kidnapping was real as the Ross police were certain that the whole affair was part of a domestic custody battle. They both had reasons. Those reasons would become pieces which would eventually fit into a logical and objective explanation for a seemingly unexplainable event: the kidnapping in broad daylight of the infant son of a well-off but hardly wealthy young mother.

The address Marguerite James had given Derek was one of the waterfront condominiums on Strawberry Point favored by up-and-coming professionals. Most of them featured a clear view of Tiburon across the Bay. Derek parked in a space marked for visitors and then set about trying to find the address. He was just beginning to swear at the mentality of builders who obviously thought it was chic to hide street addresses as far away as possible from the corresponding homes when he finally found what seemed to be the proper door. He rang the bell and the door was opened by a smartly dressed young woman in her late twenties.

"Mr. Thompson?" she said anxiously before he could speak. "I'm Marguerite James. You have no idea how glad I am to see you."

Marguerite ushered him into the condominium. The place was decorated in High Marin Yuppie, complete with a number of prints by the "right" artists. Derek guessed the culprit was any one of a dozen expensive but tastefully safe decorators he knew of in The City. Marguerite likewise was carefully stylish. Behind the designer labels, though, Derek detected uncertainty and a hint of desperation. Marguerite was younger than her age.

"Mr. Thompson . . ." she faltered.

"Call me Derek."

"Mr.—Derek—I want you to find my baby."

"Do you want me to find him or get him back from your husband—Ronald, isn't it?"

"My husband doesn't have Patrick," she said vehemently. "The police won't believe me. That's why I called you."

"O.K." Derek sighed and sat down without waiting for the invitation she was obviously too distracted to offer. "Let's start with that, but from the cops' side first. What makes the police think that Ronald's got your baby?"

"Ask them!" She was upset and letting out all of her frustrations of the past several days. When she got around to defending her side of the story, she'd be a lot calmer. "It was the first thing that awful Morelli thought of, and he's never gotten off of it! He said more than ninety percent of all kidnappings are done by relatives in a child custody dispute and when he found out that Ron and I were in the middle of divorce proceedings, I could just see his mind switch off. He found that Ron had left his apartment in New York, supposedly bound for California, two days before Patrick was taken, and that's as far as he went."

"Has he closed his case?"

"No," Marguerite said bitterly. "He told me to call him if I get a ransom note or anything—and to let him know when I finally got in touch with Ron."

"I presume you haven't gotten any ransom notes." Derek smiled wryly. "Where is Ron? Have you heard from him?"

"No. Both Detective Morelli and I have left messages with his roommate or whatever." For the first time, there was a hint of uncertainty in her voice. Unnoticed by her, Derek looked up sharply at the word "roommate."

"Why don't you think your husband has Patrick?" Derek's voice was soothing.

"It doesn't make any sense." She sounded weary now. "He left me *because* of Patrick. Why would he take him now?"

"What do you mean by that?"

She hesitated. "He left me four weeks before Patrick was born—almost two months ago—but that was just a formality. He left me mentally almost the minute I told him I was pregnant."

"Early in the pregnancy or after the first three or four months?"

"Early. Before I began to show if that's what you're asking."

Derek paused and then asked gently, "Was Patrick planned?"

Marguerite looked startled. "Yes," she said after a pause.

"Was there anyone else?"

Another hesitation. "I—I don't know. I never heard."

Derek tried another tack. "What about the divorce? Is it being contested or is it mutual? And what has Ronald said about custody?"

"It's Ronald's divorce!" she said vehemently. "Oh, now I want it too because, after what he's done to me, I'll never take him back. I'll never let him know that! I'm going to make this as expensive for him as possible to make sure that Patrick never has to worry." Derek ignored the outburst. He was beginning to recognize a pattern he had seen before.

"So what has he said about custody?"

She sighed. "He hasn't said anything for sure. At first he said he wanted fifty percent—equal custody." She turned to face Derek. "But I know that's just to hurt me, to keep down the cost of the settlement. He doesn't care about Patrick, I know he doesn't!"

Derek let the certainty hang there unchallenged. He went back over the details of the kidnapping again, carefully asking Marguerite about her habits, her activities in the weeks following Patrick's birth, and in particular her actions on the morning he was taken. He drew blanks on any suspicious persons she might have noticed. There was no one involved except her mother who seemed above suspicion and no motive for anyone she knew except the conspicuously absent husband, Ronald. It all added up to nothing— nothing, that is, except Marguerite's convictions.

After confirming the arrangements for his fee, Derek took his leave and went off to find Detective Morelli of the Ross P.D. Derek had met him once before when Derek had been engaged to buy back some stolen silver from a bunch of stoned-out kids living in Corte Madera near Ross. The silver was long gone of course and Derek had found Morelli to be particularly unhelpful, obviously more concerned with working on cases he had a good chance of solving. Derek guessed that Morelli had already classified the Patrick James kidnapping as a lost cause and had turned his attention elsewhere.

Derek found Morelli behind a clutter of reports and memos. He had the beefiness of a former patrolman, with the tired and defeated face of a man who had spent too many years in Burglary. Morelli leaned back and eyed Derek with as much amusement as he was capable of mustering. It wasn't very much.

"Well, Derek Thompson." It was a conclusion. He waved Derek into a chair. "The James kid, huh? So has the little girl convinced you to look for strangers with candy, or am I going to have to wind up arresting you for kidnapping a kid back from its father?"

"I'd never do it in your jurisdiction. You might get a conviction for a change."

"Screw you too, Thompson." Morelli slumped forward. "Besides, with the D.A. I got to work with, you might as well do it here. So why did you come in here to waste my time?"

"I'm just doing my homework so I can waste as little time as possible all around—for you, me, and my client." Derek feigned disinterest to match Morelli's, just another tired professional doing his job. "Mrs. James tends to get a little upset when you try to suggest that her husband did it. What have you got on him so far?"

Morelli's eyes narrowed. "What I got is that the guy who answered the phone in his apartment says he left two days earlier; and, no, he doesn't know where he is or when he'll be back. First he thinks he went out to the West Coast or somethin' and, when I tell him who I am, all of a sudden he doesn't even know who Mr. Ronald James is. What I got is that nine times out of ten a kid is taken by one of its own parents. What I got is that no one takes kids for ransom any more for Chrissake and perverts may like 'em young, but going through that much trouble for a kid who's three weeks old is too much to believe. *That's* what I got on Ronald James, and the little wife is too stubborn to believe it. So, you got any bright ideas?"

Morelli folded his arms and leaned back in his chair. Derek decided to ignore the challenge.

"What trouble?" he asked suddenly.

Morelli's confidence dissolved into confusion. Derek let it sit there a moment before he went on.

"You said a pervert wouldn't go through all that trouble to take a three-week-old kid. What kind of trouble?"

Morelli's face soured. "The way I figure it, it had to have been planned by someone who knew the layout of the house and how it backed up on Mt. Tam. And that someone had to know the grandmother's habits and either set up a telephone call as a diversion or was both lucky and ballsy. Again, it leads back to Ronald James."

Derek was noncommittal. "Yeah. Mind if I take a look at the reports just the same? I gotta do something to earn my keep. And who was the guy in charge of the search team?"

"I was in charge of the investigation. If you mean who handled the field work, Sergeant Dickson."

"Dickson. Can I talk to him, too?"

Morelli looked slightly irritated. "Suit yourself. He's in the back." Morelli gestured with his thumb. Derek nodded thanks and left before Morelli could change his mind.

Dickson was a little more cooperative though just as convinced of Mr. James's guilt. He pulled a slim folder from his file cabinet and let Derek look through the reports. There were interviews with Marguerite and Buffy, a statement from a Jeannie Walker who apparently had heard Buffy's screams and was the first to arrive on the scene, and a negative report from the search team. Last was a report from Dickson on his inspection of the Albertson home. Dickson had surmised that the padlock on the back gate had been broken recently. There were no recoverable latent prints on the gate and no other means of entry. Derek noted Jeannie Walker's address and phone number.

"So the search turned up nothing of interest?" he asked Dickson.

"No sign of the kid, if that's what you mean," Dickson smiled. "We found lots of interesting stuff, though."

"Oh?"

Dickson continued, "Yeah. We found everything from used rubbers to broken syringes in those bushes. Mrs. Albertson's got a lot more going on in her back yard than she realizes." Dickson paused. "Oh, I take that back. We did find a baby," he said with self-satisfaction.

"I'm breathless," Derek said.

"Of course, it was only plastic. But still it was in pretty good shape, one of those life-size baby dolls."

Derek glanced quickly at the search team's report. "You didn't note it here. Where did you find it?" he asked sharply.

Dickson looked a little uncertain. "We found it in the bushes just above the Albertson home, but I don't see how it could have any. . ." He broke off. "Actually, we didn't put it down because it just didn't match the description of the missing kid." Dickson smiled.

Derek stopped for coffee and time to think in a little coffee shop just past city hall which was frequented by cops and secretaries. He decided from both Marguerite's comments and the rather lengthy statement in the police report that Buffy Albertson could wait. He glanced again at the address of Jeannie Walker. It was only a few minutes away. Jeannie was the key if anything was. First however there was a loose end to tie up. He went to the pay phone and punched several numbers.

"Ames here." The voice on the other side was rich, almost melodic.

"Clarence. This is Derek Thompson."

"Derek! How wonderful! How's the hottest hunk west of the river? Tell me, is this business or pleasure?"

Derek winced at Clarence's style. "Strictly business. You know me."

"Oh, you're such a bore, Derek. What can I do for you, Love?"

Clarence Ames was outrageous, flamboyant, and didn't seem to care what people thought of him. He was one of the best private eyes in New York City. He could turn off his chosen style and blend in when necessary. Derek and he had met at a party in New York when they were both fledgling investigators some ten years ago. Although their personal relationship was superficial, their professional relationship had deepened over the years.

"I need some help running down a guy in your back yard, Clarence. The cops here think he kidnapped his own baby, jousting for position in an upcoming divorce settlement, but his wife is convinced he didn't do it— only she can't or won't tell me why."

"And you want me to tell you."

"Yeah. Funny thing is, I believe her that he didn't do it."

"Is that just because of your feminine intuition, or do you have something to go on?"

Derek laughed. "Not exactly a clue, Clarence. But Ronald's phone was answered by a male roommate, and his wife shows all the symptoms of a woman whose husband has left her for someone she finds a lot more embarassing than the other woman."

Clarence clucked in mock sympathy. "Derek, these days there are dozens of things that are more embarassing than the other woman, not just the one *you're* likely to think about. She has my sympathy, and you my assistance!"

Derek turned over Ronald James's address and other particulars and, after a little more banter which Clarence, true to form, sprinkled heavily with innuendoes and invitations to come to the "real" city, he rang off.

Derek smiled to himself. Clarence belonged to the Oscar Wilde school of viciously witty conversation. If you didn't rise to the occasion, you would soon be helplessly lost or, far worse, declared to be hopelessly dull.

Briefly, Derek wondered how a couple of hard-boiled cops like Morelli and Dickson would react if they overheard Derek's conversation. They wouldn't understand, that much was certain. So how safe is my job, Derek wondered, not for the first time. How much do any of them suspect about me? He was scrupulous about keeping his personal life private, except for occasions where it was useful—like just now, with Clarence. Still, any widespread rumors could destroy his effectiveness with the real world, the other ninety percent by whose rules he had to live.

He didn't particularly like it, but there it was.

Suddenly depressed, Derek went off to find Jeannie Walker.

Jeannie Walker was concerned and eager to talk. He liked her right from the start.

"I know it's supposed to have been the husband that did it, but still . . ." Jeannie shuddered. "It gives you the creeps. I mean, right there in broad daylight with all those people around. What if it had been a mugger or a rapist or something instead of a kidnapper? I had to race right to the phone and call the day care center to make sure Christopher was all right the minute the police let me go, I was so worried. I know I sound silly, but it just made me feel so insecure, you know?"

Derek said that he probably would have done the same thing. Encouraged, Jeannie went on.

"The insecurity is the worst part. I jog there every day. I chose that place because it was so safe and near so many people and houses and things, and I feel like I've been violated. Do you know what I mean? I can just imagine how that other woman felt, who was there every day with her own baby. No wonder she hasn't been back since. I mean, it could have happened to her. Wouldn't that just be an awful feeling?"

Derek looked up quickly. "What other woman? The police report said there were no other witnesses."

"Oh there weren't. I mean, no one else was any closer than me to the house when it happened. Except the kidnapper, of course. And he must have gone off in the other direction, because no one passed me after I heard that poor woman scream."

"How about just before? Who did you pass on the trail that morning?"

Jeannie thought a minute. "Just two. I got a late start, and so I think

I passed only two people: the bicycle mother and the kid. I'm sorry, I give names to all the people I see regularly on the trail. The bicycle mother is a young woman, about my age, who for a while was riding every morning with her baby in one of those carriers between the handlebars, and the kid was some guy in high school or city college, I think, who looked like he was trying to get in shape for football season or something. I think he twisted an ankle, 'cause he was limping and I ran into him just past the parking area, and usually I would pass him on my way back, much further down."

"You have a pretty good memory for details, don't you?" Derek asked.

"Yes. I do," she said confidently. "I like to be very aware of my surroundings. I believe you should stay in touch with what's going on around you. I don't smoke or drink, and neither my husband nor I take any drugs," she added proudly.

Derek studied her. She looked like she didn't eat either, but she was attractive and positively exuded health. More important, Derek began to suspect that she had a lot more to offer than Dickson and Morelli had gotten. "You say you jog there every day. Let's go back over last week, and see if you can tell me everyone you remember seeing, especially anyone new."

Jeannie talked for the next hour, interrupted occasionally by Derek asking questions about various details. The more she talked, the more a pattern began to shape itself in Derek's mind.

When she was done, Derek saw two options: either the kidnapping was totally fortuitous and the suspect got away without being seen, or the kidnapper was on what was now a relatively short list of possible suspects. Since the first option went nowhere, Derek chose the second. All I have to do ¬v, Derek thought grimly, is to put names on a bunch of rough descriptions of anonymous people in jogging suits who might have come from anywhere and go ask them if they've stolen a kid lately. Well if that was it, there was only one logical place to start.

"Would you mind if I joined you in the mornings for a while?" he asked Jeannie. "I feel an attack of physical fitness coming on."

4

*A*t the request of Sheriff Paul Oreston, Assemblyman Tyler Havening was going through all of the documents he could find at Janet and Edward Bowen's home. He started with the two-story living room, where drawers and bookshelves contained one painful reminder after another of the Bowens' lives. He found no reference to a child or to any adoption plans. Moving to the den, he searched through more items he wished he did not have to see, again without success. Finally, he reached Janet's delicate writing desk in the little landing off the master bedroom which had been her favorite reading spot. There he found the package of documents he had been looking for.

It was clear from the correspondence carefully filed in the desk's pigeonholes that the Bowens had contacted John Solomon, a San Francisco attorney, because he had been recommended to them as a specialist in adoptions. Solomon had replied, explaining that the law prohibited him from finding a child for them, but that they could easily find a child themselves if they followed the right procedures. He recommended the Parentbuilders Foundation to them. Parentbuilders, his letter said, was a nonprofit organization which could assist would-be parents in getting together with a pregnant woman who felt unable to care for a child and wished to find a good home for him or her.

There were several documents which appeared to be the standard handouts of the Parentbuilders Foundation, obviously provided in response to contact by the Bowens. They outlined how to develop a resume for distribution to spots where single pregnant women would be able to see it; they explained that Parentbuilders could act as an intermediary, so that anonymity would most likely be preserved; and they provided a great deal of information about why a private adoption, in the opinion of the writers, was far superior to an adoption arranged by an agency. Havening found a copy of the Bowens' resume, which he at first viewed only as a sad tribute to their desperate desire for a child. Upon reading it again, however, he realized that it was very carefully tailored to appeal to the emotions of a pregnant young woman trying to decide between having an abortion and giving the child up to change the life of a childless couple—or perhaps between raising the child in a poor, single parent household and sending it to a life of love and comfort in a traditional American middle-class home.

Surprisingly, there was little else. Whatever further arrangements the Bowens had made must have been done by telephone, because he could find no more neat copies of Janet's letters or carefully saved incoming mail. Only one further letter confirmed the likely identity of the child who had died: a quick note from Solomon to Ned and Janet confirming an appointment on the morning of the crash. It gave no further details.

Havening gathered up the correspondence and took it to Sheriff Oreston. He had little desire to know who the child was. His heart ached. He found it a terrible irony that his sister and her husband had been killed at the very moment they had reached the goal they had longed for all those years.

When he received the bundle of letters and brochures from Tyler Havening, Paul Oreston thought his job of identifying the child killed in the I-80 crash was nearly done. Since it was only a week after the accident, he felt good about his progress. He decided to call John Solomon, Esquire and ask him who the child was.

Oreston dialed the number on the letterhead and was quickly connected with a brisk-sounding secretary who appeared most efficient in her attempts to deal with him without disturbing her employer. Solomon, she implied, was occupied with matters of great moment.

But Paul Oreston had not been elected and re-elected sheriff of Yolo County without learning a few tricks of his own. After some sparring, he managed to get an admission that Solomon was indeed in his office, and it was all downhill from there. He deftly sidestepped the "I'm sorry, he's on his other line" ploy by offering to hold however long it might be necessary and sat back, envisioning the explanations between Brisk Voice and the lawyer. Quite soon the phone was picked up again, and a pleasant sounding male voice answered, "John Solomon. May I help you?"

Paul Oreston identified himself and gave a detailed explanation of why he had called. "So you see," he finished, "the documents in the Bowens' home all indicate that the baby in their car was picked up at your office that morning. Am I right?"

There was a lengthy silence at the other end of the line. Finally, Solomon spoke. "You do understand, Sheriff, that anything that happens between me and my client is privileged."

"Sure," Oreston replied, "I understand that as a general proposition. But we're not talking about the advice you gave them. We're talking about whether you handed them a little kid who was later killed in a crash. I don't care what you told them about adopting him. I just want to know who he is, so that the poor little thing can have a decent burial and his name on a headstone instead of lying on a slab in the morgue."

Again there was a lengthy silence. Finally, Solomon's smooth voice resumed. "Well, Sheriff, I think I can tell you this much without violating any confidences. I know that on the day they were killed, the Bowens were taking home the baby they were going to adopt. His mother had decided to give him up because she was unable to care for him herself. The Bowens called him 'Michael.' It seems to me the best thing for everybody would be for the family to honor their wishes and forget about the formalities. Bury him with them as Michael Bowen."

"That may very well be what the family will want to do, Mr. Solomon, but it seems to me that this little boy's real mother still has some say about it."

"Well, since this is an adoption matter, I can't possibly tell you anything I might know about the child's mother, Sheriff. You must understand that adoption records are completely confidential. Besides that, do you really want to torture this mother by telling her that the child she gave up to a better life is dead? Think about it! Right now, she thinks she's been selfless and wonderful by taking steps to improve her child's future and to make a childless couple's deepest wish come true, and you want to destroy all of those thoughts. For what? I think it's very merciful that I can't tell you who the mother is."

Paul Oreston knew when it was time to give up. His knowledge of adoptions law was practically nonexistent, and he could not tell whether Solomon was smoothly leading him on or telling him the truth. So he thanked Solomon for his help and hung up the phone. He decided to have another conversation with Tyler Havening.

Paul Oreston's telephone call left Tyler Havening pacing back and forth across his office in the state capitol. He had put the question of this child out of his mind. He had begun to accept the terrible tragedy and worked at getting himself back into his constituents' affairs. Then Oreston had called with his news, and now Havening didn't know what to do.

He knew something about adoptions law but not nearly enough to be able to unravel exactly who had what rights in this situation. Did they *have* to notify the child's mother of its death? Was there some requirement that the vital statistics people be informed of precisely who had died? His mind refused to deal with the questions, and he could not force himself to think calmly about the problem.

Pacing across his office a few more times, Tyler Havening decided to ask a friend for help. Like Paul Oreston he called Justice. Being Tyler Havening, however, he asked for the Attorney General himself, and thus he moved the problem one step closer to Torrance.

Charles Ezekiel Wilson was the scion of a wealthy political family, with a congressman and a governor among its members. Knowing at an early age that he wanted to run for public office, he did his best to prepare himself for the task. He did not approach the political realities with cynicism—he merely decided on the best way to do things and applied himself to doing them with a combination of luck and instinct many came to admire.

He went to U.C.L.A. where he became a minor track star popular with the local press. He knew instinctively to reject Harvard Law School which wanted him and choose Stanford which pleased the often provincial California power brokers.

During summers, he adroitly used family connections to obtain jobs with various state legislators. He found it easy to settle into his mother's socially moderate but fiscally conservative Republican stance.

Out of law school, he joined the prestigious law firm to which the family had close ties, pursued visible social causes, and waited for his chance. This came in the form of a state senate seat about to be vacated by the incumbent who had been caught with his fingers inserted in the cookie jar. What turned out to be brilliant timing combined most admirably with his well-established connections, his handsome, athletic appearance already known to the local voters, and the family money. The voters sent him to the capitol with enthusiasm.

Once in the state senate, Charles Ezekiel Wilson decided that his logical next step was to be attorney general. The then newly-elected attorney general, everyone knew, would plan to serve for eight years and, if he did well, would run for governor. When he did so, Wilson would be ready to succeed him.

He knew that the public perceived the attorney general primarily as the enforcer of the State's criminal laws, and that he therefore had to acquire a reputation as a criminal law specialist. He set upon this with the instincts and singlemindedness which had characterized his earlier efforts. He came to chair the Senate Criminal Justice Committee, he rewrote significant portions of the Penal Code under the name of the "Wilson Criminal Justice Reform Act," and he worked tirelessly on behalf of causes which showed him as the scourge of criminals, the friend of victims, and the protector of the common good.

The fact that he did all of this with genuine enthusiasm and was unusually good at it built his reputation, and when the incumbent attorney general did, as expected, run for governor, Wilson easily became the Republican candidate for the vacant office. He ran with flair and won overwhelmingly against a Democrat with far less impressive credentials.

During the campaign, Wilson began to scrutinize the existing staff of the attorney general's office. While he could and would bring trusted associates along from his senate office, he knew that he also needed a group of supportive insiders who could fill him in about the past experience and policies of the office. Relationships with a group of such attorneys were largely created and cemented at campaign lunches and fundraisers, where those who wanted to see Wilson as the next attorney general told him so and offered their help. Those who seemed best to fit what Wilson was looking for in a close associate were received into the inner planning circle and became a part of his transition team after he was elected.

Because he wanted to concentrate on criminal law, Wilson was particularly interested in a reliable personal assistant with long experience as a civil deputy in the attorney general's office. His search for such a person led him more and more in the direction of Torrance Adams.

Wilson had seen and spoken to Torrance at several gatherings, where he had noted her extensive knowledge of the attorney general's civil workload and her calm assurance that Wilson was the candidate she would prefer to see in charge of that workload in the future. Wilson could well understand her reputation as an excellent trial lawyer and a good administrator. She was a tall, slender woman, with a natural presence that was enhanced by a voice that was clear and firm. He particularly liked the fact that Torrance never criticized the current administration, as many others did. Instead, she predicted that the outgoing attorney general would become governor (she was right) and made it clear that her good relationship with him would be a benefit she did not care to destroy.

Wilson was sure Torrance would be a great political asset and when he was elected he brought her onto his transition team. When he took office, he made her Special Assistant Attorney General for Civil Matters. Her duties were to know what was going on, keep Wilson's personal relationship with the Governor and the Legislature a smooth one, keep the press happy and if possible on Wilson's side, and in general act as a high-level troubleshooter whenever the situation called for one. So far, he congratulated himself for having picked a person who did all of these things admirably and without conflict with his other executive staff. Being an elected politician, he also congratulated himself for the fact that Torrance's visibility had been noted by several women's groups which were not naturally inclined toward a Republican office holder, but which could be swayed in the direction of one who made a point of treating women fairly.

Now, when he received a call from Tyler Havening, Wilson promised at once that Torrance Adams would call Havening and give him whatever assistance he needed. Then he called his San Francisco office and happily found Torrance in.

When Torrance heard Wilson's request, she felt a sudden tension that surprised her. She gave herself a slight shake and took a deep breath. Superstition about the crash was not something she wanted to give in to. She promised Wilson she would do what she could. It was only a short time before Havening heard from her.

"This is Torrance Adams, Mr. Havening. Zeke Wilson asked me to call." Havening had briefly spoken with Torrance before in connection with legislation of interest to the Attorney General, and he noted that she always recalled Havening's personal friendship with Wilson, using his off-the-record nickname and dispensing with unnecessary titles. "I know Zeke has expressed to you how very distressed he was to hear of your sister's death, and I can only add my own sympathy. Words are inadequate under the circumstances, but from what Zeke tells me, perhaps I can be of assistance to you in taking care of some of the problems you shouldn't have to cope with right now."

Dealing with the recently bereaved was no easier for Torrance than for anyone else. She felt stiff and artificial as she spoke, distanced from Havening by his grief.

But he responded warmly. "I very much appreciate that, Torrance. I'm rather at my wits' end about whether I should be doing anything at all and, if so, what."

"Why don't you tell me briefly what the situation is, and I'll take it from there. I know only the barest details so far."

Havening explained about the child who had died in the crash, about the documents he had found at the Bowens' home, and about Sheriff Oreston's unsuccessful attempt to get identification of the child through Solomon. "Oreston called me back after he talked to Solomon and rather dropped it at my doorstep to decide what to do next. I think he feels stymied and out of his area of expertise. If I weren't an assemblyman and a lawyer, I think he would have gone to County Counsel and tried to get them to take over, but as it is he seemed to feel I should decide on the next step. Don't misunderstand me," he added quickly. "I'm not at all complaining about Oreston doing this. Maybe I sound like I'm accusing him of taking the easy way out, but I didn't mean to suggest that. He just kind of deferred to me—thought I'd have all the answers. Trouble is, I don't know a whole lot about whether Solomon is being straight or not, and I just can't bear to spend a lot of time thinking about it. After all the times I listened to Janet tell me how much she wanted a baby. . . ." Havening stopped, and Torrance could sense him fighting for control.

"There isn't any need for you to worry about what to do with Solomon, Mr. Havening," she said firmly. "Adoption happens to be something I'm rather an expert at, so I'll go over everything with Sheriff Oreston and then tackle Solomon for him. Based on what I know now, I don't think we can ignore the birth mother, even if it would be the kinder thing to do." She hesitated for a moment, trying to guess at what Havening really wanted to hear. "I'll go ahead and work with Oreston on this, and if anything significant comes up, I'll let you know. Is that all right with you?"

"Yes," Havening said quickly, letting her know she had guessed his mood correctly. "Yes, I'd like that. I don't want to be totally uninvolved, of course. You've taken a real burden off my shoulders, Torrance. Please let Zeke know how much I appreciate his asking you to do this."

After she hung up the phone, Torrance got up from her chair and walked over to the window of her office, which was open to a glorious September afternoon. Outside, steady streams of pedestrians were crossing Civic Center Plaza. As far as Torrance was concerned, real windows that actually opened to let fresh air into the old-fashioned, high-ceilinged rooms were one of the best benefits of her job. To her, the windows were better than air conditioning. She believed that Mark Twain knew what he was talking about when he quipped that the coldest winter he ever spent was a summer in San Francisco. Heat waves were such rare occurrences that she enjoyed them as phenomena, rather like comets and double rainbows, and did not complain about them like some of the other inhabitants of the old state building.

Today, however, was a day to justify neither Mark Twain nor the boosters of air conditioning. The sky was a brilliant blue, there was not a trace of fog, and only a light breeze was coming in off the ocean. It was warm enough, but not too warm. A perfect day.

As Torrance looked over the mix of purposeful walkers and lethargic baskers in the park, the tension she had felt earlier left her. Here was a puzzle for her to solve, and she loved puzzles. She always enjoyed cases that appeared like giant jigsaws when she first saw them, waiting for her to assemble the pieces. The problem the A. G. had handed her wasn't very different.

Because she had handled and supervised adoptions cases over the years, she had of necessity come to know who John Solomon was, although she had never met him. His practice consisted entirely of adoptions, and he was well known among the state and county adoptions workers—well known, and uniformly disliked.

In California, there were two kinds of adoptions. In an agency adoption, the child was given to the adoption agency by the mother (only occasionally was a father actively involved), and the agency placed the child anonymously with a family of the agency's choice. The birth parents and the adoptive parents did not know and could not find out each other's identities under ordinary circumstances. In an independent adoption, on the other hand, the child was placed by the mother herself, with no agency involvement until the adoption petition was filed. The mother and adopting parents were supposed to know each other and to have chosen each other based on that personal knowledge.

In reality, Torrance knew, independent adoptions were more and more managed by intermediaries who came perilously close to unlawfully running unlicensed adoption agencies. The birth mother and the adoptive parents often did not meet each other at all, and they might even live across the country from one another. They certainly did not choose each other personally. The intermediaries who arranged the whole thing were extremely well paid for their services, usually in the form of "legal fees" to the attorney who represented both sides.

John Solomon was such an attorney and, to judge by his apparent life-style, he was finding the practice very lucrative. From what Torrance had heard about the adoptions he was involved in, he appeared to comply carefully with the technicalities of the law while somehow managing to unite large numbers of would-be adoptive parents with the children of mothers unknown to them.

So why was Solomon stonewalling Sheriff Oreston, Torrance wondered. Solomon wouldn't have handed over the child himself—he was too smart for that, with public agencies carefully watching him for any sign of unlicensed child placement. So he was merely a witness to the transfer—not something he was prohibited from doing or disclosing. And the mother's name was not confidential in an independent placement. In fact, for physical custody of the child to change, both the mother and the Bowens would have had to sign the same document, which transferred the right to consent to medical care and such. Often the intermediary covered up the first party's name during the second signature to attempt to maintain anonymity, but Solomon could not deny the Bowens' family access to the transfer document. So why had he refused to give Oreston any information?

Torrance knew the answer might be very simple: Solomon, faced with an unexpected and unusual inquiry, might just have tried to make it all go away by being excessively cautious and asserting a duty of silence. Why not? It might just work and everyone would go away and leave him alone. At the least, he would gain time to think about it. On the other hand, the field of independent adoptions was at times volatile and prone to unexpected problems, one of which Solomon might be trying to cover up. Perhaps the mother had wanted her child back and he wanted time to cope with that. Perhaps a father had appeared on the scene unexpectedly. Perhaps there had been a financial arrangement Solomon was worried about.

Torrance decided that there was a real chance that Solomon actually had some reason for not talking. She would have to find out what it was—locate the right piece of the puzzle and turn it around and around until she knew which way it faced, and eventually it would drop into place. For a start, she knew she would have to pursue the question of the child's identity quite vigorously.

Her first step was to call Sheriff Oreston. She looked at her watch and decided that it was too late for her to do so that day. She would call him in the morning.

5

*D*erek limped painfully up the stairs to his flat. Taking with him the telephone extension, his coffee, and the morning paper, he collapsed into a chair on his deck, shook his straight black hair out of his eyes, and gazed out at The City, as San Franciscans called what was for them one of the few habitable spots on the globe. These last two mornings with Jeannie Walker had been only moderately productive, he reflected, and he was beginning to wonder if the obviously fatal damage he was doing to his knees was going to be worth it.

The first morning had been useful. Derek had timed how long it took Jeannie to run to where she was when she heard Buffy Albertson's scream, and how long it took her to get to the gate. He noted where Jeannie thought she had passed the others on the trail that morning, and how far they could have gotten before and after the scream. They followed the jogging trail past the Albertson house as far as the next point at which it intersected with a street access, a distance of over three miles, and tried following some of the myriad trails spiderwebbing across the side of Mt. Tamalpais. Finally, Derek had made a pest of himself by accosting all the regulars Jeannie pointed out to him. True to form, no one had seen anything suspicious that morning.

The second morning was nearly a total waste of time, however. Derek and Jeannie had followed more of the intersecting trails without finding what Derek was looking for, and that had meant a lot of running up and down steep slopes. Though Derek was in good shape physically and worked out regularly at the gym, running was something he had always hated, and his stamina was not what it should be. Seeing Jeannie bounce along effortlessly next to him didn't help soothe his aching muscles, either.

However, Derek was able to eliminate one possible suspect. Jeannie spotted one of the executives she had noted as a newcomer the week before the kidnapping. The fact that the man was there at all tended to rule him out as the kidnapper. Derek was finally able to put both a name and an address on one of the anonymous jogging suits when he accosted the executive with his card and his increasingly weary questions.

So far so good, Derek thought as he sipped his coffee. The only problem is, this way I'll wind up identifying everyone except the people or person who did it. The more Derek thought it over, the more it all pointed in one direction. And the two people Derek wanted to see most, the high school kid and the bicycle mother, had not shown their faces.

Derek started flipping idly through the paper when the phone rang. He answered it.

"Derek, my love! I am forever in your debt!" The voice was unmistakable.

"Hello, Clarence. Don't you have that backwards? I thought that you're the one who was supposed to be doing some work for me." Derek turned another page of the newspaper while talking.

"My dear, work should always be such pleasure," Clarence purred. "Your man finally came back to the roost, and my God, what a man!"

"Clarence. This is not what is meant by 'checking out a lead.' "

"No really, Derek. Your Ronald James is a very hot-looking young man." Clarence paused for effect. "And so, I might add, is the young man he's living with. Your suspicious little mind was right on track."

Derek's ears perked up. "You're sure?"

"You heard me. Old Clara here did not believe this scene could be true, so she did do her housework, and my dear, this story is con-firmed."

"It's called homework. You're telling me Ronald James is definitely gay?"

"A regular three-dollar bill. He's as gay as I am," Clarence said triumphantly.

"No one is as gay as you, Clarence."

"You shit. Eat your heart out. Anyway, I checked him out for a day, and he certainly didn't act like someone who had a three-week-old baby squirreled away somewhere, so I decided I might as well get acquainted. After all, any friend of Dorothy's is a friend of mine. So I gathered up my courage and bearded the lion in his den."

"That must have been rough," Derek interjected.

"Hon, it's a tough job, but somebody's got to do it," Clarence replied. "If you must know, the dear boy and I had quite a nice little chat. Not only is he not your kidnapper, it was all I could do to keep him from flying to the phone to call his soon-to-be-ex immediately. He hadn't even heard that his son was missing. Neither his wife nor that detective friend of yours out there had told his roomie why they were calling."

"You sure his surprise was genuine?" Derek asked. "Where has he been these last several days?"

"Clara knows her jewels. She can always tell the fake stuff. This," Clarence said breathlessly, "was real. As for his whereabouts, I'm afraid the boy has no taste. He was in Los Angeles the whole time. I've got addresses, times, and the names of people he was with, which I'll leave you to check out at your end, but I have a feeling that they're bona fide."

Before saying goodbye, Clarence dictated a series of names and addresses and a rough chronology of Ronald James's alleged activities over the past week in Los Angeles, which Derek scribbled into the margin of the newspaper. They would have to be checked out, Derek thought, but like Clarence he felt sure that Ronald James's story would hold up.

Derek wondered how much of all this Marguerite knew, and how much else she hadn't told him—or Morelli. He tore off the margin of the newspaper where he had jotted down his notes. As he did so, his eyes suddenly became riveted on a headline and its accompanying story:

Mystery Baby Remains Unidentified

Authorities are still attempting to learn the identity of a baby killed in the tragic auto accident on Interstate 80 just west of Sacramento last week, according to Yolo County Sheriff Paul Oreston. The baby boy was one of three occupants of a car caught in the middle of the multiple-car pileup on the busy freeway, which occurred when smoke from a grass fire suddenly reduced visibility to near zero. The other occupants of the car were also killed in the crash, which took four other lives and turned the roadway into what one bystander described as "a scene from Vietnam."

According to Sheriff Oreston, the other two occupants of the car have been positively identified as Edward and Janet Bowen of Sacramento. However, the Bowens were without children and the baby's identity is unknown. Oreston indicated that all of the other crash victims have been identified, leaving the baby the only unknown victim.

Derek studied the story and poured himself another cup of coffee. He remembered vaguely the original coverage of the freak accident. Mentally, he counted back the days since the crash to last Thursday.

Thursday. The day Patrick James was kidnapped. Derek calculated how long it would take someone to drive from Marin to the Yolo Causeway between Davis and Sacramento. You could stop for breakfast and still get there in time for the accident, he thought grimly.

"This is impossible," he said aloud and punched directory assistance for the phone number of the Yolo County Sheriff's Office. He had no sooner told the receptionist the purpose of his call than he was put through to the Sheriff himself.

"Paul Oreston." The Sheriff's gruff voice had that trace of rural twang Derek often encountered among residents of the small farming communities scattered throughout the Sacramento Valley. Derek was never sure how much of it was a genuine relic of their Midwest heritage and how much of it they deliberately maintained to establish themselves as different from their citified neighbors in the Bay Area and Sacramento. Derek particularly suspected the accents of elected public officials.

"Sheriff, this is Derek Thompson. I'm a private investigator in San Francisco. I'm calling you on a real long shot, but I believe in covering all the bases." Derek outlined the case he was working on and then concluded, "I know it sounds crazy, but the question I'm asking myself is whether there's any chance that the baby killed in that big I-80 crash you had up there is the same kid I'm looking for."

"A kidnapped kid?" Oreston sounded genuinely surprised. There was a long pause. "Well it is an interesting coincidence, but I doubt that we've got your kid here."

"Okay, keep talking."

"Well actually, it's not that we don't know where the kid came from, it's just that we don't know who he is, or was, rather. It seems the kid was in the process of being privately adopted. We know the agency the parents got the kid through, and it's all on the up and up. So at this point, even though we can't seem to find out who the kid was or who or where his real mother is, I think we can be pretty sure he wasn't just snatched out of someone's back yard."

"I figured you'd have information that the papers weren't reporting," Derek offered. "I guess this is one time I'm glad that a lead didn't pan out."

"Yeah, I can see your point. Well it was a pleasure disappointing you."

"The pleasure was all mine, Sheriff. Thanks again." Derek hung up and went back to his coffee. In Yolo County, Sheriff Oreston put down the phone and shook his head at all the weird phone calls he'd been getting ever since the wire services had picked up the story of the unknown Baby Boy Doe. After a moment's reflection, he jotted down Derek Thompson's name and information in his note pad, just in case.

Derek spent what remained of the morning following up on Ronald James's alibi, chasing down the various names Clarence Ames had given him. A couple of the names Derek knew to be pillars of the closeted Los Angeles high society gay community. They were the kind of men you saw everywhere at fundraisers and charity balls. They were invariably surrounded by stylishly attractive women—except in the privacy of their own homes.

Shortly after noon, however, Derek was satisfied that Ronald James's alibi was solid. He finished jotting a few more notes to himself, leaned back in the chair, and admired his handiwork. Not bad, he thought.

He put down his notes and let his eyes wander through the room at the front of his flat which served as his office. Like the rest of the flat, it was furnished in a comfortable and uncluttered style. Derek's general predilection was for simplicity and function, but above all he insisted on surroundings that made you feel welcome.

Derek let out a deep breath. He had almost succeeded in filling the empty spaces left behind when Doug had suddenly moved out, without warning, some ten months ago. The one space he couldn't fill was the self-doubt the incident had planted. It sat in Derek's mind like a little black hole slowly draining his energy. He would never get over the feeling that he had done something wrong—or that he, the great private detective, should have sensed Doug's impending departure.

After six years, he couldn't believe he knew Doug so little. After six years, Derek thought he deserved more of an explanation.

Scattered about the flat were a few carefully chosen antiques, paintings, and sculptures he and Doug had quietly collected for years, even before they could afford them, the signs of a hobby Derek liked to pretend was an investment plan. Doug obviously hadn't felt that way, since he'd simply left them all behind—one more event that was inexplicable.

More for therapy than for any other reason, Derek had finally added to their—his—collection. This latest acquisition, a large, bronze, nineteenth-century Nepalese Buddha, sat serenely on a table against the wall across from him, glowing in the afternoon sunlight, a hint of a smile on its face.

Derek studied the Buddha. One finger of its left hand rested lightly on the earth, while its right hand was held up, palm outward. Derek always imagined this meant that true enlightenment would stay grounded in the everyday world. He didn't know if his interpretation was accurate, but it somehow seemed to fit in with the way he approached much of his life and his job in particular. At this thought, his mind came back to earth. He stood up. It was time to find out what else Marguerite Albertson-James hadn't told him.

Three days had done a lot for Marguerite James' composure. She received Derek coolly and professionally in her front room. She was dressed for an afternoon function, and her dress and makeup had brought her apparent age back up to her real one. Derek ignored her question about his progress.

"I understand you've heard from Ronald."

Marguerite turned cold. "Yes, he called this morning right after your colleague finished browbeating him. He's very worried about Patrick."

"Mrs. James, I'm going to be very blunt. You seemed very sure that your husband hadn't taken Patrick, but you never told me why. The fact is, you knew from the start that Ronald wasn't interested in obtaining custody of Patrick. He wasn't even pressing you on anything except minimal visiting rights. If anyone's been using Patrick as leverage in the divorce proceedings, it's you. Now if you want me to find your kid, you're going to have to be more up-front with me about the inside maneuverings of your divorce. It may or may not be relevant, but if I'm going to do my job, I'm the one who has to decide that."

"He's lying!" Marguerite was outwardly composed, but her fingers dug into the arms of her chair. "Do you believe him? I don't know what kind of story he's telling you, but I swear he wanted *equal* custody of Patrick—equal!"

"And what did his new boyfriend want?"

"What?" Marguerite stopped as if struck. Then she sagged back in her chair.

"You knew your husband was gay, didn't you?"

Marguerite nodded.

"That's why he left you, isn't it?" Derek pressed. "He could handle living with you until you got pregnant, and then he suddenly realized that he didn't want to be pinned down to the straight life-style. Your pregnancy forced him to come to terms with who he really was and, when he figured it out, he left. It's an old story, especially for this part of the country. So why the charade?"

Marguerite rubbed her forehead with her fingers. "It's not an old story for me. Or for my family, or for our friends. It's cheap and it's disgusting. I really loved Ronald, once. I thought I could help him." Marguerite looked up at Derek, pleading. "I thought that having Patrick could make a difference; could bring him to his senses."

Derek smiled wryly. "Well, I guess you were right on that count."

"I guess so." Marguerite gave a bitter little half laugh.

"The two of you fought."

"Yes. We fought." Marguerite was regaining her composure. "We fought, and when I told him he could change and begged him to stay he got really mean. He sneered at me and threw in my face all the horrible things he had done, been doing, even while we were married! He deliberately tried to hurt me! I resolved then that he wasn't going to get off easily. He wasn't going to leave me with a child without adequate support. His family has money. He makes a good living! I'm established here. I've got social obligations and respectable friends, a lot of whom would be disgusted if they knew the truth about him. He can't just run away and cut me off and expect me to give that all up."

Derek sat back. Marguerite's attitude was familiar, and he knew enough to close his mind to it for the present. "So you were threatening to expose him in order to get the settlement you want, only you couldn't tell your friends and the cops the real dispute between the two of you, so you made like the two of you were really fighting over Patrick's custody, is that it?"

Marguerite's impassive face signalled assent.

"And now Patrick's kidnapping puts a whole different angle on the story you've been telling your friends. Your friends are probably expecting that this will bring the two of you back together." Derek paused. "Tell me, Marguerite. At this point, if Ronald wanted to come back, would you have him?"

Marguerite looked away and stared out her front window. A small flotilla of sailboats glided slowly across the Bay and disappeared from her view. "If he really came back, yes," she said finally. "I guess that sounds silly." She turned back to face Derek, her face fighting for control. "I mean, he hurt me—he really hurt me—but I loved him . . . and I love Patrick, and I want them both back."

For a few seconds, Derek's mind was flooded with thoughts about his own life during the last ten months. Just as quickly, he pushed them aside and stood up to go. "Nothing like that ever sounds silly," he said finally.

He went to the door and, as an afterthought, turned back to Marguerite. "By the way, do you by any chance own a bicycle?"

"Of course," Marguerite stammered. "What does that matter?"

"Just asking," Derek replied. "It's such a nice area for biking here. Do you go out riding often?"

"I haven't been riding since I was pregnant with Patrick," Marguerite replied distantly.

"Too bad," Derek replied. "I was just thinking of getting back into it myself."

He left her staring out her window at the Bay.

6

*L*ater that afternoon, Torrance leaned back in her chair and groaned. She had been trying to find time for a call to Sheriff Oreston, but another crisis had kept her occupied. She rubbed her left ear and grimaced. Once again she had spent too many hours with a telephone receiver pressed to it. She really was going to have to learn to hold the phone to her right ear occasionally. O.K., Torrance, time for new habit training, she said to herself, and attempted to feel comfortable with the receiver held to her right ear as she pushed the buttons for Oreston's number.

She did not know Oreston personally and had no idea how he would respond to being offered a volunteer assistant from the attorney general's office. Particularly a woman volunteer, she thought wryly. Some of the older law enforcement types still had a whole lot of trouble coping with the concept of equal employment opportunity for women or, as they were wont to put it, "females."

The timing of her call turned out to be lucky. Not only was Oreston in, but it took her very little time to convince the dragons at the gate (as she thought of them) to allow her to talk to the boss himself.

Oreston had a no-nonsense style. He came on the phone with a brief "Paul Oreston."

"Sheriff, this is Torrance Adams. I'm an assistant attorney general. On the civil side. One of my jobs is to take care of some things the A.G. personally wants done. The reason I'm calling you is that Tyler Havening asked for the A.G.'s help on the matter of this baby that died along with Havening's sister and brother-in-law. I'm probably the best adoptions expert in the office, so the A.G. thought I might be able to be of assistance to you.

This isn't by any means an official approach, you understand. We wouldn't want you to think our office is sticking its nose into this thing unless you want us there."

Oreston laughed unexpectedly. "Hell, I'm not going to get my nose out of joint because the A.G. lends me an expert to keep me from screwing up a case that involves my local assemblyman. More power to you. Did you say your name is Florence Adams?"

"No, Sheriff. It's Torrance. As in the city of."

"Oh, sorry. Unusual name. Not like Paul." He laughed again. "O.K. Torrance, what do you want me to tell you about this mess?"

Over the next half hour, Torrance and Oreston reviewed everything he knew about the death of the Bowens and the baby they had with them—which wasn't overly much when it came to the baby. Most of what Oreston knew Torrance had already heard from Havening. She was pleased to find out that Oreston had obtained the services of Tim McDonald to footprint the baby's body. The prints were ready to be compared to the birth prints of any child tentatively I.D.'d as the Baby Doe in the Yolo County morgue.

"I got one more thing," Oreston finally said. "I'm sure it doesn't relate to this, but you may as well know. I got a call from a private investigator out of San Francisco named Derek Thompson. He's working a case that involves a kidnapping of a two-week-old baby out of a back yard in Marin County. It happened just about when our Baby Doe was killed. The local cops are guessing that it was the lady's husband who walked off with the kid, so they're not giving it a lot of time. This Thompson is sure it wasn't her husband, though, so when he saw in the paper that we had a Baby Doe the right age, he called to check. He's being thorough, I guess, but I can't see how it could possibly connect. I told him we know pretty much where this kid came from. Even if we didn't, I can't see Tyler Havening's sister ripping him off from a back yard in Marin."

"You're right, it doesn't sound like anything more than a coincidence. But I'm glad you told me. You never know where an odd fact will fit in, so I feel a lot safer not ignoring anything until the case is over."

"I wish I could teach some of my young deputies to think that way."

"So does the A.G., but wisdom often comes only after bitter experience. Don't give up hope, Sheriff." She paused briefly and continued in a more serious voice, "Do you have anything else I should know about?"

"No, I think you've got everything. What are your thoughts about what we do next?"

Torrance liked the "we." In fact, she liked Oreston a whole lot so far. "Well, the first thing is for me to get hold of a copy of the documents Havening gave you. So if you could get those to me quickly, it'll help. Then

I'll call Solomon. He tried some things on you, and you backed off because you weren't sure about the law. But he won't be able to give me a snow job about confidentiality, so I'll at least find out his real position—whether he'll cave in once somebody pushes back or keep up the defense. If I don't get anything more than you did, I think we'd better assume he's got something to hide and talk about getting a court order. If he comes right out and tells me where the baby came from, it should be a piece of cake from there on."

She had no idea how wrong she was about that.

The next morning Derek finally found what he was looking for. He let Jeannie run on by herself as he continued to scour the upper trails behind the Lagunitas Country Club. The morning's cool marine air swiftly gave way under the late summer sun as Derek climbed and repeatedly circled the many ridges and knolls, always curving back to the slope above Buffy Albertson's house. Then, finally, he saw it.

He was walking along a path he had been on several times before when he noticed for the first time a little-used track leaving the main trail and curving down into a small grove of trees. A jumble of rocks hid the point at which it branched off.

Derek followed it down. The stony ground resisted footprints. Crouching, he pushed his way under the low-hanging branches of the grove of trees. Suddenly, they gave way. Derek pitched forward onto his hands and found himself looking straight down over the edge of a steep slope.

Taking a deep breath, Derek backed away from the cliff, sat back on his haunches and looked around. To his right was a little clearing at the top of a knoll, hidden from up above by the trees and from below by the natural contours of the land. Carefully, inspecting the soil as he went, Derek crawled over to the clearing.

The clearing had been used repeatedly. From what Derek could make out, the use had been by a single pair of a very popular brand of running shoes, about Derek's size. The prints were devoid of any unique characteristic, except the sharp-edged newness of their tread. There was a place where it appeared a fabric bag had been repeatedly laid and, just to the right of it, what looked like the imprints of someone's knees. Derek placed himself in the depression left by the prints, brought his field glasses up to his eyes and looked down.

He found himself practically staring through Buffy Albertson's patio door.

Astonished, Derek scanned the hillside below him without the binoculars for a moment. The vantage afforded by this knoll was almost beyond belief.

Derek picked up the field glasses again and began picking out critical points in the trail which led along the top of Buffy Albertson's yard. He followed along the trail, marvelling at the view it gave him of the various joggers below. One of them, a hefty young kid probably still in high school, was jogging back toward the Lagunitas parking area that Jeannie used.

"Shit!" Derek cursed, as he focused quickly on the rapidly disappearing back. "The kid!"

Derek jumped to his feet and shouted, "Hey! Kid! Don't go away!"

The kid moved on without breaking stride. In a panic, Derek realized that the kid was wearing earphones. He couldn't hear Derek any more than he had heard Buffy's scream.

"Damn!" Derek cursed again. Turning, he shoved his way back through the brush, ignoring the branches scratching his face. He scrambled up the steep slope on all fours and burst onto the main upper trail. Blindly, he tore down it, crashing through the shortcuts he hoped he remembered and cutting off switchbacks until suddenly he half-stumbled out onto the lower trail. Turning left, he raced as fast as he could in the direction in which the boy had disappeared, the blood slowly beginning to rise in his head, blotting off his vision.

Down at the parking area, the high school kid finished stretching out his calves and pulled off his now-soaked sweatshirt, revealing a tank top and the new muscles he hoped would help him win first-string on his school's football team. He popped the cassette out of his portable player and slid it into the dash of his car, put the key into the ignition and turned it. The car roared to life simultaneously with the tape. He rolled down the driver's side window, slid the car into gear, and smoothly backed into a turn with one hand. He paused to retrieve his dark glasses from the seat next to him, shifted into first, and suddenly slammed on his brakes.

With a thud, a face dripping with sweat, blood and dirt landed on his windshield.

"Jeesus, what . . .?" The kid threw the car in park and leaped out, not sure if he should be ready to fight or render first aid.

"Don't . . . leave," Derek gasped. Give me . . . few minutes." He sagged against the kid's car.

The kid glanced worriedly at his paint job. "Hey mister, you all right? What happened to you?"

Still gasping painfully, Derek pulled his wallet out of his pocket and handed the kid one of his business cards. The kid stared at it open-mouthed.

"Five minutes," Derek wheezed. "I need to talk to you. Just let me catch . . . my breath." While the kid was still staring incredulously at Derek's card, Derek painfully peeled off his own sweatshirt and began mopping his face and sides. The world was slowly beginning to reappear. Derek took a deep breath and shook his head to clear it.

"Hi," he said, holding out his hand. "I'm Derek Thompson. I'm a private investigator working on the Patrick James kidnapping."

Numbly, the kid shook Derek's hand. "I'm Jason Walters," he blurted.

Derek had more or less fully recovered from his headlong dash down the side of Mt. Tam. He and Jason Walters stood side by side, leaning against Jason's car, which at Derek's suggestion was parked in a patch of sun at the top of Lagunitas. Jason was obviously awed by Derek's sudden appearance and introduction, a state of mind that was heightened by Derek's opening question.

"By any chance did you sprain your ankle out here a week ago Thursday?" Derek had asked.

Jason could only stammer, "Yeah." Every television and movie stereotype about the prowess of private investigators was irrevocably confirmed in his mind.

"I want you to think back to that Thursday," Derek was saying. "I want you to remember everyone you saw that morning on the trail."

"I dunno, I'm really not sure I could remember any day from the next," Jason replied unhelpfully.

"Let's back up a little, then. When did you first start jogging here?"

For the next five minutes, Derek patiently took Jason through the full history of his jogging, from Jason's first having established a regular workout routine, to how he began jogging from the Natalie Greene Park access, through Jason's progress up to the present, including his sprained ankle. As he talked, Jason began to remember details, things he had seen along the trail and people he ran into. The details began to fit into a rough chronology, and Derek noted with pleasure how Jason's details and descriptions began to converge with Jeannie Walker's. When Jason mentioned a woman with her baby on a bike, Derek was careful not to express any heightened interest, lest he drive the memory of any other possibly important details from Jason's mind. Finally, Jason was through, and Derek circled in.

"Now let's go back again to the morning you sprained your ankle. You've hobbled back to the car, and you're sitting in the front seat, rubbing your ankle, trying to decide if you should take your shoe off or not. You haven't seen anyone since you got hurt. But someone does come down off the trail then and gets into a car, right? Maybe you just gave her a passing glance because you were working on your ankle. . . ."

"That's right! The woman with the bicycle. And her baby!" Jason brightened with the recollection. "Yeah, she came back, packed up and went off."

"Is there anything at all that struck you about her—anything that stands out?"

"Well, she was really in good shape, you know, and kind of foxy—for an older lady, like in her twenties or thirties or something." Jason hesitated.

"And something else?"

"Yeah. Yeah, I just remembered. It was real funny 'cause she puts the bike on this rack on the back of her car all right, but then she just sticks the baby carrier on the floorboard of the car in the front seat. I mean, that's really weird, you know, like here's this lady with her new kid and this state law and everything requiring your kid to be in a car seat, and she just sticks the car seat on the floor with all the heat and fumes and stuff. Can you believe that? Is that weird or what?"

"In this case, I believe it," Derek answered. "I don't suppose you were so offended that you happened to take down her license number, were you?"

"Hardly!" Jason laughed. "I guess I'd never make it as a private eye, huh?"

"You're not doing so badly. Do you remember what kind of car she drove?"

"Oh that's easy," Jason replied. "She was driving an old Pontiac Grand Prix sedan, '73 or '74, blue, pretty clean. Fix it up, it could be pretty radical, you know. You could make some real money on it in the Mission district."

"Yeah. How'd it sound?"

"Don't know. I was wearing my earphones, remember?"

"Sorry, I forgot. Is there anything else that strikes you about the car, any other detail that could help identify it?"

Jason thought a minute. "Yeah, there is one thing. I remember 'cause it was so funny."

"What's that?"

"A bumper sticker. I saw it when she drove off with her kid sliding around on the floor, and I laughed 'cause it was just too weird."

"So what'd it say?"

Jason shook his head thoughtfully. "Something about parents, Man. Something about . . . 'parent builders'! That's what it said! 'Parent builders.' Can you believe that?"

"Pretty weird," Derek said.

"Too weird," Jason agreed.

Derek stood up to go. "You've been a big help. You've got my card. If you ever see her or her car again, give me a call, will you?"

"Sure! And this time I'll get a license number," Jason said eagerly.

"You might make a private eye yet," Derek winked. "Just remember one thing: it doesn't matter how good a scam it is, people will always leave tracks behind them. There's always a clue. All you have to do is keep digging until you find it. And be smart enough to recognize it."

"So, did I give you a good clue?" Jason said with a mischievous twinkle.

"Yeah, you gave me a good clue," Derek laughed. "All I have to do now is figure out what the heck it means."

7

Very early on Tuesday morning, just as the sun was beginning to tint the sky gray, a fog was covering the lower reaches of San Francisco. A high-flying bird would have seen the spiky top of the Transamerica pyramid and the external steel skeleton of another supposedly earthquake-safe skyscraper sticking above the fog, along with the tops of the Golden Gate and Bay bridges and some other landmarks. But the people of The City were submerged in the chill blanket. On the slope of Telegraph Hill, in the dove and slate gray Victorian as well-kept as its equally stately and historic neighbors, Torrance Adams woke up to the sound of her alarm clock.

She sat up against the headboard of the king-size bed and ran a hand through her short brown hair. Looking past her feet, she smiled at the dark lump at the foot of the bed which she was just barely able to see in the dim light coming in from the street. Her two Burmese cats were piled one on top of the other as usual at this hour, undoubtedly opening one eye each at the sound of the alarm, only to go back to sleep until there was something to be gained by getting up. Torrance turned on the bedside light and looked around the large and airy bedroom, which had a comfortable sitting area to one side, next to glass doors leading to a greenhouse-roofed patio with a view. She felt good, at home, comfortable with the room, and she suddenly asked herself whether she had become used to living alone, whether the ache of waking up without her husband next to her would finally stop.

She got up, turned on the heat in the upper part of the house, and stood under a hot shower while the room warmed up. When she emerged from the bathroom in a bottle green fleece robe, her hair curling damply, the cats suddenly became wide awake, stretched, and preceded her downstairs to the kitchen. When she and Harry had acquired the two sable Burmese shortly after moving into this house, Harry had quickly decided that their names were Jade and Buddha. Torrance was initially appalled at the thought.

"Harry," she pleaded, "cats have to have wonderful, unusual, personal names. Why on earth Jade and Buddha?"

Harry had a simple answer. They were Burmese cats, weren't they? Well, all he knew about Burma was that there was Burmese jade and a lot of Burmese Buddhas. So those were the only authentically Burmese names he could give them. Torrance finally gave up and accepted the names which Harry was unlikely to relinquish. Amusingly, the cats eventually came to fit them quite well, with Buddha growing into a large and placid male, given to lengthy periods of seeming contemplation of the universe, and Jade becoming a slim and playful female who expected to be treated like a precious jewel.

As Torrance fixed her own breakfast and fed the cats (they observed her with the greatest indifference, but would have demanded vociferously to be fed had she forgotten), she went over what she planned to do that day. Yesterday, she had received the documents relating to the proposed adoption which Tyler Havening had found at the Bowens' home and reviewed them closely. She had decided that her best approach was still through Solomon, with the Parentbuilders Foundation as a fallback resource. She was used to dealing with lawyers, and a lawyer would understand her position quickly and presumably cooperate unless he had some very good reason not to, a fact which would then be notable in itself. So she had called Solomon's office, identified herself to his secretary, and asked for an appointment.

Solomon was apparently either curious or willing to cooperate because she was offered a time the following afternoon. Now she considered her approach and decided that she would begin by talking easily and in a chatty fashion about her legal experience, apparently without suggesting any direct relevance to the case. This would let him know he could not easily hoodwink her, yet she would not appear too threatening or demanding. From Sheriff Oreston's description of Solomon, she thought this approach might get her the most information.

She dressed carefully for the appointment in a fashionable tweed suit and silk blouse. She was satisfied as she looked at herself in the mirror. No stereotypical state bureaucrat here, she thought. She wanted Solomon to see her as the equal of the professional women he'd meet in the financial district. With a quick check of her watch, she headed for her bus to the office. She loved driving her Porsche, but not on the steep streets in town. Besides, the parking spot assigned to her was neither particularly secure nor particularly close to her office, so she might as well keep her car safe at home.

Torrance spent the morning coping with a small portion of the flood of letters, memos, and phone messages that went with her job. When she joined a deputy she knew for lunch at a small Thai restaurant near the office, she found herself once again rubbing her left ear. Damn, she thought, I've broken new habit training already. At least the afternoon would be taken up with her appointment with Solomon instead of phone calls.

Solomon's office was located in the shadow of the Transamerica pyramid, in an area of buildings antedating the 1906 earthquake. Originally, these three-story brick buildings had been warehouses and small industrial enterprises, but they had become the subject of historical preservation and had been refurbished into stylish offices inhabited mostly by professional firms and some very exclusive sales rooms, with an occasional fashionable restaurant thrown in. The entire small neighborhood glowed with scrubbed brick, brightly painted woodwork and well-polished brass, looking as though gaslights and hansom cabs would be more fitting than the congested automobile traffic and the towering skyscrapers of the financial district next door.

Torrance located Solomon's office, which was on the third floor of a building shared with several other lawyers, a firm of architects, and an office with a clientele presumably so exclusive that its brass plate announced only the firm's name. She announced herself to the secretary-receptionist, a motherly-looking woman in her fifties who nevertheless exuded an aura of competence and had a no-nonsense, take-charge style. She told Torrance to be seated, Mr. Solomon would see her shortly.

Apparently, Solomon was one of those individuals who felt it necessary to assert himself by making even the most on-time visitor wait the requisite ten minutes in his anteroom, because Torrance was ushered into his presence twelve minutes after she arrived, with no one having left in the interim.

Torrance disliked Solomon the moment she saw him welcoming her with a broad smile and a hand outstretched across his desk, but she recognized just as quickly that many people would be drawn to him and find him persuasive and comforting. He had the style of a Sunday-morning television evangelist who projected his powerful personality at his audience, convincing them that only by sending their money to his church would they gain the many things they lacked in their lives. There would be many responding to his charisma with trust and confidence. Torrance responded to it with instant suspicion of charlatanism, which she recognized might or might not be deserved.

She shook hands with Solomon and sat down in one of his comfortable client chairs. The office was decorated in traditional legal office style, with leather, dark wood, and law books the outstanding features of the decor. Solomon himself, behind his massive desk, was of middle height and middle age, dressed slightly less stylishly than Torrance would have expected from his office address. He had a build that suggested the weight he carried was muscle rather than fat. As he beamed at Torrance, he projected an image of self-confidence and openness. Sensing that he would immediately attempt to find out why she was here, she rushed forward at once.

"Mr. Solomon, I do hope you'll forgive me for taking up your time," she exclaimed in the closest approximation she could manage of a socialite collecting for her favorite charity. "I thought I should come and talk to you myself since I'm familiar with much of the work you've done in the adoptions area. I remember when you handled the *Bobby L.* case, we were all watching to see whether the Supreme Court would agree with you. It always seemed to me that the real question was whether they understood independent adoptions or not." Her ploy worked. Solomon, obviously not devoid of ego when it came to his cases, embarked upon a discussion of recent adoptions decisions which allowed Torrance to display her thorough knowledge of the law while she appeared chatty and unfocused on her real purpose. Finally, she found the right stopping place and moved on to business.

"Well, I guess we could go on like this forever," she said, "but your time is probably short and I did come to ask for your help in connection with the death of Mr. and Mrs. Bowen and their baby." She watched Solomon carefully as she said this, and he gave her a slightly pained smile, which might just have been his way of acknowledging untimely death. Otherwise, he remained apparently untroubled as she went on. "Since Mrs. Bowen's brother is Assemblyman Havening, my office is providing some courtesy assistance. I thought it would be helpful if I came to see you myself to get the information you have about the child's birth parents." There, she had laid it out. Would Solomon forget his earlier arguments and give her the information, or would he do it the hard way and make her go to court?

The pained smile deepened on Solomon's face. "Have you ever had a case with which everything has gone wrong, Miss Adams? I've never lost an adoptive parent before, or a child, and suddenly here I've lost both in the same tragic accident. And right after I found that out, I found out that the birth mother had disappeared. I knew she was sort of a free spirit, but I expected her to stay put long enough to sign the consent. I tried to impress on her how important that is to the adoptive parents, and therefore to the future of her child. But apparently she didn't care. She's gone, and I have no idea where to."

Torrance sat very quietly, her mind racing through the implications of this disclosure while her face and body gave nothing away. Where did she go from here? "Did the mother know the Bowens' names?" she finally asked. "Could she have read about their death and disappeared because of it?"

"No," Solomon answered, "she insisted that the actual names be covered whenever documents were signed. She did know a good deal about the Bowens, of course, just not the actual identity and address."

Torrance knew that this might or might not be true, but that Solomon would insist on saying it to maintain the fiction that the mother herself had chosen the potential adoptive family. After a moment, she said, "I assume you have a copy of the birth certificate."

"Of course," Solomon responded, his salesman's smile back on his face. "Would you like me to have a copy made for you?"

Torrance nodded, and Solomon buzzed his secretary, who appeared and efficiently extracted a document from a case file, which she took away with her. She returned a moment later and handed Torrance a photocopy of a birth certificate. Torrance read it slowly, trying to weigh each item to see what importance she might be able to attach to it. The mother's name was Jane Robertson. A common name, perhaps a pseudonym? Her address was given only as General Delivery, Ferndale, which Torrance vaguely remembered as a small town on the north coast. The father's name was given as "unknown." A true statement by a "free spirit" or an attempt not to involve a known man who had fathered the child? The child was named Russell John, which gave Torrance no clue she could think of. But the final item of information was the most striking. Russell John had not been born in a hospital. The birth was registered as a home birth. It was acknowledged by Dr. Albert Moorehead, who had attended it. The place of birth was given as Fernbridge, California.

Torrance was stunned by this information. She had been counting on having a reasonable chance at identifying the dead child based on his footprints. To have prints taken at birth, however, a child had to be born in a hospital. There was no provision for printing a child after a home birth. So here was a child with no mother who could be found, no hospital record, and no footprints. How convenient it all was.

She knew that she needed to withdraw and think, discuss this with some other people in her office, and form a new plan. She asked Solomon a number of deliberately inconsequential questions and inquired about any other documents he might have with predictably negative results. Then she thanked him for his help, chatted a bit more to cover her consternation, and left as soon as she could without appearing alarmed.

All the way back to her office, Torrance turned the facts she knew over and over in her mind. A woman who may or may not have been named Jane Robertson gave birth to a little boy named Russell on August sixteenth, slightly more than three weeks before the Bowens took him home. That in itself was unusual. Most mothers who choose to give up their babies want to spend as little time as possible with them, in order not to get attached to them. Usually, the baby goes home from the hospital with the prospective adoptive parents. Of course, when the baby wasn't born in a hospital, that routine would be disrupted. Still, two or more weeks was a long time. She wondered whether the baby had been staying with the mother or with someone else but hadn't been ready to ask that question of Solomon, not knowing how the answer would fit in and not wanting to alert him to her doubts.

She also knew that the mother had given the father's name as unknown, something that happened often when children were given up for adoption. Again, it was a statement that was not necessarily true. Torrance was aware that attorneys sometimes advised mothers not to name the father to avoid any possibility that he or his family might claim the child. When the mother had never told him of her pregnancy, this usually worked well for her and for the prospective adoptive parents, but of course it deprived the father of any opportunity to claim custody and raise the child himself. The question of the unmarried father's rights was a hotly litigated one in California, with the Supreme Court itself split between those who saw him as no different from a married father and those who stated that a "casual inseminator" should have no rights. Torrance decided that one of the options she had to keep in mind was that this adoption was originally set up to avoid giving away the identity of a father who might claim the child.

By the time she returned to her office she was sure that there was ample reason for her suspicion that the facts she had been given were entirely too convenient for Solomon and the Parentbuilders Foundation. She was unsure of what they were hiding, but all her instincts which she had learned to trust over the years were ringing alarm bells. To test these reactions, she called an old friend, the adoptions supervisor in the local office of the California Adoptions Service.

Louise Sandowski had been involved in public and private adoption agency work for twenty-five years. Anything about adoptions that Louise had not come across or thought about was, in Torrance's opinion, probably not worth knowing. For her part Louise had long regarded Torrance as her favorite lawyer, finding her sensitive to the people and issues involved, while incredibly tough and hard- working when it came to getting her client's point across. The two became far more than professional acquaintances a year ago, when Torrance's husband of fourteen years was killed by a drunk driver. Louise took it upon herself to pull Torrance back from the utter misery she was sinking into and, while desperately searching for a cause she could get Torrance interested in, pushed her in the direction of the attorney general's campaign. These days, Louise thought back upon that decision with an ironic smile. Little had she suspected that it would result in Torrance no longer handling any of Louise's cases. It was a rare thing now when Torrance called on business, and Louise was thrilled to be asked for advice on the Bowen baby case.

Torrance gave Louise a rundown of all the facts and asked her to voice all the suspicions she could come up with. Louise's mind worked like Torrance's. She worried about the real identity of the natural mother, since there was no hospital record to confirm it, and the mother had disappeared; she thought of a possible plan to avoid an interested father; and she wondered whether a large sum of money had changed hands in return for this baby which the parties did not want to disclose.

"Then you don't think I'm being paranoid when I wonder that there may be something funny going on here?" Torrance asked. Louise laughed. "Torrance, my dear, you have never been paranoid in your life. You just have the kind of mind the bad guys wish that people in law enforcement didn't have. But no matter how suspicious you've been over the years, it has always turned out that the people involved were fully deserving of your mistrust."

By the time Torrance was through with the call, it was after five, and after she dealt with a few more items on her desk she decided to call it a day. When she reached her home soon after six, she saw light streaming from the ground floor windows, and heard a Mozart horn concerto when she unlocked the street door. Monica was obviously inviting her for dinner.

Torrance smiled and walked through the open door into the ground floor apartment. Monica was in the kitchen, wearing a vaguely Turkish-looking purple garment and preparing what appeared to be a Middle-Eastern meal.

"It's about time you got home," Monica said matter-of-factly. "I'm too busy to uncork the wine."

Torrance laughed. "You just can't wait to hear the next installment. Let me run and change, and I'll be down with some good new stuff."

While Torrance climbed the stairs to the second floor, she thought fondly of the unconventional woman who was so good at making her feel wanted. Since Harry's death, Monica's presence had made it pleasant for Torrance to come home. Monica never intruded, but she always seemed to know when to come upstairs to offer a glass of wine or beg a cup of sugar. She guessed that Torrance wasn't eating properly (an accurate deduction) and began to offer her more than an occasional meal. She was so subtle she almost had Torrance convinced that it was *Monica's* loneliness that was being assuaged. When she played her favorite classical music and left the inside door open, it was her signal that Torrance was invited to come in and eat with her if she cared to do so. Torrance usually accepted unless she was too tired.

Torrance opened the door to the top of the house to find Buddha lying immediately behind it waiting to have his belly scratched, and Jade approaching to rub against her legs. "You guys are getting a treat tonight," she told them, since they loved to be talked to after a day alone in the house. "You can inspect downstairs while I have dinner with Monica."

Dressed in jeans and a sweater, she returned to Monica's apartment and uncorked the wine. While Monica finished the dinner, Torrance did what Monica loved best: she told her all about the interesting case she was working on. Monica was an excellent sounding board. She listened well, quickly grasped the issues, and readily offered her sometimes outrageous but always insightful opinions.

Predictably, she really perked up when Torrance told her about the call from a detective who was looking for a kidnapped baby. "There you have it," she exclaimed. "The reason for all of this funny stuff is that they kidnapped the kid and sold him for a lot of money to someone who didn't care where it came from!"

"Now Monica," Torrance chided, "the Bowens were the most reputable people in the world. You have to remember that I read all of their correspondence. There isn't the slightest hint that they were involved in anything other than a straightforward adoption."

"All right," Monica conceded reluctantly, "so they weren't in on it. But what about that lawyer you talked to? You said you didn't trust him."

"Yes, but I meant that he may be a little devious in his lawyering, not that he's a kidnapper! The man has been practicing adoption law for years and making a very good living at it. Why should he do something risky like stealing a child?"

Monica looked at Torrance with disgust. "Honey," she said, "you're naive if you believe that anyone like him is ever going to think he's making enough money. And where's the risk? You can't prove who this kid is, right?"

Torrance, who would have dealt severely with anyone else who called her "honey," did not even blink. She was well used to Monica's ways by now, and there wouldn't have been any point in fighting it anyway. She sat for a while, deep in thought. Monica's comments made it clear to her that, unlikely or not, there was one thing she should check out. She had the dead baby's prints. Surely that kidnapped child was born in a hospital, and if luck was with them the mother would be able to provide Torrance with a usable set of his footprints.

8

*D*erek settled back in his car seat, feeling mildly stupid and decidedly irritated. The two things he hated most were long shots and wasting time, and here he was combining both in one stakeout.

The Monday following his meeting with the high school kid he spent on the phone with every social worker and family counselor he knew, trying to find out who would put out a bumper sticker with "parent builders" on it and what it might mean.

It was shortly after noon when a gay social worker Derek knew in the welfare department made the connection. "It's 'Parentbuilders,' " he said. "One word. It's a private adoption agency—excuse me, it's a private foundation that helps *facilitate* adoptions. They aren't licensed as an agency. Their office is somewhere here in The City, I think. I'm not sure they're in the phone book. Let me see if I can find out where they are. I'll get back to you." That afternoon Derek had an address on outer Clement, where old residences were just starting to be converted to commercial use.

Once again he thought about how much of his success he owed to his network of friends and acquaintances in San Francisco. The gay community cut across all social boundaries, ethnic groups and occupations, giving Derek access to people and information not available to most of Derek's straight competitors without a lot more footwork.

Friends often asked him how he always seemed to find a conveniently-placed member of the "fraternity," as he sometimes put it. "There are really only thirteen of us," he would respond mysteriously. "We just keep changing disguises."

A short time later, he was sitting in his car parked strategically across the street and less than half a block away from an old, peeling three-story frame house apparently long ago converted to flats and now changing over to offices. The building which housed the Parentbuilders Foundation (as it seemed to be called) had no garage or parking lot of its own that Derek could determine. That put him in a particularly bad mood. He had hoped there would be an employee's parking lot so that he could see if any of the cars matched the description given him by the high school kid.

That was a long shot, since the woman on the bicycle might be a former employee or a disappointed customer. Or she might take the bus or walk to her job at the Foundation. Or the car might have been purchased from a past employee. The possibilities were endless.

Derek's problems were multiple. He would have to watch the various people entering and exiting the Foundation's doorway, note their descriptions, and follow them to their cars. He had already scouted the several blocks around the building, looking unsuccessfully for a blue '73 or '74 Pontiac Grand Prix which, of course, would undoubtedly still have a bicycle rack on the back, a brightly-lettered "Parentbuilders" bumpersticker, and a kidnapped baby in a carrier sliding around loose on the front passenger side floorboard.

What made Derek even more sour was the knowledge that this was such a long shot that he couldn't in good conscience bill Marguerite for the time he spent—unless, of course, lightning struck and something actually came of all this.

On the other hand, Derek was faced with the reality that he had essentially run out of leads. This case was turning out to be quite frustrating. Several smaller cases had come in during the past week. If nothing happened soon, he would have to take a break from the James case later this week, he decided. The new cases would bring in some quick cash and keep him from going crazy.

A change of pace might also help clear his mind and let him see something new that he had overlooked or misinterpreted. When he ran out of leads, there were three things he could do: pursue long shots, carefully and meticulously checking them off; do something else for a while and then approach the case again with a fresh mind; or, if all else failed, throw some kind of monkey wrench into the machinery and wait to see what fell out.

In the present situation, Derek mused, you would go boldly into the Foundation office announcing you're a private investigator working on a kidnapping, describe the woman and her car, and ask a lot of questions about the Foundation's present and former employees and customers. Then you would sit back and wait to see if anyone panics. Even if such an approach wouldn't be productive, he reasoned, it usually would be amusing. More often than not, however, the "monkey wrench" technique succeeded in breaking open a stalled case—with wildly unpredictable results.

Derek was pulled out of his reverie by the appearance of a large woman with short dark hair in the doorway of the building which housed the Parentbuilders Foundation. He swore at himself for the brief spell of inattention which had caused him to miss seeing which door the woman had come out of. In any event, she was too large and too old to match Jeannie Walker's description of the woman with the bicycle, and her glasses were more suggestive of a society stalwart than a woman who would be out exercising every day.

These thoughts took only a second or two to pass through Derek's mind, and he was beyond them almost before they started. Instinctively, he reached for the movie camera the moment he saw the woman. Within seconds, he shot a few feet of film, including a zoom closeup of the woman's face for possible later identification, duly noted the time and description of the woman in his note pad, and then watched where she was headed. She walked up Clement and got into a white 1985 Cadillac Seville. As she drove past Derek, he noted the license plate number and vehicle make in his pad. He put back the camera and pad and heaved a sigh.

Derek hated surveillance. He was very good at it because he was sensitive to how a particular subject was going to act and how he should blend in, but he hated it nonetheless. He often described surveillance to his friends as hours of total boredom followed by a few split seconds of semi-boredom.

The woman's abrupt departure was a case in point. The time from her appearance in the doorway to the moment she drove off was not more than sixty seconds. A momentary diversion could easily have caused him to miss her entirely. Taking a break to go to the bathroom was courting disaster. Derek decided to see how things went at closing time and then give it two more days.

Torrance was more efficient than most people because once she made up her mind on the best course of action, she did it with the least possible delay. This was not a conscious effort on her part but an instinctive reaction. When she was turning a problem over and over in her mind, she was endlessly patient. But once she decided what to do next, she found procrastination unbearable and at times almost physically painful.

When she reached her office the next morning, she went straight to the notes of her conversation with Sheriff Oreston and found the reference to the investigator who had called about the kidnapping in Marin. Torrance had a vague recollection of having read about it in the papers, but she was unsure of the exact date and could not recall many other details.

Her notes gave her Derek Thompson's name with a San Francisco phone number. She had not heard of Thompson before but found that hardly surprising since, when her work involved investigators at all, it was usually Department of Justice special agents or police of one kind or another.

Before dialing the number, she took the local Yellow Pages from a shelf and opened them to "Investigators." She found both a line entry with Derek Thompson's name and state license number, and a small ad on the same page. The content of the ad was unremarkable. It failed to tell her whether "Derek Thompson Investigations" was one or more persons. It included only a fairly typical brief list of services offered and ended with a post office box and a telephone number. The ad somehow stood out from the others nearby. It was done in two type styles, both unusual, and laid out in a way which caught one's attention through the effective use of the small space. It had class the other ads didn't have. As Torrance reached for the telephone, she wondered whether Thompson had the insight and artistic sense the ad implied or was just the recipient of good advice.

A polite female voice belonging to an answering service took Torrance's message efficiently and suggested that Mr. Thompson would likely return the call that morning. Obviously, Torrance told herself, a private detective couldn't get anything done if he sat around waiting for the phone to ring. She reached for an analysis of a new piece of legislation she had begun writing the day before and soon was focused on the intricacies of yet another proposal to restructure juvenile court procedures. Her phone began to ring with the usual demands on her time. She had almost forgotten her early morning preoccupation with Baby Doe when Derek Thompson called on her direct line.

"You told my answering service only that you're with the attorney general's office, Ms. Adams," he said in a pleasant, rather deep voice. "But I have to confess that I have an organization chart of your office, and I looked you up. I don't recall having had the A.G.'s attention at such a high level before." He laughed briefly. "Am I being investigated or recruited?"

Torrance couldn't help smiling. "I hate to disappoint you, Mr. Thompson," she said. "I just called to ask for your help. You have a client in Marin County who says her son was kidnapped."

Derek paused to absorb this message. "True, but I'm curious to know how you came to hear about that. I thought the Ross police weren't paying too much attention to it."

"Well, if you can't believe that they would have called this office, you're right. It was Sheriff Oreston in Yolo County who gave me your name."

"The baby killed in the I-80 crash," Derek answered quickly. "I thought that was all taken care of. Was there something Oreston didn't tell me?"

"No, he was straight with you. The baby was to be adopted by the couple he was with—the Bowens—and Oreston thought when he talked to you that the identification would be pretty routine. But it didn't turn out that way. I have some real questions about the origins of that baby. Enough to want to be absolutely sure that he couldn't have been the one you're looking for. When was your client's baby taken?"

"That same Thursday as the crash; about six hours earlier. That's why I called Oreston to begin with. Are you saying there's something else that suggests the two babies are the same?"

Torrance could feel her heartbeat quicken. What if Monica was right? But she kept her voice under control and said, "Only the fact that this baby seems to have been unusually anonymous. That and my chronically suspicious mind. But the reason I called you, Mr. Thompson, is this: do you know whether the baby you're looking for was born in a hospital?"

"In a hospital?" Derek was dumbfounded by the question, and it showed in his voice. "I have no idea. Why would it matter?"

Torrance explained. "If the baby was born in a hospital, there are almost definitely footprints available. In fact, the mother should have her own copy— they would have offered her one. If the nurse who took the prints did a decent job, we should be able to compare the two sets of footprints and tell whether the kidnapped baby you're looking for is or isn't the dead baby. I really have no reason to think it is," she continued quickly, "I just want to be sure, and it seemed like this is one loose end I could eliminate rather easily."

Derek Thompson didn't answer right away, and Torrance gave him time to think. When he spoke, he sounded subdued. "For my client's sake, I liked it a lot better when Oreston turned me down. It's kind of tough to have to reconsider the possibility that I might have to tell Mrs. James I was only able to find her son's body. I don't suppose you have any idea how I can get those footprints from her without telling her what you're working on?"

Torrance ran her mind over the possibilities and didn't like any of them. "None that she's likely to buy."

"Yeah, that's what I thought, too," Derek answered. "Once I get the prints to you, how long will it be before you can give us an answer?"

"Two days, maybe three. I have to send them to Sacramento on the courier and our print specialist has to do the comparison. If he's available, it won't take any time at all once he has them. I'll do my best to speed things up once you tell me the prints are on their way."

"I'll try to get them for you by tomorrow. Shall I call you or just drop them by your office?"

"Call me first so I can try to be here when you stop by. But bring them in whether I'm here or not. I'll leave instructions for them to go to Sacramento right away. "

"In that case, I'll be talking to you again, Ms. Adams. I appreciate your calling me, even if you didn't exactly have good news. Goodbye."

"Goodbye," Torrance answered and hung up. She sat for a minute and thought about Derek Thompson. He sounded like a nice person. She had always thought that real private investigators, unlike those on television, were brash and sleazy. Come to think of it, even some of the ones on television were brash and sleazy. But Thompson didn't sound like that. She remembered his ad and decided he matched it rather well. Maybe that's just his telephone manner, she thought. He's probably a retired cop with flat feet and a big gut.

Having asked Derek Thompson for the prints, Torrance felt restless again. She had another loose end she hadn't taken care of yet, and she could think of no good reason to wait. From the file of materials Tyler Havening had sent her, she took the documents with the "Parentbuilders Foundation" letterhead and stared at them. The address was not one she could easily reach by public transportation. If she went there, she would have to use her car.

As she often did when she wanted to think, Torrance got up and went to stand by the window, a habit which occasionally got her accused of daydreaming. The Parentbuilders Foundation would have to be approached no matter how the footprint analysis turned out. She might as well do it right away. She wondered whether to call them first or just drop in. She didn't know anything about the Foundation, but it was likely to be modeled on similar enterprises she had heard of. There were several groups of private adoption facilitators, which were based on a genuine desire to help childless couples and sometimes an equally genuine wish to make money doing so. They could not legally charge for procuring adoptable babies, of course, so they depended on fees charged for passing on their expertise, or on the solicitation of "voluntary" contributions to the cause.

Would Solomon have called the Foundation to advise it of her interest? She decided he surely must have done so, since he knew them well enough to have recommended their services to the Bowens. So they were likely to know her name. She wasn't an undercover investigator and couldn't approach them as anyone other than who she was. All things considered, she couldn't think of any reason why a surprise visit would be to her advantage. Besides, they might not keep regular office hours—in fact, they might not even have a regular office.

Torrance returned to her desk and remained in thought for a few more moments. Then she reached for her telephone and called the number on the Foundation letterhead.

After several rings, a woman answered, "Parentbuilders Foundation. Can we help you?" The voice was friendly and cheerful. Torrance tried to picture herself as a potential client ambivalent about calling the Foundation and decided that she would be pleased with the tone.

"This is Torrance Adams at the Attorney General's Office," she said in a tone that tried to match that of the speaker at the other end. "I've been talking to John Solomon about the baby Edward and Janet Bowen were going to adopt." She dropped the cheerful component and went on, "I'm sure Mr. Solomon has told you about his tragic death." In spite of the silence at the other end, she steadfastly refused to go on and waited for a response.

"Yes. Yes, he has," it finally came.

"I wonder whether I might be able to come and see you tomorrow to go over some things Mr. Solomon and I talked about." Again the silence. Torrance wondered whether the speaker had instructions from Solomon about what to say if Torrance called. Perhaps not. She seemed unsure of how to deal with the call.

"We don't talk to third parties about our clients, Miss Adams," the woman finally said. Torrance felt like answering that Solomon had already tried that line, but she restrained herself and kept her voice friendly.

"I'm not asking for any information that I don't already have, although . . . I'm afraid I don't know your name."

"It's Shirley Robusson."

"Well, then, Miss Robusson . . . or is it Mrs. Robusson?"

"It's Mrs."

"Mrs. Robusson. Are you the person in charge of the Parentbuilders Foundation?"

"Yes. Yes, I am. We're a very small organization. We don't have anyone who just answers the phone."

"Then you're certainly the person I should see, Mrs. Robusson. Can you manage some time tomorrow?"

"I guess you can come over at ten if you want to. I really don't see what good it will do you to talk to me."

Torrance finally assured Shirley Robusson that she knew how to find the address of the Parentbuilders Foundation and got off the phone. Well, at least things were moving. She now had two balls up in the air and, one way or another, it would be interesting to see how they came down.

9

At 9:15 the next day, Torrance left her never-quiet telephone in the capable hands of her secretary and walked to her parking spot. She had carefully dressed for the occasion, deciding that a glen plaid dress and a grey blazer projected the kind of image Mrs. Robusson might be comfortable with. As she drove to outer Clement Street, Torrance listened to the local news on KNBR radio. The City was its usual self. A stall on the Bay Bridge, a proposed Muni fare hike, and another controversy about AIDS antibody testing.

The Parentbuilders Foundation was close to where Torrance guessed it would be. She drove past the old three-story frame house, in good repair but somewhat in need of paint, and noted that the Foundation displayed its name (nothing more) on a sign in one of the first-floor bay windows. Luckily, this was a neighborhood where curb parking was not impossible to find. Torrance parked two blocks away and walked back along the row of older residences, trying to guess which of them would be the next to give in to the advance of the commercial district and which would resist to the end.

The house she was looking for had steps leading up to an open entryway, where a variety of doorbells and speaker boxes were located. Small businesses and residential tenants appeared to share the premises. A neat brass plaque above a brass bellpush announced the Parentbuilders Foundation. Torrance rang the bell, and a buzzer announced the unlocking of the inner door. The hall inside was like the house's exterior—basically well-kept, but ever so slightly shabby with age. To the right, a door with a pebble glass upper panel bore the same sign that appeared in the window outside, with a "Please Come In" below it. The Parentbuilders Foundation obviously did not count on a walk-in trade. Those who came to see it were expected to know what it was.

The room Torrance entered through the inner door was typical of a small reception room on which not too much money had been spent. There was a desk with a telephone and a clutter of papers, some shelves with various books and directories, and a seating area with a sofa, two chairs, a table full of popular magazines, and a somewhat dusty dieffenbachia in a pot. A woman appeared. She was in her late forties, wearing a dress that had been well chosen to look fashionable on her large-boned but not overweight figure, with horn-rimmed glasses below thick, dark brown hair that had been cut short by someone who was very good at it.

Torrance smiled her best smile and stepped forward with her hand out. "Mrs. Robusson? I'm so glad to meet you. I'm Mrs. Adams."

Shirley Robusson was obviously unsure why Torrance would claim to be glad to meet her, but she was well-mannered. She invited Torrance into her office, which was more personal and comfortable than the reception area, but not overly so. One wall was decorated with two large collages made up of pictures of smiling couples with babies or young children.

Torrance ignored Shirley Robusson's invitation to sit in one of the comfortable-looking chairs facing her desk and went to stand before one of the collages. "How wonderful!" she said and turned toward Mrs. Robusson. "Are these your success stories?"

For the first time, Shirley Robusson's smile looked genuine. Here was someone who was clearly proud of the job she was doing. "Yes. Yes, these are all children we have helped to unite with parents who want and love them."

"Do you usually assist couples who want children in finding someone who wants to give up a baby, rather than the other way around?"

Shirley Robusson drew herself up and launched into a lecture she had clearly given before. "Virtually no one wants to 'give up' a baby, Mrs. Adams. That is why adoption agencies don't come close to filling the very real need for help in this field. If a young woman is pregnant and feels she is personally unable to raise her child as she would like, she nevertheless wants to be instrumental in choosing her child's future. She wants to assure herself that the people who will raise her child will give her or him a good life. And she wants to feel that this good life is the result of her own efforts. Agencies don't understand that. They want the poor girl to leave it all in their hands, which is the worst thing for her psychologically." Mrs. Robusson paused as if trying to recall what Torrance's question had been. "We teach adopting parents how to understand these things," she went on, "and we show them how to go about finding young women who may want to choose them."

Realizing that both of them were still standing due to her detour toward the picture collage, Torrance took the previously proffered chair, and Shirley

Robusson sat down behind her desk. She was in her environment, clearly happy to be explaining a job she believed in. Torrance decided to plunge ahead.

"I assume that's what you did for the Bowens after they contacted you. I've seen some of the information you provided them with. It seemed very helpful."

Mrs. Robusson was obviously not above responding to flattery. She appeared not to notice that the conversation had gone from general to specific. "Well, yes, we did try to help them as best we could. They were very typical of our couples—so happily married and ready to give a child a wonderful home, but the good Lord had not blessed them with one of their own. I told them that it's couples like them whom God has specially chosen to help young women who make mistakes but have the maturity to know what is best for their babies." She stopped and looked firmly at Torrance. "We deal only with couples, you know. I've heard that some adoption agencies will place with single people and even with people in relationships that should not be observed by children. I think that's disgraceful. Here, we believe in the family. We have helped couples of every race and creed, but we do expect that those who come to us for help will offer the child a *real* family."

Torrance smiled the same smile she would have given a witness whose testimony was necessary to her case, however much she might have disagreed with its content. "The Bowens obviously followed your advice very well."

Shirley Robusson suddenly seemed to recall that the Bowens had died, and her face fell. "Yes, they did. They did. But they weren't meant to have the happiness of that child. It was awful for us to learn about the accident. Awful."

Torrance allowed her the pause she seemed to need to contemplate the tragedy and then gently asked, "Could you explain to me why the baby was more than two weeks old when the Bowens picked him up? That's unusual, isn't it?"

Shirley Robusson looked at Torrance, and something seemed to close off in her face. There was no change that Torrance could have described, but in some way the outgoing expression that had previously been there disappeared. Torrance could feel her own internal tension in response, but she maintained her relaxed look, and continued to look at Shirley Robusson with mere curiosity.

"Do you have a copy of the child's birth certificate?" Mrs. Robusson asked.

"Yes," Torrance responded. And I would bet you perfectly well knew it all along, she added to herself.

"Then you know he was born at his mother's home up there in the

Redwood Country somewhere." Mrs. Robusson waved in a general northerly direction. "His mother saw herself as a child of nature. She wasn't able to organize herself enough to arrange a smooth transition." Suddenly, she seemed to recall that she had previously praised mothers who gave their babies to her Foundation's clients as displaying maturity. She sighed. "For her, of course, given her background, doing as much as she did was extraordinarily responsible. She contacted us after the child was born." A sharp look at Torrance questioned whether she found this statement objectionable.

Torrance only smiled. "I see. The Bowens used your address for anonymity, I assume."

"Yes," Shirley Robusson smiled in return. "It's one of the services we provide."

"The birth mother—Jane Robertson—how did she come to use the services of the Parentbuilders Foundation?"

"Someone referred her, someone who had dealt with us before. I really can't recall . . . ." Torrance had to admire the utterly innocent, vague look that Mrs. Robusson gave her.

She tried one more tack, recalling the physician's name on the birth certificate. "Was it Dr. Moorehead?"

Shirley Robusson didn't so much as blink. "Dr. Moorehead? I don't think I know that name."

"He was the doctor who attended the baby's birth, according to the birth certificate."

"Oh yes! I do recall that now. He *is* familiar with our Foundation, I think. But I really don't remember whether he was the one who told Jane about us, I'm sorry."

Torrance suddenly knew that she would get nothing further from this woman. Except for that one moment of what (tension? fear? concern?), Shirley Robusson had given nothing away. Either she was exactly what she seemed to be—an arranger of private adoptions with somewhat rigid moral views, or she was well coached and prepared to tough out any inquiries. There was nothing further to be learned from her right now about the child the Bowens had been trying to take home.

After extricating herself politely from the conversation and thanking Shirley Robusson for her time, Torrance left the Parentbuilders Foundation office and walked back to her car. She was trying to decide what she really thought of Shirley Robusson. She would not have noticed Derek Thompson watching her, taking careful notes on her arrival and departure, even if she knew what he looked like.

10

When Torrance saw Derek at the door to her office the next day, the first thing she thought was that he was young, attractive, and certainly didn't have a large gut. As she got up and walked across to offer him her hand, she had to suppress a giggle, because she suddenly wondered whether or not he had flat feet. After all, even attractive, physically fit men in their thirties could have flat feet, couldn't they? Because of the incipient giggle, her smile was more friendly than the one she gave most strangers who came to see her.

The second thing she noticed was the funny way he was looking at her—as though he were extraordinarily surprised by her appearance. He stayed at her door where her secretary had left him. Torrance stopped halfway across the room and wasn't sure what to say. The internal grin finally reasserted itself, and she simply stared back.

"Forgive me if I'm coming up with a line you've heard before, but you're forcing me to rewrite my most treasured prejudices about what a private investigator looks like."

Derek tore himself from his reverie. He gave her a small bow and grinned back at her with a slightly crooked grin. "The secret of my success, my dear Ms. Adams, is to fool all but the right people about who I really am. In fact, sometimes I fool myself. Yesterday, I thought I was running surveillance on a suspect, and it seems I was tailing an Assistant Attorney General."

Torrance tilted her head slightly to one side, a look of puzzlement on her face. "Perhaps we had better sit down and go back a few steps in your story." She offered Derek one of the four chairs arranged around a table at one side of her office and sat down there herself, rather than returning behind her desk. "But before we do that, were you able to get the prints?"

Derek held out a manila envelope in which Torrance found a stiff card. On it were the tiny footprints of Patrick Albertson-James.

"Mrs. James had already asked for a set from the hospital, and she kept them," Derek explained. "I'm afraid I told her a bit of a lie. I said I was going to send them to the National Clearinghouse for Missing Children to register Patrick. Since I *will* do that as soon as you return the prints to me—if they don't match, of course—I suppose it wasn't that big a lie after all." He sat back in his chair and smiled that same smile Torrance had seen before, which made him look ever so innocent and guileless.

Torrance studied him for a moment and then returned her attention to the prints. "They seem quite good to me, but that doesn't mean very much. I'm hardly an expert. Are you?"

Derek shook his head. "No, not at reading prints. But you're right, they look like the detail's good. No smudges, and the foot wasn't pressed down so hard that the smaller lines were wiped out."

"I have Tim McDonald standing by Monday to compare these prints with those of the dead baby. He's a baby footprint specialist. Apparently they're a lot harder to do than adult fingerprints." As she said this, Torrance looked at her own fingertips as though scrutinizing their usefulness for prints, then shrugged slightly and ran her hand along the edge of the fingerprint card. "I'll have these prints put on our regular courier. It's overnight, but since it's Friday afternoon, Tim will have these between ten and noon on Monday."

Derek listened with increasing interest. Torrance was knowledgeable and obviously had the confidence of the Attorney General. He smiled at her as she rose, envelope in hand, to buzz her secretary.

"Now then," she said after the envelope had been taken away, "are you finally going to tell me about how you were tailing me?"

"Yes. Well frankly, I'm as curious about that as you are," Derek replied. He paused and looked at his watch. "Have you eaten lunch yet? I think this may require a proper setting."

He was pleased when Torrance readily accepted his invitation. She was a contact worth developing, regardless of how this case turned out. This was his chance to make himself memorable.

Half an hour later they were seated in the upstairs balcony of Kimball's Restaurant just behind the Opera House. Derek was chatting easily. Torrance found herself responding, forgetting her usual strict separation of business and personal matters. After ordering the trout, she mentioned her cats.

"Jade and Buddha?" Derek repeated with some amusement. "Did you name them? You don't strike me as a child of the sixties type. Next you'll tell me that you have two little tow-headed kids named Jason and Snowplow, and I'll have to throw out all *my* preconceptions about state attorneys general."

Torrance saw the mischief in Derek's eyes. "They're Burmese cats," she said in mock defensiveness, "and those are proper Burmese names. Actually, my late husband named them. I would have chosen names more befitting a cat's dignity—like Mungojerrie and Rumpelteazer," she added quickly and was pleased when Derek immediately showed a sign of recognition.

"I always liked the Gumbie Cat best," he replied. "Did you see *Cats* here or in New York?"

"Unfortunately, neither. I seem to have had a hard time finding someone to go out with, ever since Harry died. But I have lots of time to read."

Derek noted that this was the second mention of her late husband. He wondered if this belied the apparent coolness with which Torrance had spoken of the subject. "I'm afraid I don't go out as much as I would like to either, though I have a friend who can usually get me house seats to various plays and reviews if I'm desperate. I can't afford the opera."

"Who can?" Torrance agreed. Her trout suddenly appeared in front of her. She sat back as the waiter served Derek his blackened redfish and topped off their glasses of Chardonnay. The dishes looked and smelled wonderful, and she was pleased that, contrary to her usual practice on a working day, she had let herself be talked into the bottle of wine.

"Actually," said Derek, poking absent-mindedly at his redfish, "I'd bet Buffy Albertson has her own box there." He looked up. "Patrick James's grandmother," he explained.

"Which brings us back to the subject at hand," Torrance smoothly picked up the opportunity to turn the conversation to a more serious tone, wondering as she did so if Derek's cue was deliberate. "So when were you following me, and did I do anything interesting?"

Derek laughed. "Yesterday morning. If the truth were known, I wasn't actually following you, but, yes, you did do something very interesting. You visited the office of the Parentbuilders Foundation on Clement Street."

Torrance raised her eyebrows. She was aware of her heart beating just a little faster. "Were you there because of the James baby kidnapping?" she asked, afraid of the implications of the question and even more afraid of the answer.

"Yes. And you?" Derek replied.

"The I-80 crash," Torrance said quietly. She let out a long breath as Derek's mind raced to the same conclusions as hers. Both suddenly knew that the two or three days before the prints could be matched would be interminable. "How the hell could you wind up getting involved with the Parentbuilders Foundation starting where you did?" Torrance finally asked. "You'd better start at the top and give me the details."

"It seemed strictly a long shot at the time," Derek answered, "but I was fresh out of leads." He then proceeded to tell Torrance what he had pieced together of the details of the kidnapping, his suspicions about the woman on the bicycle, and his conversation with the kid, ending with the bumpersticker on the bicycle woman's car and his subsequent stakeout of the office on Clement. Torrance was fascinated both by his painstaking technique and the incredible implications if the "bicycle mother" was a Parentbuilders Foundation employee. She suddenly realized that she had barely noticed the second half of her meal. Recalling the animation with which Derek had related his tale, she bet that he hadn't tasted much either.

Derek came back to the present just as Torrance did, and both of them decided to make up for their lost attention to food when the waiter produced a dessert tray. They agreed that whereas they almost never ate dessert, the occasion somehow demanded dessert and coffee. Torrance ordered a raspberry-chocolate mousse, while Derek splurged on a black-bottom pie. Immediately abandoning their pledges to pay attention solely to the food, they plunged back into their discussion.

"I can see where you thought the whole thing was terribly farfetched. I don't suppose you've seen the woman with the bicycle coming or going."

"You were the closest one to fitting the description Jeannie gave me. Imagine my disappointment when you drove off in a Porsche instead of a Grand Prix."

"I don't own a bicycle either. I live on Telegraph Hill."

"That's probably just as well. I have a feeling I'd much rather be working with you than against you." Derek meant it but couldn't help noting that Torrance seemed pleased by this remark. "So now it's your turn. What took you to outer Clement?"

"The Bowens got their baby through Parentbuilders. From the baby's birth certificate, I got only some very minimal information, so I was going out to the Foundation's office to see if I could pick up something additional. They must know a great deal about how the baby came to be placed with the Bowens. I'm afraid I didn't get very far, though." Torrance then related her conversations with John Solomon and Shirley Robusson.

"It seems like a pretty neat little bundle," Derek concluded when she was done.

"That's what's wrong with it," Torrance answered. "It's too neat. Too convenient. I'm not saying a supposedly high-class private foundation like

Parentbuilders would get mixed up in a kidnapping, but I can't help feeling that there's something about the birth mother of the Bowens' baby that they'd just as soon hide."

Derek nodded. He and Torrance certainly seemed to think alike, he mused. He liked to find orderly patterns in events, but when things which should be a little disorderly didn't have any loose ends, Derek got suspicious and began to look around for a larger, more hidden solution.

"So now we wait for the prints to be compared," he said. "If they match, then Parentbuilders has a lot of fast explaining to do. If they don't, it's back to square one for both of us. Are there any other possibilities?"

"Just this. There's a fair chance we might not have a good enough print of Patrick to be able to draw a conclusion either way. In that case, I'm not sure what we do then."

"In that case, it appears that our paths will continue to run together for a while. Maybe even long enough to have lunch again." He gave Torrance another slightly crooked grin.

"I guess I could handle that possibility," Torrance replied with a smile and reached into her purse to pay her half of the tab.

11

*M*onday morning found Torrance in a state that was rare for her. She tended to some of her routine work in a halfhearted fashion and kept breaking off to fidget and look at her watch. Finally, at ten o'clock, she took a deep breath, got up, and took a walk around the maze of corridors that led through the quarters of the attorney general's office. There was no point to this walk other than to try to work off her restlessness.

She had spent the weekend trying to make sense of the Baby Doe situation with occasional help (or hindrance?) from Monica. On Saturday, she had driven up to the far side of Mt. Tamalpais and hiked halfway down to Stinson Beach on one of her favorite trails. While she was many miles from the scene of the Patrick James kidnapping, she acknowledged to herself that her choice of hiking trail was probably influenced by the thought that this pilgrimage to the Tamalpais nature area might help her get her thinking in better order.

As she sat in a spot sheltered from both the bright sun and the fresh wind off the ocean, she asked herself for perhaps the hundredth time whether she really believed the child who died with the Bowens was likely to be Patrick James. She looked out at a fishing boat headed north along the coast and leaned back against the trunk of her shade tree. If she couldn't answer that basic question, she couldn't unravel the threads leading up to the final solution. She would just go around and around, uncertain of which assumptions she could legitimately make. She finally got up and started back up the steep slope to where she had left her car, pushing herself to a training pace that startled a squirrel, several birds, and a peacefully strolling couple she met along the way.

When she got to the top, with her heart pounding and her legs and lungs aching, the certainty that "Michael Bowen" was the kidnapped baby suddenly rushed in upon her. She dropped down on a rock bordering the turnout where her Porsche was parked and contemplated this sudden thought while her breathing returned to normal. She was used to exertion bringing sudden clarity to her mind. Was this an example of that phenomenon? Or had she just allowed her desire to focus on a single solution get the better of her?

By the time she was ready to go and get a cold Seven-Up from the cooler in her car, she decided that her insight was genuine. There were too many coincidences, too many funny things that didn't quite fit otherwise. Solomon and the Parentbuilders Foundation *must* have been involved in something they were trying to hide, and the Marin County kidnapping was a perfect fit. So the whole thing would be resolved when she got the footprint report from Sacramento.

On her way home, Torrance thought about Derek Thompson and the effect this result would have on his case. She rather liked Derek. He was bright, attractive, and hadn't been the slightest bit sexist toward her. Nor had he been intimidated by her title, although he knew she was near the top of her office's power structure. She met very few men who dealt with her simply as another human being without automatically subjecting her either to condescension or to fawning.

If she had to tell Derek that the footprints matched, it would bother her, knowing he would have to tell his client that he had been unable to find her baby alive. The death had nothing to do with him, of course, the child had died accidentally before Derek was hired. But that wouldn't make the truth any easier. And Derek would associate her unpleasant message with the messenger. He'd thank her for her help and wish she'd never gotten involved in his case. The thought made her unexpectedly sad. There had been something so exhilarating about their lunch, putting their heads together to try to figure it all out; she really hoped they could go on working—no, *thinking*—together.

It was these thoughts that went through her mind again and made her restless on Monday. This is the classic approach-avoidance conflict, she thought. I want to be right, but I don't want to have to tell Derek I was right. She finished her round of pacing and returned to her desk to wait for Tim McDonald's call.

It came in typical fashion. She just returned a call from a legislative staffer whose goodwill the Attorney General needed when her incoming line began to ring. She had to stay with her call and let her secretary answer. So what she got was a brief message carried in to her: "Tim McD. says it's definitely not the same kid."

Torrance was stunned. This couldn't be true. She had been so absolutely sure that the facts fit together somehow: that Patrick Albertson-James was kidnapped in order to be handed to the Bowens as a child available for adoption, and that his fictitious mother had "disappeared." She went to her window and stared out at the Plaza without seeing it. Had she been all wrong?

But the certainty that had come to her on Saturday was still there. She remained sure that her case and Derek's were connected. She must have come up with too simple a solution. There was obviously more to this than they had come across so far. What she wasn't sure yet, but the existence of a connection was as firm in her mind now as it had ever been.

She called back Tim McDonald just to be sure that there was no mistake. There wasn't. The two sets of prints were both clear and utterly incompatible. No answer for her, and no answer for Derek.

Torrance dialed Derek's number. She felt tongue-tied, not knowing whether to apologize for her hunch being wrong or to express pleasure that Derek did not have to give his client bad news. As it turned out, Derek sensed her ambivalence at once and saved her from her struggle.

"You must be trying to tell me that the prints don't match."

"Well—yes, I am. I didn't know it was that obvious."

"Simple human nature. Us famous detectives know how to take advantage of it every time. If you'd had an answer that meant real news, you'd have told me fast."

Torrance realized that he was right and laughed. "If you find me that easy to figure out, I'm glad we're on the same side." More seriously, she went on. "I don't consider this the last word on our discussion, Derek. I thought about this a lot this weekend, and I came to the conclusion that Solomon and Parentbuilders are definitely hiding something. I was sure that it is connected to the child you're looking for, and somehow I'm still sure of that. It's just not as simple as we thought it was."

"Far be it from me to criticize someone's instincts, Torrance, but are you sure you aren't refusing to give up on a theory you've become attached to? God knows, I've done it often enough myself to know how easy it is."

Torrance recognized his attempt to take the sting out of his expression of doubt and responded less defensively than she might have. "I've gone through all the facts over and over again, and there isn't any way I can convince myself that the case is totally straightforward. And if something funny was going on with the Bowen baby, there are probably other funny things going on, too. You tracked down that Parentbuilders bumpersticker at the scene of your kidnapping. It has to mean something. I don't believe that someone from that outfit happened to be in the neighborhood when a newborn was kidnapped. There just aren't very many kidnappings of newborns. Why should I believe in a coincidence like that?"

Derek sighed. "I don't know. I bought your idea before. The timing was perfect; the method seemed possible; there was a clear motive. But now that we know the two babies weren't the same, what makes it fit?"

"I'll tell you what makes it fit. You have a kidnapped newborn who wasn't taken by his father, and there's been no ransom demand. Nor, thank God, has anyone found a body. That tells me that the most likely explanation is that someone simply wanted a baby—to keep. I can see two choices: the kidnapper is a disturbed woman who wanted it for herself, or the kidnapper wanted to sell it. Babies are worth a lot of money these days—one of the side effects of the legalization of abortion. So, can we tell which of the two choices is more likely? I think we can. From everything you've said, from everything you believe, this kidnapping was very well executed. It was meticulously planned. That's not the kind of pattern I'd expect from a disturbed woman. She's more likely to grab and run on impulse. The amount of planning that went into this is probably beyond her. Are you with me so far?"

"Yes, I am. But I still don't see how that connects your case to mine."

"Look at it this way. Kidnapping children for adoption isn't a very common crime. I can't think of a single instance that's ever become known in California. So what are the chances that there are two outfits doing it in the same place at the same time?"

"Wait a minute! Aren't you assuming the solution in order to prove it? How do we know that your case has anything to do with kidnapping at all?"

"Well, maybe not kidnapping, but definitely something fishy, which comes to the same thing. I don't believe in two separate adoptions rackets. If Solomon is selling illegally acquired babies, I'll bet you Patrick's kidnapping somehow fed into his system." Torrance suddenly realized that she had not spoken with the circumspection that was required when you had absolutely no proof. She didn't normally pour out her unsubstantiated suppositions to someone who was virtually a stranger. If Derek were to quote her in the wrong place (such as to a newspaper), she would never see the end of the resulting trouble. "Derek," she went on in a suddenly subdued tone, "I hope you heard all the 'ifs' in what I just said. I'm not telling you that I know any of this."

"Torrance, you don't have to worry about talking to me. I make my living by protecting my sources. Even if I didn't care about getting you in trouble, I wouldn't want to waste you as a resource. So your speculations are safe with me." Derek's voice was light and joking, but Torrance could tell that he meant to reassure her. All the same, she had to get to know him better before being too indiscreet, she thought.

"Well. I've given you my arguments. That's all there is. I think there's more to be found by tracing the background of the Bowen baby. So that's what I'm going to do next. Do you want to stay involved?"

"I don't know." Derek paused, considering his options. "What exactly do you see as the next step?"

"There's only one choice. I have to go talk to the doctor who says he attended the child's birth. In Fernbridge, of all places."

"Fernbridge? I've never heard of it."

"It's just south of Eureka, where the road for Cape Mendocino takes off on Route 101. There's a lot of back country around there. I haven't been through that area in years, but if I remember it correctly, it isn't as attractive to tourists as the parts of 101 with access to the ocean."

"That sounds like one hell of a drive."

"Actually, I was thinking of trying to get on a plane to Eureka. I don't know if I can still get a seat tomorrow, but I thought I'd try."

"Have you called the doctor for an appointment?"

"No, I haven't. I thought that dropping in on him would be more effective. I did check to see that he actually exists; there does seem to be a doctor by that name up there."

Derek didn't say anything for a minute or two. What did he have to gain from finding the origins of the Bowen kid? Nothing. It couldn't possibly lead to Patrick. But as he went over what Torrance had said about the chance of two similar rackets, he had to admit that it made sense to him. Besides, what if Torrance was right and she went off all by herself and cracked his case for him. He wasn't sure he liked the idea of explaining to Marguerite that he had turned down an offer to be there. He sighed. "I can't say I buy your whole theory, Torrance, but the only choices I have right now are to park outside of the Parentbuilders offices for God knows how long or to follow your train of thought. Would you mind if I went to Eureka with you?"

Torrance smiled at the telephone. "Not at all. I'll be glad to have you along, even if you aren't willing to give my ideas your unqualified endorsement. I'm planning on a day up there, but I thought I'd take an overnight bag just in case things get interesting. O.K.?"

Derek thought he might be slightly crazy, but he agreed. When Torrance offered to have her secretary try to get plane tickets, he accepted. As he began to arrange his other affairs so that he could be away, he was still unsure whether he had allowed himself to be swayed by her persuasive style rather than by reason or logic. Maybe he had been sold the middle tower of the Golden Gate Bridge by a person who made a living selling her point of view.

His thoughts about Torrance suddenly became more personal. He found himself liking her—a lot. She was the type of coolly competent, professional woman who appealed to him. No bubblehead to worry about, he thought.

But the idea of spending one or more days with her in some remote town made him slightly nervous. He hoped that his judgment of Torrance was accurate—that her interest was in the job, not in him. Derek hated awkward situations and felt that he didn't always handle them very gracefully.

Oh well, he thought as he picked up the phone again, at least it'll be an interesting trip. Maybe I can pick up some tips on bridge-selling.

With a good piece of the afternoon left, Derek found that he had done all he needed to do before leaving for Fernbridge. He didn't have enough time left to start on something unrelated to the case, but he knew that if he sat around and went over the James kidnapping, he'd get grumpy. He thought about it and decided that there was still some action he could take by himself. He'd promised Marguerite that Patrick would be listed with the National Clearinghouse for Missing Children. Even though Patrick's prints were on their way to Sacramento, he did have a good photo of the child that Marguerite had given him. He decided to list Patrick as missing.

After a few minutes of rummaging around in the phone book, Derek was on his way to an organization that described itself as a local affiliate of a national missing children's center. The affiliate's office was in an upscale, gentrified building on Fillmore, less than a block from Union Street, in the heart of high-rent chic. The sign on their door was a large brass plaque. Feeling his natural cynicism rise, Derek vowed that he would keep an open mind.

He was met by a young and attractive woman as he entered a small reception area. She hung earnestly on Derek as he explained his reason for coming. She had the amateur actress' habit of expressing a strong emotional response to every shift in Derek's story, punctuated by exclamations and meaningless syllables. She wanted to let him know that she was listening attentively.

Derek finished his story. She registered a little surprise as she realized that he had stopped talking and that some kind of action was called for on her part. She closed her mouth thoughtfully for a moment and said that Derek should probably see the Director, Mr. Thomas, himself. Derek noted irritably that she probably could have made that determination when he began his story, but he recalled his vow and quickly put the thought out of his mind.

In a few seconds, Derek was ushered into Mr. Thomas's office, and all of his vows crumbled. The office was spacious and well-appointed, with large leather wing chairs facing an even larger desk. About the perimeter were huge, professionally-done displays of missing children: smiling faces from old photos, newspaper ads and posters, some printed over with the large red stenciled letters "FOUND," and shelves full of milk cartons and shopping bags. On one side was a tall display with statistics, charts, and maps, obviously suitable for television visuals. In the middle of all this stood a tall, lean, good-looking man in his early forties, who strode forward to meet Derek with his long arm outstretched and the intense smile of the believer among his brethren. Derek noted wrily how much Mr. Thomas resembled the well-known state legislator who had recently been making his reputation by putting his name on missing children legislation and who had started the milk carton and shopping bag campaigns by very publicly calling together the top executives of California's biggest supermarket chains.

"Mr. Derek Thompson? I'm Bradford Thomas, Northern California Coordinator of the Missing Children Coalition. My friends call me Tom. Cindy here tells me that you're a private investigator." The statement hung there like an accusation.

Derek found it hard not to back away. He toyed with the idea of causing a scene and ruefully dismissed it. He had his client to think about.

"That's right, Tom—if I can call you that. I have a problem and I need your help. I've got a distraught young mother over in Marin whose newborn kid was snatched in broad daylight, and the police are helpless."

That pushed the right buttons. "That's a tragedy. That's a tragedy," Thomas repeated. "This is a national scourge, and the helplessness of the authorities to stop it is the reason we have had to form the National Clearinghouse and its affiliated networks. The utter uselessness and helplessness of the taxpayer-funded authorities in the face of this epidemic amounts to nothing less than a national scandal."

Derek was having a hard time remembering that they were talking about missing children, but he advanced bravely. "Well, Tom, that's why I'm here. I don't know how well your system works for an infant since to me they all look pretty much the same, but I do have a good picture of him, and I can get you his footprints if that will help. Is there anything your outfit can do?"

Tom Thomas shifted into high gear. "My dear Derek, we do everything that can be done! Of course we could do much more if the authorities and the law gave us better cooperation and better tools to work with." Thomas then launched into an outline of the various levels of "exposure" they could give Patrick James, in much the same way that a salesman would pitch the options for a new car. Most important, Thomas said, baby Patrick would be in their national computer bank of missing children, along with his footprints, once they were provided.

Of course, Marguerite Albertson-James's name, address and donor status would be in someone's computer too, Derek thought cynically, hoping that his face did not betray his thoughts. The speech and pitch over, he patiently answered Tom's questions while Tom filled out their "Data Questionnaire." Some of this information, Derek was told, would go into the Clearinghouse's national computer bank of missing children, and some information was needed "so as to get to know a little better the folks who turn to us in time of need."

That done, and Patrick's photo duly turned over, Derek extracted himself from Tom's office as quickly as he could. Back on the street, he took a deep breath and cleared his mind. He gazed up at strips of fog streaming overhead. Eureka was looking better all the time.

12

*E*arly the next morning, Torrance and Derek met in the PSA terminal at the San Francisco airport. Torrance's secretary had performed her usual miracle and found two adjoining seats on a plane bound for Oregon with a stop in Eureka. The Boeing 727 was one of the better choices for the short flight, preferable, in Torrance's view, to one of the small commuter planes which could occasionally give their passengers an exciting tour of the local air pockets.

The plane took off over the bay and headed north toward San Francisco. There was a lingering morning fog, but it lay in capricious patches, and for a while Derek and Torrance were both caught up in watching the familiar sights—glimpses of the sparkling bay and boats, the Bay Bridge resting on Yerba Buena Island, the hills and towers of The City itself, then Alcatraz, a piece of the Golden Gate Bridge, and the Marin headlands sheltering Sausalito and its houseboats. Torrance tried unsuccessfully to point out her house to Derek and, as Mt. Tamalpais came into view, Derek tried equally unsuccessfully to show her Buffy Albertson's home and the fateful trail that ran past it. By the time the plane left Marin County behind and flew northwest over seemingly endless ridges covered with varied patches of trees, shrubs, and buff-colored grasslands, the two of them had re-established their earlier easy camaraderie.

After they examined the column of smoke marking an uncontrolled brush fire which had been in the news the last few days, Derek turned to Torrance and leaned back in his seat. "O.K., now—how about letting me in on your plans once we get to Eureka?"

Torrance also leaned back and gathered her thoughts. "I reserved a rental car at the airport. I'm planning to pick it up and drive to Fernbridge. Once I get there, I'll look for the doctor whose name was on the birth certificate. Since I don't have any idea what information may be out there, I'll have to play it pretty much by ear." She turned to look at Derek. "I thought that initially you could just ride along with me. If we get too many leads for one person, we can always split up." The tentative grin that went along with the last statement betrayed her disbelief in the overwhelming likelihood of such an outcome. Derek agreed both with the plan and with the unspoken doubts. At least if he didn't have to rent his own car, his expenses wouldn't be totally out of line. He didn't voice this last sentiment to Torrance though, since he didn't want to let her know how much he doubted there was a connection between their two cases.

Instead, he brought the conversation back to their earlier banter about Torrance's house, which they had tried so hard to identify. He admitted he admired the neat rows of restored Victorians that characterized several San Francisco neighborhoods. "I have some friends who have spent a lot of time and money restoring one particularly nice one facing Golden Gate Park. I'm jealous of them whenever I go there. I'm not quite rich enough to be able to afford a whole house to myself in The City."

"Neither am I. On my salary I can barely afford to keep the place up. But my husband was a doctor—an oncologist. He added a good pile to the family income. Besides that, he came from a pretty rich family. Harrison James Adams—it sounds very Boston Brahmin, doesn't it? The 'James' was a family last name, too, incidentally, nothing as plebeian as a first name for the Adamses." She laughed and looked slightly sheepish. "I guess my prejudice is showing. I feel a little guilty for finding the whole family rather hard to take, since I was more than pleased that Harry inherited a little of great-aunt Dorothea's money and used it to have work done on our house when we first bought it."

"You don't have to apologize to me for not getting along with relatives," Derek responded. "There's a whole group of mine I find hard to be in the same room with."

"Your own, rather than in-laws?"

"Oh yes, all my very own. I've never been married, so I'm safe from in-laws."

"Well, that's both good and bad. No in-laws but no second wage-earner either. Since you're pleading poverty, I assume you don't have a rich live-in lover."

Derek gave her a questioning glance and saw only humor on her face. She caught his look and shook her head slightly, her eyes turning serious. "I'm not prying, Derek."

He shook his head in response and smiled. "No, I shouldn't have thought you were. And your diagnosis is correct. No current live-in, rich or otherwise. I pay the rent all by myself. I had a—roommate—up until a few months ago, who helped with the expenses. Things have been a little tighter since then."

"If you're able to afford a totally useless trip to Eureka, your firm must have had some favorable growth."

Derek gave Torrance a startled look and found her smiling at him questioningly, her head tilted to one side. Dammit, he thought, she's been reading my mind! Then he had to laugh at being so plainly caught. "I didn't want to let on how little I believed in this trip. How'd you figure it out?"

"If you really believed we were going to find something, you'd be sitting there speculating about what it was. Since you've been sitting there talking about everything else but, I concluded that your faith in me is severely limited." As Derek started to protest, Torrance smiled, putting a hand on his arm. "You don't have to worry about offending me. I'll just have more fun being right." Her face fell into a comically pained expression, "Assuming the whole thing doesn't fall apart the way you expect it will."

Just then the sound of the plane's engine changed, announcing the approach to Eureka. The 727 left the coast and flew in an arc out over the ocean, banking and descending toward a bluff north of the coastal plain on which Eureka and Arcata could be seen. It flew straight at the precipitous coastline and touched the ground almost immediately after reaching land. Before they had quite recovered from the suddenness of the descent, passengers for Eureka-Arcata were invited to deplane.

Torrance and Derek emerged from the plane into a sunny morning chilled by a fresh wind off the ocean. Huddled against it, they crossed to the terminal and approached the Hertz counter. Torrance's reservation got her a sporty little Ford with a stick shift which obviously pleased her. Derek thought it was a lot smaller than what he would have chosen, but told himself not to look a gift horse from the state in the mouth.

Torrance had to drive, of course, since she was on official business and had charged the car to her office. Derek sat back and watched as they pulled onto U.S. 101 south to Eureka. He had never been in this part of California before and found it very different from the coast further south. Route 101 was a freeway here and swept quickly through Arcata, a town that owed its fortunes and decline to the state of the building industry and thus of the lumber market. South of Arcata, he noted the turnoff for Samoa, a town on the spit of land sheltering Humboldt Bay from the north.

Torrance told him about her confusion at a news report she had once heard on the local radio about "two fishermen from Samoa" who were missing and were being sought by the Coast Guard near Point Reyes. "I was picturing these poor South Sea Islanders who had drifted across the Pacific Ocean. It took a long time before it came to me that they meant Samoa, California."

They reached the edge of Eureka, where the freeway ended. The road ran through town on two parallel one-way streets, making its way past a profusion of motels, restaurants, fast-food shops and gas stations, with a series of traffic lights keeping the traffic to a crawl. Derek imagined that this would be an unpleasant bottleneck during the summer tourist season. It was bad enough now, he thought. At a stop light, he rolled down a window and breathed the distinctive smell of Eureka—a combination of wet seaweed, fish and lumber, overlaid with traffic fumes and a chemical smell which hinted of paper production.

Torrance laughed at his wrinkled nose, and pointed to a rather ugly modern building coming up on their left which seemed taller than anything else around. "That's the courthouse—also the county clerk, county recorder, county sheriff, and anything else we might need. You might as well know where it is in case we have to split up." Derek figured he could easily find the building again, but he made a note of the cross streets from force of habit.

Shortly thereafter Eureka ended, and the road became a freeway again. They sped past the smokestacks of the Pacific Gas and Electric Company's Humboldt Bay Power Plant and began to cross lush meadows bordered by eucalyptus and cypress with dairy cattle grazing here and there. A pronounced eucalyptus smell freshened the air. To the right, between 101 and the ocean, appeared Fields Landing, a total contrast to Eureka. It was a small, neat town of well-kept frame houses with no commercial development in sight. Derek began to like the view more now and said so.

"There are some very nice parts of Eureka," Torrance countered. "You just don't get to see them from the main thoroughfare. Don't be too down on it yet."

After passing more fields and the campus of the College of the Redwoods to their left, the highway began to climb. From the top of a rise there was a sudden view of the wooded hills of Cape Mendocino behind a surprisingly large flat area lying along the Eel River estuary. Just as the view opened up, an exit sign for Fernbridge and Ferndale appeared. Torrance felt a surge of excitement as she steered the car off the freeway and down a hill to a small cluster of buildings.

After one look at Fernbridge, she realized that she would have to pull off the road and stop to avoid leaving it before she had seen it. At first it looked as though there were no homes at all. They passed a restaurant set off by itself outside of town, and saw the Humboldt Creamery (a large dairy plant) which shared one side of the road and railroad tracks with the Barnes

Tractor and Equipment Company, while a store featuring fishing tackle, beer, wine, groceries and videocassette rentals was most prominent on the other side. Behind the dairy, the bridge which presumably gave Fernbridge its name led across the Eel River and according to a sign to Ferndale.

Torrance pulled off the road near the grocery store and they got out of the car. "You actually have an address in this town?" Derek asked, his voice reflecting sincere doubt.

Torrance reached into her purse and handed him a photocopy of Russell John Robertson's birth certificate. The attending physician's address was a number on Fernbridge Street, Fernbridge, California. The mother's address was c/o General Delivery in Ferndale. "Do you think this is Fernbridge Street?" Torrance asked, looking to the left and right.

Derek shrugged, "It doesn't seem there are too many other choices, unless the town continues on the far side of the bridge." This seemed unlikely to both of them, since they could see only widely spaced farms in that direction. Fernbridge Street ought to be right here near the little sign announcing the town's name, the only clue to the fact that they had arrived at their destination.

Trying to find a number on the store or one of the adjoining buildings, Torrance and Derek walked away from the car. It was only then that they saw a lone street sign at what first appeared to be a driveway but was really a narrow street running up a steep hill toward the freeway. A few more steps brought them close enough to see that the sign said "Fernbridge Street." Not only that, their walk had given them a clear view up the hill, where they saw six or eight houses of varying sizes.

Torrance gave Derek a little bow. "Eureka!—or Fernbridge, as the case may be," she announced and laughed at the expected pained expression on Derek's face. They returned to the car and made their way up Fernbridge Street.

The street was even narrower than it had looked from below. Not quite two lanes wide, it wound up the hill, leaving Torrance unsure of where the street went and where driveways turned off it. But just as she slowed down in confusion at another turn, Derek pointed to a mailbox ahead. It had the number they were looking for painted on its side, and it went with a smallish stucco house set in a well-tended patch of garden. A car standing in the driveway was a promising sign that the house was occupied.

Torrance parked in the little patch of driveway left free, and she and Derek approached the house. A neat sign below the doorbell said "MacDonald." Derek raised an eyebrow. "The doctor's name was Moorehead, wasn't it?" Torrance nodded as she rang the bell, "Nothing to do but ask."

A friendly-looking woman in her forties, dressed in a calico dress and wiping her hands on an apron, answered the door. She was obviously surprised to see someone she didn't know. "Oh, I'm sorry," she exclaimed, smoothing down the apron with still-damp hands, "I was expecting a neighbor. I'm in the middle of making a batch of tomato sauce for our church supper." She faltered, not knowing how to cope with strangers.

Torrance tried to help her out. "I'm so sorry to bother you when you should be tending to your cooking. If you need to run back in and make sure nothing burns while you talk to us, we'll be perfectly happy to wait here for a few minutes."

The woman smiled and tucked a stray strand of hair behind an ear. "Oh no, please, do come in and sit down. I'll just be a moment." She stepped back to let Torrance and Derek into a colonial-style living room which was barely separated from the front hall. Like the woman herself, it was cheery and comfortable. The two seated themselves while their hostess returned to a bright kitchen which could be seen across a dining area and a pass-through counter. She stirred and rattled dishes for a few moments, clicked off stove burners, and took off her apron before returning to the living room. She sat down across from her visitors and smiled.

"It's safe to talk now. No disasters from the kitchen will interrupt us." She looked at Torrance and Derek, trying to gauge why they would be visiting her. "I don't get very many strangers here. It's not the easiest place to find."

Torrance smiled and acknowledged that it had been a challenge to locate the house. "We were looking for Dr. Albert Moorehead but we noticed that wasn't the name on the door. Has he moved?"

For the first time, the woman seemed less than pleased with their presence. She looked nervous, perhaps suddenly afraid of who they were. Torrance thought that this was the time for introductions.

"I'm sorry—we just started talking, and you don't even know who we are. I'm Torrance Adams and this is Derek Thompson. I'm here on behalf of the state trying to get some information from Dr. Moorehead about a baby he delivered who later died in an accident. There have been some technical problems with positive identification."

As Torrance spoke, the woman looked more worried and then more relieved. "I see. Well, I'm Edna MacDonald, Dr. Moorehead's sister. He did live with me for a short time, but we really don't have a lot of room to put someone up permanently. He's rented a house in Ferndale and lives there now." She seemed somehow apologetic that her brother was not living with her in the neat little home, which was undoubtedly too small for more than two people.

"Did he live with you in mid-August?" Torrance asked, recalling the date on Russell's birth certificate.

Mrs. MacDonald thought for a moment and nodded. "Yes, that was just before he moved to Ferndale." She looked up with an anxious expression. "He did tell the state he moved. I don't understand why you're looking for him here."

Torrance pulled the photocopy of Russell's birth certificate from her purse and handed it to the woman. "We just went by this, Mrs. MacDonald. Since so little time has gone by, I thought it would be most helpful to start here. I didn't check on Dr. Moorehead's current address with the Medical Board. The County Medical Society told me that he's listed locally."

Mrs. MacDonald nodded and handed back the birth certificate after looking at it for a moment. "You're not from the Medical Board, then?"

"No, we're not. I'm from the Attorney General's Office, assisting the sheriff of the county where this baby was killed in a traffic accident."

Mrs. MacDonald seemed strangely relieved by this disclosure. Torrance wondered why she had displayed such disquietude at the thought of the Board of Medical Quality Assurance. It was a loose thread that she would have to follow up on later. In the meantime, she got Dr. Moorehead's current address from Mrs. MacDonald, and she and Derek said polite goodbyes.

As Torrance was backing the little car out of the MacDonald driveway, Derek looked at her and said, "She doesn't like the B.M.Q.A."

"You noticed that too? I thought it was fear as much as dislike. Maybe the good doctor's had a run-in with the board. I should have thought to check."

"We'll do it later. Ferndale first, I think. Maybe Mrs. MacDonald won't scare the rabbit out of its hole before we get there."

13

*T*orrance drove slowly as she crossed the long bridge across the Eel River, and both she and Derek looked down at the clear turquoise water. "The Eel is one of my favorite rivers," Torrance said. "I've camped along it several times and rafted some stretches of it. It's beautifully clear and runs through some wonderful redwood groves."

Derek tried to imagine himself rafting this river and camping in redwood groves. While theoretically he could see its attractions, he had no practical experience to rely on. His life had always been tied to one city or another, with little time spent in anything resembling wilderness. Even the kind of country they were now crossing was strange to him—lush green meadows with dairy cows.

As they passed a large farmhouse that appeared on their right, Torrance drew his attention to it. "Look at that house, Derek. It's Victorian gingerbread all over. I can't remember ever seeing an area before where the farmhouses look like this. Eureka has a lot of Victorians in its old town, but I didn't expect to see buildings like that out here."

Derek looked at the other farms they passed and noted that many had a distinctly Victorian appearance. As their car approached what seemed to be the edge of a town, a large billboard announced "Victorian Ferndale."

"I had no idea this was out here!" Torrance exclaimed. "Why would there be a Victorian town this far from anywhere?" And a genuine Victorian town it surely was, there couldn't be any doubt about that. The large house coming up on their right wasn't something that had been built recently to attract the tourists.

Only a little way into town, a sign appeared pointing to a historical marker on their left. Torrance pulled the car over. "I have to look, Derek," she explained.

"Weren't we on our way to do something terribly important?" Derek asked mildly as he followed her out of the car.

"Don't give me a hard time. I have to find out what this strange town is all about. It'll only take two minutes."

Torrance quickly crossed the street and walked through the grass of a small park to a bronze plaque set under a little bandstand-like covering. Derek followed, shaking his head but smiling in spite of himself. He looked at the marker over Torrance's shoulder. The plaque told them that Ferndale was founded in 1852 to provide dairy products to a growing San Francisco. Known as "Cream City," it was a transportation and shipping center in the late nineteenth and early twentieth centuries.

Torrance turned around with a puzzled expression. "Do you think they shipped milk out of here by sea? There wasn't a railroad up here in the 1850s, was there?" Derek shrugged and shook his head, and Torrance laughed. She put a hand on his shoulder and turned him back to their car. "O.K., we're on our way to the good doctor's house. No more history lessons."

In spite of her promise, Torrance was focusing mainly on the architectural treat presented by Ferndale as she drove on down Main Street. On the left was the First Congregational Church with its pointed spire, and opposite it was the Shaw House Inn, white with blue and white gingerbread trim, hidden in a lush garden. A bit beyond it was the Ferndale Inn, another bed and breakfast place, this one in yellow and white. Beyond that, there were several blocks of uniform Victorian buildings, a number of them with false fronts facing the street.

A building on the right that Torrance particularly admired held a store called "The Gazebo". It was pale green, decorated in ornately carved wood painted beige, tan, brown, dark green and gold. The decorations were most intricate surrounding the second floor's twin bay windows. Competing with it across the street was a pink building with deep mauve trim that held "Gepetto's Nostalgic Gifts," its picture windows filled with puppets, dolls and other delights.

Torrance was sorry she had to turn left off Main Street, following Edna MacDonald's instructions. But when she turned right again on Berding Street, she was rewarded by the sight of the Gingerbread Mansion, an extraordinarily ornate residence aptly named. Even Derek joined in her exclamations. As they continued down Berding Street, however, the houses became smaller and less well kept, although mostly still old. Derek spotted Dr. Moorehead's house first—a plain cottage in need of paint and repairs, surrounded by a neglected garden. Torrance parked across the street, and she and Derek walked up to the front door.

There was a small hand-lettered sign tacked next to a bellpush, with the words "Albert Moorehead, M.D." and "Please Enter" beneath that. The office hours were listed as ten to noon and two to four. "Busy man, isn't he," Derek muttered. Torrance looked at her watch. It was 12:10.

"Well," she said, "I wonder if he's ready for us. But then again, are we ready for him?" She gave Derek a quick smile and pushed at the door.

The door was unlocked and opened into what could have passed as a reception and waiting area, although it had no place for a receptionist to sit. It looked more like someone's front living room and gave the impression that perhaps it did double duty as both. There was no one in sight.

Derek and Torrance looked around without saying anything. The room had a musty, stale odor, as though the air had not been changed for many months. The furniture was sparse and almost shabby. A well-worn sofa with a slightly broken back leaned against one wall, its cover the obvious victim of too many hours of sun, too many spills, and God only knew what else. A small end-table, an overstuffed chair almost in poorer shape than the sofa, and two decidedly uncomfortable straight-backed chairs completed the picture. There wasn't even a plant to soften the dismal assemblage.

Torrance turned to Derek who was looking at the walls where only one object, a cheap print of a redwood grove, broke the colorless monotony. "Hmmm," he said as he returned her look, "he doesn't even bother to hang up his license." He began to crane his neck toward a door which stood partly open at the back of the room, trying to see whether he could get a view without pushing it open. Just then Torrance noticed a little bell sitting on the end table, walked over to it, and rang it sharply.

There was a hint of sound from the back room and then silence. After a moment, Torrance rang the bell again. "Maybe he's not here. . ." she started to say when suddenly through the slightly open door they heard several deep emphysematous coughs, rich with phlegm, and the unmistakable sounds of someone rising and coming to the door.

A short, owl-faced man peered out of the back room. He quickly stepped through the door and just as quickly, almost guiltily, closed it behind him, but not before Derek had caught a glimpse of litter on the floor and a table seemingly covered with ash trays, glasses and bottles. As the door closed, the musty odor got stronger for a moment, as if the back room were the source of the staleness they had felt.

The man looked plainly startled and glanced back and forth from Derek to Torrance.

"Are you Dr. Moorehead?" Torrance asked.

"Yes. . ." he answered slowly. "Can I help you?" His initial alarm faded into confusion, as he recognized that Derek and Torrance did not fit the mold of those who were likely to come to him as patients.

"I'm Torrance Adams and this is Derek Thompson. I'm an Assistant Attorney General working on an adoption matter. You delivered the baby boy involved in this adoption, and we'd just like to ask you a few questions about him, that's all. Derek doesn't work for the state; he's been retained by a private party."

Dr. Moorehead's face ran the full gamut of emotions during Torrance's statement. Derek noted his sudden rigidity when Torrance mentioned she was an Assistant Attorney General and the immediate relaxation when she mentioned an adoption. When he heard her say that he had delivered the boy, however, he straightened and his face closed in on itself. Derek didn't know if this was the result of a sudden wariness or simply the assumption of a professional demeanor now that there were to be professional questions in need of answers.

"Certainly. Why don't you sit down?" Dr. Moorehead replied after a long pause, pointing at the sofa. Torrance, her mind working much like Derek's, wondered whether his deliberate hesitation stemmed only from a long professional habit of appearing wise to his patients.

She sat down on the sofa, while Dr. Moorehead took the one chair that was upholstered and cushioned, with a familiarity that marked it as his regular spot. Derek, instead of sitting on the couch as directed, took one of the stiff-backed chairs to the side, from where he could study the doctor unobserved.

As Torrance began to explain about the accident involving the Bowens and the baby they had planned to adopt, Derek studied the doctor. Dr. Moorehead's owlish head was surrounded by a circle of thin wisps of gray hair. He was about five feet four and stout through the lower rib cage (was swollen a better word?), but his arms and hands were slender, almost delicate...effeminate. He kept his hands folded in front of him, and would slowly and delicately bring one up to his mouth every few minutes when he would again produce that rich cough. On one of those occasions, Derek noted that his fingertips were yellowed with nicotine, and his nails looked as though they had not been cleaned.

But it was his face that caught Derek's interest. Dr. Moorehead looked at Torrance with the remnant of a well-practiced professional calmness, almost a total passivity, his lips curled up ever so slightly (and ever so kindly) at their edges. He sat with his head inclined, so that he could look down at his questioner (and surely at his patients) through half-lidded eyes below thin and delicate raised eyebrows. But his eyes, like his hands, betrayed him. Derek noticed at once the deep redness of their rims and the yellow rheuminess in the corners, which the doctor had either forgotten to wipe off in private or had ceased to be conscious of.

His survey completed, Derek noted that Torrance had moved on from telling the background of their visit to asking questions. Dr. Moorehead was proving to be rather difficult. His answers came about as quickly as those of a C.I.A. spokesman being interviewed on national television.

At first he was insufferably vague about whether he had ever had a patient named Jane Robertson who gave birth to a boy named Russell John. Derek was sure that the confidentiality of the doctor-patient relationship was about to be raised, when Torrance opened her purse and drew out the birth certificate she had earlier shown to Edna MacDonald. "Dr. Moorehead," she said firmly, "I'm not asking you whether Jane Robertson was your patient. This birth certificate says she was. Is this your signature as the attending physician?"

Moorehead looked at the document and paused. "Yes," he said, trying for firmness and finality.

"So she was your patient for the delivery?"

Again there was a pause, followed by a weighty "Yes" and a cough.

"Can you tell us where she lives?"

This was obviously too large a step. There was an even longer pause, a more thoughtful demeanor. "I don't think she has a permanent residence of any sort."

"She must have given you some kind of address."

Another pause. "Ah...yes, she did. It was very vague."

Torrance tilted her head to one side and raised her eyebrows. "A temporary address? One where she was staying until she had the child?"

Moorehead seemed to like the question. Derek wondered briefly whether he saw it as an opportunity for evasion. "She was a hippie," the doctor said meaningfully. "She lived with other hippies. We get that sort around here."

Torrance's face was wonderfully sympathetic, and she leaned forward slightly. "But I'm sure you know where they stay when they come," she said with a hint of approval in her voice.

Moorehead paused nevertheless. "Ahh..." he started again and paused. "There is a place they stay sometimes." He stopped and looked at the ceiling. Finally he gave Torrance another below-the-lids look. "Sanctuary House, they call it. A big house full of hippies. On the road toward Centerville."

"Was Jane Robertson staying there when she came to see you?"

"Well...ahh...as to that...I can't totally be sure. But I do seem to recall she was."

Torrance suddenly looked firmer. "Do you have her medical records?"

Once more, Derek expected an appeal to confidentiality, but again it didn't come. There was a cough and a frown. Dr. Moorehead reached for the birth certificate, which had remained on the table next to him, and stared at it for a while. "I was living at my sister's house then. In Fernbridge. I kept records there. Then I moved." He looked up at Torrance with a look that was undoubtedly intended to be firm, but missed slightly. "I haven't had time to sort out my earlier records. Not for patients who came to see me and then disappeared. Regular patients would be a different matter."

"Did Jane Robertson come to see you only to have her baby?"

Another pause. Torrance sat patiently still. "Ahh...yes. Just then. She wasn't a regular patient, as I've told you."

"Can you describe her?"

Moorehead seemed startled by the question. Derek wondered if it was the question about Jane Robertson's looks that surprised him, or the broader concept of being asked to describe *any* of his patients.

"Looked like?" the doctor repeated. "Well...she was a young girl. Long hair. Funny clothing. They all look like that."

"What color long hair?" Torrance asked.

"Ahh...nondescript. Must have been...ahh...brown, I think."

"How much did she weigh?"

"Weigh?...I don't recall."

Surely you must have weighed her."

"Well, yes. Yes...but you can't expect me to remember."

"How tall was she?"

"Oh...ahh...sort of medium, I guess."

"But you did measure her?"

"Well, yes...that's my practice...I would have done that, of course."

"Dr. Moorehead," Torrance finally confronted him. "How many regular patients do you have?"

"Oh...I have a few, those who know me...I'm really semi-retired. Don't have much of a practice any more these days."

"But you can't remember this woman who came to you to have a baby less than two months ago?" Derek noted a slight fraying of Torrance's hitherto perfect air of equanimity. "How many times did you see her?" A new, pointed look accompanied the question.

The cough came again, and another pause. "Ahh...just that once."

"At the time of the delivery?"

Dr. Moorehead gave Torrance another look he undoubtedly meant to make him look wise. "Mmmm...." " was all he said.

"Did she come to see you?"

"Ahh...yes."

"Did she come alone or did someone bring her?"

"I don't think...no...she must have come alone. I don't remember anyone else."

Torrance leaned forward slightly and looked straight into those red-rimmed eyes. "Where did you deliver the child?"

"Where?" He looked slightly startled, his professional demeanor slipping just a bit. "I was at my sister's home then. I saw her at my sister's."

"Did your sister help with the delivery?"

"Ah well . . . well . . . no . . . My sister wasn't there. She was visiting relatives. She was gone then."

Torrance leaned back, and Derek saw her take a deep breath. "What state was Jane in when she got to your sister's house?"

Moorehead looked puzzled. "State? What do you mean?"

"Was she in labor?"

"Well yes, that's why she came to find a doctor. She was beginning labor."

"How fast were the contractions coming?"

"Surely you can't expect me to recall that without my records. I really don't have any idea."

"Was she dilated when you first examined her?"

"Well . . . . I think she must have been . . . . I don't recall that it took all that long . . . . but I can't really say for sure."

Torrance threw a pained glance at Derek. He nodded and cleared his throat, which prompted Dr. Moorehead to turn around, as though he had forgotten Derek's presence.

"Dr. Moorehead," he began, "just how many babies have you delivered in the last year?"

"Babies? . . . I can't say exactly . . . a few . . . two or three at least."

"I'm surprised you can't remember any more details about the one we're talking about." Dr. Moorehead coughed and shrugged his shoulders.

Torrance stood up to go. "Well, we may be back to ask you some more questions later, Doctor. Right now, I think we'll go out to the Sanctuary House. I appreciate your cooperation and helpfulness," she added, almost too sweetly. In what seemed like an afterthought, she reached into her purse and produced a business card. By habit, Derek pulled one out of his wallet. "This is in case you remember any more details which might help," Torrance said, handing both cards to Dr. Moorehead. He glanced at them dispassionately, though his eyes widened a little when he saw Derek's. Then he placed both cards carefully on the side table, one above the other.

14

When Torrance and Derek left Dr. Moorehead's house, she got behind the wheel of their car and looked at her watch. "Past lunchtime," she said. "How about we eat and regroup?"

Derek nodded and Torrance drove back to Main Street, where she remembered having passed the Fern Cafe. She found it again and parked in front of it. They walked through the door, which sported a sign warning of a microwave oven in use, into a pleasant interior hung with—appropriately—ferns. They had a choice of tables and took one on the side opposite two fiftyish ladies with a guidebook who were debating the relative merits of the local art galleries. After a quick perusal of the menu, Derek waited for Torrance to finish reading. "You're a pretty good interrogator," he said. "I'd love to see you on cross-examination."

Torrance suddenly looked shy. "They were just the obvious questions," she shrugged.

Derek smiled and pushed the hair out of his face in a gesture Torrance was coming to recognize, then looked up at the arrival of their waitress. When they had ordered sandwiches and drinks, Torrance got back to the business at hand. "O.K.," she started, "what do we think of the story the good doctor told us?"

Derek thought back to the interview for a while. "I didn't like the way he told it at all," he finally said. "He sounded very evasive, very much like a person with something to hide. But it could be what he's hiding has nothing to do with you or me or our problem. He's not in good shape professionally or personally. Maybe his nervousness comes from that. He might think we're here with some ulterior motive, like his sister did. As far as the basic story is concerned. . ." Derek gave it thought. "It sounded plausible to me, but I'm disturbed by his lack of memory about details I would expect he'd have right at hand. Provided, of course, that his brain isn't too pickled," Derek added sourly.

Torrance smiled. "You caught that too? But I agree with you. There wasn't anything wrong with what he said happened, although I haven't yet made all the pieces fit. The kind of person he described as Russell John Robertson's mother could very well have acted like that. My main reservation, aside from his incredibly bad memory, is that we now have a situation even more convenient for anyone trying to hide the identity of the baby: a crash pad for dropouts, a mother who drifts in and out of town, no known father, a doctor who seems to have no staff for an independent check of the facts and has no memory for them either. As you said, the man was terribly uncomfortable talking to us. Do you agree that we should find this commune sort of place where he says Jane Robertson lived?"

Derek nodded and sat back to allow their lunches to be placed before them. As they ate, they agreed that they should go directly out to Sanctuary House, since the commune was near Ferndale and, according to their map, in the opposite direction from Eureka; besides, the information to be found there might be crucial to their investigation. They paid for their lunches and asked the waitress for directions to the Centerville Road.

Having returned to their car, Derek and Torrance proceeded once more down Main Street. They went straight through town. Derek noted some nice window displays in the art galleries they passed, while Torrance admired the Rexall Pharmacy, its pale green background attractively highlighted with dark green and white trim on the complex decorative woodwork.

Near the end of town they found the yellow and white building of the Bank of Loleta which marked their turn to the right. The street they followed brought them to the crossroads they had been told to look for. To the left a steep curvy road, barely wide enough for two-way traffic, headed up into the lush vegetation covering the side of the hill that marked the edge of the estuary plain. It was the way to Cape Mendocino, Petrolia, and Honeydew. Torrance, a fan of narrow roads heading off into the hills, felt a momentary sense of loss that this was not their route. Instead, she followed a sign that pointed toward the ocean and promised "Centerville Beach" in five miles.

This road was not particularly wide either, and it headed curvily along the very edge of the plain. On the right were flat meadows housing dairy cattle, and on the left was a brush and fern-covered hillside occasionally broken by a steep-sided valley. A few sheep and the occasional horse could be seen on both sides of the road. The local residences varied greatly. A few of the Victorian farmhouses which continued to dot the fields had been lovingly refurbished and carefully kept up. They looked prosperous, and their surroundings were neat and clean. Others were so run-down they looked as though no one had taken a hammer to them in this century. Between the widely scattered farmhouses tucked up into the little valleys heading off to the left were many trailers, sometimes surrounded by collections of more or less derelict possessions, from cars to baby buggies.

As Torrance drove on toward the shore, she and Derek could see the low rise of sand that marked the edge of the land, but the ocean itself was invisible from their low vantage point. They were three or four miles from the edge of Ferndale when a mailbox on their left alerted them. The mailbox was painted in psychedelic colors, somewhat weathered at this point, with "Sanctuary House" written on it in a flowing script. It stood beside a driveway leading into one of the valleys breaking up the hillside.

This one gave shelter to a large Victorian farmhouse surrounded by a porch trimmed with gingerbread. While a coat of white paint seemed to have been applied to the house in the not too distant past, the amount of attention given to the underlying material had been minimal, and pieces of gingerbread and window trim that had fallen off had not been replaced. The area surrounding the house was fenced, and two cows, three sheep, three goats and a pony were visible in the enclosure. A somewhat derelict barn was obviously used for storage as well as for the animals' needs, and the stored goods overflowed into a sort of lean-to attached to one of the barn's sides. But the clutter was confined to that area, and the rest of the yard was reasonably neat, with what appeared to be a children's play area under some shade trees to the left of the house.

Derek got out to open and shut the gate across the driveway in order to let the car through. He grinned as he got back in. "Even a city boy like me knows the animals get out if you don't keep the gate closed." Torrance smiled. "They've got a nice little collection. I wonder if they milk the goats and make goat cheese."

"If they do, I hope they have enough sense to sell it in San Francisco for huge amounts of money rather than to eat it themselves. Given the price of goat cheese since it became the in thing to have on your salad, they could probably live off the proceeds."

"You don't know yet how many of them there are. For all you know, this place contains dozens of free spirits."

"You'd better watch your choice of words, Torrance. I like to think I'm a free spirit myself."

"O.K., what do we call them? Flower children?"

Derek laughed and looked around. "This isn't quite Haight-Ashbury, but maybe it's where what's left of the old Hashbury crowd ran off to to escape urban redevelopment. I feel like I'm in a time warp."

Torrance parked next to an ancient pickup truck in the area just in front of the steps leading up to the front porch. She and Derek got out and approached the house. As they did so, the front door opened and a woman of enormous proportions emerged. She was at least six feet tall and incredibly wide. In spite of her shapeless, floor-length gown, the bulges of her body were obvious. Her hair was black, streaked with gray and hung straight down past her shoulders. But with all of that it was still her face that was distinctive. It had character in spite of the excessive flesh, and it gave an impression of friendliness and calm. This was the sort of person little children should have for their mothers, Torrance thought. The woman looked at Torrance and Derek and smiled.

"Hi, what can I do for you?" she asked in a pleasant voice.

Torrance noticed Derek hanging back a bit and took the cue. She stepped forward, offered a hand, and introduced the two of them by name without appending titles. The woman shook their hands amiably.

"We were sent here by Dr. Moorehead," she said. "We went to talk to him about a baby who died in an automobile accident. The baby was given up for adoption, so there's been a problem with identification. It gets kind of complicated, but the reason we're here is that Dr. Moorehead said the mother lived here at the time he delivered the baby at his sister's house in Fernbridge. Can you help us?"

The woman folded her arms across her enormous breasts. "Well, I'll certainly try. My name is Jasmine Free. I've been the coordinator for Sanctuary House for the past two years. Come on in and sit down."

Torrance and Derek followed her down a bare hallway faintly scented with marijuana smoke to a room that was furnished with a variety of sofas and armchairs, none of them matching. The windows looked out at the playground across the gingerbread veranda. Jasmine pointed out seats and offered to bring them something to drink before proceeding. Torrance politely declined, saying that they had just finished a late lunch, and Jasmine lowered herself into a giant-sized armchair that Torrance and Derek both suspected was her usual seat because it could hold her bulk without collapsing.

"So, tell me what it is you need to know," she prompted, looking peaceful and comfortable in her chair.

With Derek still giving her the lead, Torrance explained that they were looking for a woman named Jane Robertson who had borne a child on the sixteenth of August and lived right here in this house at the time, according to Dr. Moorehead, who attended the birth. "We're looking for Jane Robertson," Torrance explained. "She was going to give the child up for adoption, but she hadn't signed the papers yet. That means he was still her baby when he died." She saw Jasmine's frown and responded to it. "No one else is available to identify the baby. We have to find the birth mother. The couple who wanted to adopt him died in the crash, too."

This seemed to satisfy Jasmine and her frown disappeared. She leaned back, closed her eyes, and swayed back and forth gently. "Jane Robertson . . ." she muttered. It doesn't mean a thing to me. Not a thing . . . ." She sat up and looked at Torrance again. "We don't really use names here very much. Not the names that people use out there." She pointed vaguely in the direction of Ferndale and Eureka. "When someone comes to stay here, they tell us what they want to be called. That's what we call them. Other names aren't relevant. I suppose we could have had a Jane Robertson here, but if we did, I didn't know that was her name."

"But this woman was pregnant. Have you had pregnant women here?"

Jasmine closed her eyes again and considered Torrance's question. "Yes. We've had pregnant women now and then."

"Jane Robertson would have been pregnant the beginning of August. Until August sixteenth."

"August sixteenth," Jasmine Free repeated slowly, then looked at Torrance. "What date is it now?"

"It's September twenty-ninth." Jasmine still looked vague. Torrance went on. "She gave birth about six weeks ago."

"I don't remember having a pregnant woman here six weeks ago. No. I'm pretty sure of that. Six weeks ago I would remember. There wasn't anyone like that."

Torrance nodded at Derek who had been sitting by quietly. "Do you know Dr. Moorehead?" he asked Jasmine.

Jasmine looked at him calmly and inclined her head slowly. "Sure," she answered. "People around here pretty much know him."

"If someone here needed a doctor, might they go to Dr. Moorehead?"

Jasmine rocked a little and closed her eyes again. "Well, if someone needed a prescription in an emergency, or something like that, sure, they'd go to see him. He's convenient. Not like going to the clinic at the hospital."

"Well, what if a woman were pregnant? Would she go to Dr. Moorehead for the delivery?"

Jasmine rocked herself some more and looked warily at Torrance and Derek in turn. "We don't really view pregnancy as a medical problem here," she finally said.

Torrance made a tiny gesture at Derek, out of Jasmine's view. "I certainly agree with you there," she said.

Jasmine sat up straight again and gave Torrance her full attention. She looked benign, motherly. "Childbirth is a natural process. It worked very well long before there were doctors."

Torrance smiled in a reassuring way. "Women are lucky to come here if they're pregnant, then."

Jasmine gave her a long look, which seemed to satisfy her. "We take care of our own here. If they don't want a doctor when they're not ill, we don't force one on them. We don't force them to submit themselves to procedures they don't need or want."

"And you don't remember anyone six weeks ago who wanted a doctor when her baby came?"

Jasmine shook her head emphatically. "No. There wasn't anyone like that. I couldn't possibly have forgotten. It would have been very unusual."

At Torrance's quick look, Derek took over again.

"Maybe Dr. Moorehead was mistaken about the place where Jane Robertson was staying. Are there any other places around here where a young pregnant mother might have taken shelter?"

Jasmine brought a hand to her chin and rubbed it for a while. "There is only one other place like this," she said. "Well, not really like this, but a place where a dropout might be welcome. I've heard of it, but I don't know exactly where it is." She looked at Derek and then at Torrance. "I don't really ever leave here. The people who come to stay do the shopping and run errands. I take care of the children and the animals."

Torrance looked back. "But you have heard of another place."

"Yes," Jasmine answered. "It's out on the estuary, over toward Loleta. Another big old Victorian farmhouse. That's all I know about it. . . . Oh. . . . I've heard the name I think. Now what what was it?" She concentrated on the ceiling for a while, then said, "Rainbow House. That's it."

Torrance reached into her purse and came up with one of her business cards. Derek followed her lead and handed her one of his. Torrance took a few steps toward Jasmine Free and held the cards out to her. "Thank you for talking to us," she said with genuine sincerity. "Here are our cards. If you think of anything else that will help us, would you please call one of us and let us know?"

Jasmine looked at the two cards and heaved an enormous sigh. "You aren't here just to identify a dead baby," she said. "There's something else that you're not telling me."

Torrance gave her a level look. "There are some other questions. But if you've told us everything, they don't have anything to do with you or with your place."

Jasmine struggled out of her chair and gave Torrance one of her enormous hands. "I'll remember that," she said and shook Derek's hand in turn before following the two of them out of the room. As they walked down the hall, a sudden noise erupted from upstairs, and a pair of young children came bounding down the staircase from the floor above. Jasmine caught them and hugged them, and whispered to them, obviously delighting them. She followed Torrance and Derek down the hall and out the front door towing the two laughing and bouncing children behind her. As Torrance and Derek got into their car and turned it into the drive, they saw Jasmine lead her two charges to the edge of the playground, where one of the goats was advancing on the threesome, bleating at them as though it was quite sure of being understood.

For a while, Torrance and Derek remained silent. They turned back down Centerville Road toward Ferndale and reached the edge of town when Torrance finally looked at her watch and spoke. "It's getting late. Back to Eureka, I think, and find a place to spend the night. We had an early start, and I'm getting pretty tired. You agree there's more to be done here, don't you?"

Derek nodded, sending his hair tumbling back over his forehead. "Yeah, I do. There are some odd things we've come across—and so far, we have no idea why they're odd." He paused for a while. "I still agree with what we said at lunch. Dr. Moorehead's story may be plausible on the surface, but it's unsatisfactory as hell. Either he has the most terrible memory, or he has something to hide. The question is, what is he hiding, and what does it have to do with me—or with you?"

"I keep going back to that story he told about the delivery at his sister's house. There were some things about that story. . . . It didn't hang together."

Derek pushed his hair back again. "I'd like to talk to the good doctor again myself, that's for sure, but before we do it, we need some more information. Let's do some more digging before going back to him." Torrance voiced her agreement and drove on for a while in silence.

Derek suddenly asked, "What about Jasmine? What about her story? Is she dealing with us straight?"

"Well, she's either telling the truth or she's an excellent and honest-faced liar."

"I agree, but I have a hard time being suspicious of her. What reason would she have to hide anything from us?"

Torrance smiled. "Remember that speech she gave us about home births, after I suggested I was in sympathy with her views? My guess is that she works as a lay midwife which is illegal in this state. If by some chance the baby was actually delivered there at Sanctuary House, and Moorehead only signed the certificate to hide that fact and protect Jasmine, she would have every incentive to lie to us. And besides, she would feel virtuous and come across as calmly and honestly as if she were telling us the Gospel truth."

Derek ran a finger along his jaw as he thought this over. "Hmmm, that would account for the doctor's funny story about his sister, too, wouldn't it? Too bad. I do like Jasmine. And unlike you, I have no professional duty to root out the unlicensed practice of midwifery."

Torrance managed to look indignant and amused at the same time. "I only want the facts, and we'll worry later about what I may want to do with them. Meanwhile, here's the Red Lion Inn. O.K. with you? We can check in and I'll show you a good place for dinner. We can decide what to do tomorrow while we have wine and appetizers."

Later that evening, Derek and Torrance were relaxing at a corner table at Lazio's, sipping a decent Chardonnay and enjoying an appetizer of dry-smoked salmon which the restaurant purchased from the local Indian tribes. Torrance put down her glass with a sigh of pleasure and squared her shoulders. "Tomorrow," she started pointedly.

"O.K., you first," said Derek and closed his eyes while swirling the wine under his nose.

"How can I be sure you're listening?"

Derek opened one eye momentarily. "My ears are wide open."

"Well then, here goes. There are some things I want to check up on back in Sacramento, things I have access to more easily than you. I'll do that first thing in the morning, so they'll be able to get back to me. Also I want to look at public records of births at the county's vital statistics office. I have some ideas what to look for there. On the other hand, we have some leads still to be checked out in Ferndale."

Derek nodded, giving Torrance a sparkling look. She thought he must have been forgiven for almost any mischief when he was a child.

"I can rent a second car and see if I can find that other commune. Private eye stuff, you know. And I'll try to find a forwarding address for Jane Robertson at the Ferndale Post Office. Then we need to get together again. Where do you want to meet?"

"How about back at the Fern Cafe? We know where that is, and we like the lunch. Since we know we probably will want to talk to the doctor again, it'll be convenient."

"That's good," Derek agreed. "Let's meet just after noon, and if either one of us is delayed, we'll leave a message back at the hotel. So call in if you think I've left you sitting alone too long."

15

After dinner Derek politely walked Torrance to her room and agreed to meet her for an early breakfast. He gave her a little mock bow and a wave and disappeared down the hall. Torrance looked after him for a moment. A damned attractive man, she thought, and wondered what kind of roommate he had been talking about on the plane.

The next morning at breakfast, Torrance was bright-eyed and eager to get going. She laughed at Derek's demand for intravenous coffee and jumper cables before he could turn into a human being. "I don't do mornings," he said with a slight shudder.

After coffee and ham and eggs he brightened considerably and professed a readiness to go to the airport to pick up another car if Torrance drove him there. He had already checked on the time the rental counter opened. (Obviously, Torrance thought, that sleepy-eyed morning act didn't get in the way of his doing his job.) His proposal fit in well with her plans, since she wanted to call her office in San Francisco before doing anything else, and the average deputy there was even more adamant than Derek about not being a morning person.

Having dropped Derek off, she returned to the hotel and pulled out her telephone credit card. Now to find out what good old Dr. Moorehead had against the Board of Medical Quality Assurance.

Torrance had no direct contact at B.M.Q.A., so she called back to her office. First, she checked in with Lynda, her secretary; as usual, she received two phone messages she absolutely *had* to return that morning. She briefed Lynda on progress on the Bowen baby case and asked that it be passed on to Sheriff Oreston. Then she asked for a deputy who often represented the

Medical Board on its cases and explained what she wanted to know about Dr. Moorehead and why. Since she wouldn't be near a telephone, she promised to call back before noon to find out the results.

Now for vital statistics, she told herself, and gathered up her belongings to move on to the county building. She and Derek had decided to check out and go home that night, no matter what, since neither had come prepared for spending more than two days.

Having presented her badge and I.D. folder to the vital statistics clerk, Torrance was given room in which to work and a horrible-tasting cup of coffee which nevertheless represented a social cohesion she wouldn't reject. Thus armed, she dove into the file of birth certificates. She worked quickly, yet carefully, aware that overlooking even one certificate of importance might cause her to miss the pattern she was hoping to find.

An hour and a half later, Torrance leaned back, appalled at the number of babies born in Humboldt County during the last sixteen months. But she had found her pattern. Before her she had copies of three birth certificates. One was Russell John Robertson's. He was born on August sixteenth. A second belonged to Corey Daniel Johnson, born August twelfth, mother given as Mary Johnson, General Delivery, Ferndale, father unknown; and the physician attending Corey's home birth was Albert Moorehead. Then there was the third. It registered the birth of David Richard Marawik, born June second, to Carol Esther Marawik. The father was also listed as unknown, and the birth was stated to be a home birth attended by Dr. Moorehead. But there was an address for the mother. It was a street address in Fields Landing, the little town between Eureka and Fernbridge that Derek had admired the day before.

Torrance sat back for a moment and thought about what she had found. She looked in her cup, noting that the few sips of coffee left were cold. She could think of nothing else to do here. Now for a telephone and a call back to San Francisco.

The deputy who had promised to contact the Medical Board on her behalf was not in his office, but after Torrance patiently waited while he was paged, he came on the line.

"You were right about Dr. Moorehead having had a run-in with B.M.Q.A. The doctor is—or was—an alcoholic. He was disciplined for bad patient care about four years ago. He voluntarily went into an alcohol diversion program and got three years probation with limited supervision. Promised to go to A.A. and that sort of stuff. He completed it successfully and went off probation about a year ago. With him up on the north coast, I suspect they had little idea whether he was really on the wagon or not."

"He may have been, but I doubt that he is now," Torrance commented.

"Anyway, your doctor is now off probation and free to practice as he wishes. Have you got a new complaint on him?"

"I can't tell yet. His practice does seem to be a little substandard, but what I'm looking into may be more serious. Do you have any details about what kind of patient care problems he had?"

"Yes, I had them read me the charges over the phone, since I didn't have time to get our file out of archives. It sounds like general sloppiness—missing simple diagnoses and failure to order tests or follow procedures that any up-to-date physician would consider routine. One of his patients even died. It had to be due to negligence, but there were apparently some problems with the evidence, and they couldn't pin it on him."

"I assume that even though he got probation last time, his history sets him up for serious problems if he does anything else that B.M.Q.A. frowns on."

"Yeah, I'd say so. Anything more you need?"

Torrance thought for a moment, but nothing additional came to her mind. "No thanks. I appreciate your help. I may have to get back to you again, though."

"That's O.K., your problem sounds more interesting than what I'm working on anyway. So feel free."

After hanging up the telephone, Torrance looked at her watch. The morning was almost gone. She had better head back for Ferndale. She thought that Derek would be pleased with the progress she had made. At the very least, she had two new names to follow up on, and a basis for rattling Dr. Moorehead's cage a little.

After Derek left Torrance, he rented a car and drove down to Ferndale. He drove quickly, something he did often when he was uneasy or irritated. Mentally, he added up the cost of the car rental and hotel room and reviewed the cases he had just taken on that he had left on his desk. Cases he should be working on. Cases that would bring in money. Instead he was miles away, piling up expenses on a wild goose chase which he couldn't possibly bill to his client. And for what? Why had he done it? Boredom? Intellectual curiosity? Had there really been some serious possibility that this trip was related to his case?

At least the trip was something new and unpredictable, Derek mused. Maybe that's why he had agreed to come. Maybe it was as simple as that. Even as he smiled to himself and settled back for the rest of the drive into Ferndale, Derek thought that it was not that simple. There was something else that had brought him here—a nagging doubt that had caused him to intuitively go with Torrance's offer.

As Derek drove into Ferndale, he had a strong feeling that he was overlooking something important and should be doing something else. It distracted him so much that he missed the post office and had to go around the block. Irritably, Derek told himself to get back to the job at hand. He parked and entered the post office with his mind finally focused.

Jo Travers, the Postmistress of Ferndale, walked slowly around to the counter where Derek was standing, holding the card Derek had presented to the lone clerk on duty. She was short and round, with tightly curled, graying hair wrapped around a little ball of a face. Her eyes, peering at Derek over the top of black, plastic-rimmed half-lenses, betrayed her excitement even as the rest of her was trying very hard to look and act official. The clerk stood a discreet distance away, having just found some terribly engrossing paper work that needed her quiet attention.

"My. A real private investigator from San Francisco. What can I do for you, Mr. Thompson?" This last question was delivered in her best official tone.

"I need some help trying to find a young woman who lived here last August. Unfortunately, all I have for an address is general delivery." Derek lowered his voice, but not so much that the hovering clerk couldn't overhear. "Her aunt lives in San Francisco. She has no children of her own and well, frankly, the young woman I'm trying to find was the only one of her nieces and nephews who visited her and wrote her over the years without ever asking for anything in return. Last Christmas, her niece sent her the most beautiful handmade macrame angel. She made it herself. And now her aunt is in the hospital. It doesn't look good, I'm afraid." Derek shook his head. "She asked me to find her niece. All she had was the return address on the package with the angel and the most recent letter, which was mailed last August."

"And that was general delivery, Ferndale." Jo finished the story herself.

"The niece's name is Jane Robertson," Derek nodded. "I was hoping that you might know whether she is still in town, or perhaps you still have a forwarding address for her after all this time."

Jo shook her head thoughtfully. The clerk, having given up all pretense of her paper work, did the same.

"The name doesn't recall anything. Does it to you, Madge—Jane Robertson?" The clerk continued to slowly shake her head.

"Why don't you fetch me the forwarding address book?" Jo commanded.

As the clerk brought back a large old leather-bound folio, Jo explained, "The post office came out a few years ago with this new machine that prints up forwarding address labels automatically. You just type in the name of the addressee. We're only supposed to keep a forwarding address in the machine for six months, so that's what we do.

"But actually," Jo added conspiratorially, as she opened the heavy book, "Madge and I don't trust the thing. It makes mistakes and, besides, this is a small town. People expect a little more personal service here. So Madge and I have kept up our old forwarding address book, just like we used to. And things don't get lost or thrown away. Let's see, Robertson...." Jo ran her fingers backwards up the pages, beginning with the last entry.

"Robertson, Robertson..." she muttered to herself. "You see, I can go back several years with this. I thought we should at least go as far back as last Christmas, just in case." She resumed her finger search. Derek tried to look over her shoulder as she went, not entirely trusting her to be as observant as he would be.

At last she looked up, shaking her head worriedly. "Well, I've gone all the way back to just before last Thanksgiving. I don't see any forwarding address for a Robertson. But then, folks who use general delivery don't always expect a lot of mail. Most times they forget to leave us a forwarding address." Jo pushed the book away from her.

"Would Jane have been likely to use general delivery if she lived at Sanctuary House or Rainbow House?" Derek asked. Jo looked up, surprised.

"You know something about our community here, I see," she said. "Maybe, if she didn't want people to know she was there. The only mail the Sanctuary gets is from welfare, plus a few magazines. Rainbow—well, if she was at Rainbow, she'd have a reason for not wanting her family to know she was there. And she'd have fallen into some bad company, if you'll excuse me. Nothing but pot-growers there."

Derek smiled as the little round face spit out "pot-growers." Soothingly, he said that from what he knew of Jane Robertson, Rainbow House sounded like a very unlikely place for her to be. An idea suddenly came to him.

"Do you suppose we could look through the mail you're holding in general delivery? Maybe something could have come in for her, and I could get a lead from the return address."

Jo hesitated, calculating. Then she obviously thought of a macrame angel on a Christmas tree, and a poor old lady in the hospital. "Well, it's not according to regulations, but let's look. So long as it's only the outside of the envelope, I imagine it won't hurt to take a peek."

She returned in a few minutes with a bundle of mail and some loose pieces in a cardboard box. "We're only supposed to keep unclaimed mail for thirty days in general delivery but, as I said, this is a small town." She put the bundle on the counter in front of her. "Folks expect us to treat them like people, not like numbers." Derek smiled his agreement with her philosophy, as Jo sorted through the bundle.

"Here's something!" Jo said suddenly, tossing to the side a long official envelope with the return address of the Vital Statistics Section of the State Department of Health Services. Through a window in the envelope, Jane Robertson's address showed on what was clearly some kind of official document.

"That's the mother's copy of a birth certificate. We get a lot of them through here. See? Here's another one." She showed Derek a similar envelope, addressed to a Mary Johnson and postmarked just a few days before Jane Robertson's. She dug through the rest of the pile. "No, nothing else." Suddenly Jo looked up at Derek suspiciously.

"You didn't say she was married and had a baby," she said sharply. "Are you working for the husband? Is this a divorce case?"

"I don't take domestic cases," Derek said flatly, glad to be telling the truth for once. "No, this surprises me as much as it does you," he added, indicating the envelope. "She may have had a kid, but I'm pretty sure she wasn't married." He looked at his watch. "Well, I've taken enough of your time. I know her aunt appreciates it, and so would Jane, if she knew. You have my card. Please, call me collect if by chance you hear of any news." Derek made ready to leave.

"I will, Mr. Thompson," Jo replied. "By the way, what is the aunt's name? Just in case it might come up, of course."

"The aunt's name?" The question caught Derek off guard. He seized on the first name that came to mind. "Uh, Robusson. Shirley Robusson." As he said it, he immediately regretted it.

"Shirley Robusson," Jo repeated. "Funny, but that name does ring a bell. Wrong context, though." She shrugged it off. "Oh well, if I hear anything, I'll let you know."

An hour and a half later, Derek was back in the Fern Cafe, sipping a cup of coffee. He smiled and stood up as Torrance came in, looking somewhat pleased with herself.

"I have a surprise for you," she said, beaming. "But you first. What have you come up with?"

"Humph!" Derek snorted in mock indignation. "If you insist. Actually, I did come up with something. Nothing as convenient as a forwarding address, of course, but I'll come back to that." He waited for Torrance to settle down and sipped his glass of water before continuing.

"I didn't bother going out to the Rainbow House," he said offhandedly, watching Torrance's reaction. When he got a look of amused interest, he went on.

"It seems the place is inhabited by some local marijuana growers. I had a nice time discussing it with the police chief. I figured they probably knew more about it and its residents than I could find out in a week, and I was right. The chief could assure me in no uncertain terms that there has been no Jane Robertson or any woman resembling her condition or age at Rainbow in recent months. Though he told me very mysteriously that he couldn't tell me why he was so sure."

"Oh, the chief has an undercover informant then?" Torrance grinned.

"So it seems. It's a little late for the marijuana harvest; their crop has to be in by now. My guess is that if the chief hasn't busted them yet it's because he's hoping for something bigger, like breaking up the distribution network or getting the financial backer behind the whole operation. Anyway, it made my job simpler." Derek paused as the waitress came by for their order.

"The rest of the morning was a total waste of time, except for one little thing," he went on when the waitress had left. "I think we should ask Dr. Moorehead about his patient Mary Johnson, and see if he remembers anything more about the birth of her baby than he does Jane Robertson's."

Torrance suddenly sat up very straight. "How did you come across that name?" she asked sharply.

Derek told her about the two envelopes from Vital Statistics. "The way I figured, if Jane Robertson was the type of girl Moorehead said she was, the pieces didn't fit. If either Jane or this Johnson character were really 'hippies' and were living at the Sanctuary or some similar place, they'd use their real address or at least come in to pick up the birth certificate. After all, unless they're unusually big on honesty, they'd want it for the welfare department. Even if they'd given up their kids for adoption, there are plenty at the Sanctuary they could borrow if they had to, with the social worker none the wiser.

"Until I came across that second birth certificate," Derek went on, "I was coming to the conclusion that our Jane Robertson was the daughter of some well-to-do Ferndalian who had paid Dr. Moorehead to keep his mouth shut. But with a second birth certificate for Mary Johnson, I have to throw that theory out the window. It's hard enough accepting one 'free-spirited' mother with a home birth in Ferndale who disappears from the face of the earth. I can't believe two."

"How about three?" Torrance said with devilish smugness. Derek nearly choked on his sandwich. Gleefully, she recounted her expedition through the files of the county's vital statistics office and coming across the three home births attended by Dr. Moorehead. She showed Derek the birth certificates.

"The thing that is interesting," Torrance said as Derek was inspecting the certificates, "is that home birth is fairly popular in this county. There were even a few out at Sanctuary House. Those didn't give the name of an attending practitioner." Torrance paused meaningfully. Derek looked up. "Most of the rest gave the name of a local nurse midwife or this one doctor who practices out of a hospital in Eureka. And virtually all of them listed a father.

"Going back for a year and a half," Torrance continued, "that was the pattern...until last June, when Dr. Moorehead suddenly decides to try a home delivery himself. And then, after several more months of nothing, he suddenly has the good fortune to deliver two babies within four days of each other."

"At least one of which he can't remember a thing about," Derek interjected.

"Which doesn't make any sense," Torrance went on, ignoring him. "He was not known in the community as an obstetrician, homebirth or otherwise, and it was only about a year since his license was restored."

Derek started. "Excuse me?"

"Oh, didn't I mention that?" Torrance smiled innocently. Derek sat back in his chair and scowled. He had to admire her timing.

"Dr. Moorehead's license was put on probation by the Medical Board for three years. It seems that he missed a few diagnoses. One of his patients died, though the Board couldn't clearly prove the death was due to Moorehead's negligence. I guess that's why the Board didn't revoke him outright. He was a drunk, and the Board decided to give him a second chance. They ordered him into their alcohol rehabilitation program." Torrance paused and took a sip of water.

"Anyway, when he went off probation over a year ago, he was apparently judged to be dry. After that, he dropped from sight."

"And fell off the wagon," Derek added. "But how did he get hooked up with Parentbuilders? And how does that fit in with Mary Johnson and— what was the other mother's name?"

"Carol Marawik. She's the only one who doesn't sound like a fake." Torrance paused. "I don't know, but we certainly have a lot more questions to ask Dr. Moorehead. I want to find out why his story and Shirley Robusson's don't match, and which one—if either—is telling the truth."

At the mention of that name, the unease that Derek felt earlier returned. "Let's go see the doctor," he said and waved at the waitress for a check.

16

*T*hey left quickly in Torrance's car. Torrance found Derek's sudden tension contagious, and they drove in silence the few short blocks to Dr. Moorehead's office.

At the sight of the quiet, shabby house, looking the same as it had the day before, Derek and Torrance relaxed slightly. Torrance walked up the steps first. "This is one cross-examination I'm going to enjoy," she smiled grimly and opened the door.

They entered the front room. The door to the back living quarters was slightly ajar, as it had been yesterday. "Hello. . . Dr. Moorehead?" Torrance called.

There was no answer. The room had the same stale, musty smell, which seemed to emanate from the back. But there was something else—a thick, foul redolence seemed to hang on the edge of the air. Derek couldn't quite place it, but his internal alarm bells began to ring.

"Hello?" Torrance called again. She turned anxiously toward Derek, just as he pushed past her. He threw open the back door, which led to an elongated kitchen with a dining nook converted to a sitting area.

"Christ!" he exclaimed, nearly gagging. The smell of stale wine and cigarettes was overpowered by the thick stench of urine and feces. Derek stared at the source of it in the middle of the seating area.

Dr. Moorehead was sitting up in an old shabby armchair, surrounded by an overflowing ashtray, several empty bottles of cheap wine scattered about, and a half-gallon bottle with only a few inches gone squatting to one side. A glass lay spilled in the doctor's lap. A dark patch of wetness ran from it to join a larger stain which spread from the doctor's crotch to soak the seat between his legs. His delicate hands sat limply on his knees, palms up. Derek caught his breath.

Moorehead's eyes bulged open, staring blankly ahead from his grotesquely distorted owl face. A dark necktie was knotted tightly around his neck, digging deep into the flesh.

"My God," Torrance said quietly. She had come up behind Derek and was staring, horrified, over his shoulder. Derek started to tell her not to look and just as quickly decided not to bother. His stomach gave a lurch. The two of them locked eyes, trying to decide what to do.

It was Torrance who broke the spell. "I'd better call the police. Is there a phone in here?" She and Derek looked about. She saw a phone on the kitchen counter and moved toward it.

Her action snapped Derek back to awareness. "Wait!" he said sharply. Torrance looked at him, puzzled.

"The minute the cops get here, we won't be able to touch a thing." He looked at Torrance and then nodded his head in the direction of the corner behind Moorehead's chair. Torrance followed his glance. There stood an old metal filing cabinet.

Torrance shook her head. "I'm sorry, Derek. I'm here on official business, and I work for the Attorney General, remember? I can't be a party to tampering with evidence of an obvious crime."

Derek hesitated a moment; then he gently took Torrance by the shoulders and turned her around. "Then you'd better not touch the phone in here," he said. "I'm sure I saw a telephone out there. Maybe you should go look." Pulling a handkerchief from his pocket and stepping carefully over the spilled bottles and ashes, he threw a quick glance back over his shoulder.

Torrance held her breath and shut her eyes. For a few seconds, she stood there undecided. Then she let her breath out slowly.

"You're right. I think I did see a phone in the front room. I'll see if I can find it."

After a few minutes Derek heard her call out. "I'm sorry, I can't find another phone. I'll have to use the one in the kitchen whether we like it or not."

"Wait a minute," Derek answered. He closed the file drawer he had been searching and turned around. "O.K., here's something you can cover the receiver with to protect any fingerprints."

Torrance came in and approached the phone, avoiding the armchair where Moorehead still sat. She took Derek's handkerchief, folded it over the headset, and called the police.

Several hours later, an exhausted Derek slumped in the chair in Torrance's hotel room. An equally tired Torrance lay on her bed, her head propped up on both pillows, staring at the ceiling. Derek ordered a double Scotch from room service, and Torrance, upon his insistence that it was medicinal, agreed to a similar-sized brandy. After it became clear that another night in Eureka was necessary even in the absence of clean clothes, Torrance called her office and Derek called his answering service. They managed to change their plane reservations to noon the next day.

The Chief of Police in Ferndale was cooperative, obviously having decided that Derek's association with Torrance made him at least semi-official. But the investigation had not proven particularly fruitful so far. The killer had worn gloves, or at least there didn't appear to be any usable fingerprints. The proprietor of a local grocery store had seen Moorehead shortly after lunch the day before. He had used the pay phone and then bought a couple of bottles of jug wine, the three-liter size. None of the neighbors had seen or heard anything suspicious.

The only remotely helpful clue came from an old woman who lived a block away from Dr. Moorehead's residence. She had been awakened about one a.m. by a car door slamming in front of her house. Curious about the noise, she looked out her window in time to see a large black sedan make a U-turn and drive off. From her second-story vantage point, she couldn't see the driver. Make, model or license plate was out of the question.

The coroner agreed with Derek's initial assessment that Moorehead had probably been very drunk by the time he was killed. The signs of an advanced binge were everywhere and virtually no sign of a struggle. They would have to wait for the pathologist's report, however, to fix the time of death and know for certain just how drunk he was. Meanwhile, the police were going to start checking pharmacy records. The Chief of Police was convinced Moorehead's death was somehow related to the diversion of prescription drugs.

"He must have started hitting it pretty heavily after we left," Derek sighed. "I guess we really shook him up. I assume he kept drinking well into the evening, and then someone stopped in to see him." He tried to blot out the image of Moorehead's swollen face.

"He phoned someone," Torrance said flatly, "and the person he phoned killed him."

"At least the killer was nice enough to bring Moorehead that half-gallon of wine. I wonder how long it would take the doctor to drink a couple of inches worth."

Torrance sat up a little straighter and rearranged her pillows. "Probably not long, in his state." She took another sip of her brandy, which was beginning to do the job it had been intended for. "You still haven't told me what you found."

"Are you allowed to know?"

She let out a deep breath. "Not really, but so long as I don't know how you found it, I guess I can rationalize satisfying my burning curiosity."

Derek laughed softly. "Actually, it was what I didn't find that was most interesting." He took another long sip of his Scotch. "His patients' records were in the top two drawers of his file cabinet. The bottom drawer was mostly junk—and a lot of black bag stuff. Most of the records were in old brown folders that looked like they hadn't been touched in a long time. He had a set of newer manila ones at the front of the top drawer. They weren't in any particular order, and most of them were a real mess."

"How so?" Torrance asked.

"Just that they were real disorganized. Progress notes on scraps of paper, lab reports just tossed in, stuff like that." Derek finished his drink and offered to order another round. When Torrance refused, he decided to go along with her. The Scotch was beginning to numb him just enough.

"I did find Carol Marawik's file. In fact, it was one of the best organized of the bunch. The narrative report of the birth read like something out of a textbook. He even used full sheets of lined paper." Derek smiled. "When I was done with hers, I went looking for Jane Robertson and Mary Johnson."

"And they weren't there," Torrance said with resignation in her voice.

"You guessed it," Derek sighed. "The killer must have taken them." He looked up at Torrance. "Only now I can't tell the Chief of Police that they're missing, can I?"

Torrance shook her head. "We could always suggest that he look for them, just to see if they're related to the murder. And then when he can't find them, maybe he'll get suspicious and come to the same conclusion."

"Yeah. Just as soon as he's checked every pharmacy and drug wholesaler from here to Crescent City."

"I suppose you're right. Did you find anything else of interest?"

"Nope. That was about it. I did appreciate your thorough search for the phone."

"It took some effort to spend any time at all looking around that room. I went three times around the lamp table." She stopped. "Derek!" she said quietly, suddenly sitting up all the way. "There was nothing on the lamp table. Do you remember? Dr. Moorehead put our cards on the lamp table in the front room."

Derek looked at Torrance thoughtfully. "Moorehead didn't have them on him," he said finally. Torrance looked up sharply. "I searched his pockets," Derek added, as a slight wave of nausea ran through him. Maybe he should have ordered that second drink.

The next morning, Derek drove back out to Ferndale to see what else he could find out, and Torrance started out with a call to Sheriff Oreston. She briefed him on recent events and filled him in on her various theories. "There's one thing you can do for me while I follow up on some loose ends up here," she finally said. "We haven't been able to tie the Bowen baby to the Marin kidnapping, but the theory still seems a good one. Maybe we just don't have the right kidnapping. Could you ask Justice to do a computer run on all kidnappings of newborns in the last year? I know it's a pretty rare crime, so there won't be more than a handful. It should be easy for them to give you the details." Torrance laughed somewhat self-consciously. "It may seem a funny request, since I work for Justice, but C.I.&I. doesn't seem to consider lawyers a part of legitimate law enforcement. They'll give you far better service than I could get."

Oreston promised to put in an urgent request for the information Torrance wanted. Privately, he sincerely hoped she wouldn't uncover anything that linked the Bowens to a stolen baby. Assemblyman Havening wouldn't like that at all.

Having put that particular line of inquiry in motion, Torrance took her car out to Fields Landing to look for Carol Esther Marawik. The weather had deteriorated, and ragged grey clouds were moving in from the northwest, driven by a damp, chill wind. On the edge of town, a stocky man of military bearing, wearing a tightly-belted raincoat and an Irish tweed hat pulled well down his forehead, was braving the elements to the evident delight of his golden retriever. Torrance asked him for directions and was sent to an isolated house on the edge of town.

As she pulled her car up in front of the well-kept cottage set back behind a garden in which late flowers were still blooming, Torrance felt a chill, as the image of Dr. Moorehead's dead body suddenly came to her mind. She tried to tell herself that it was just the Alfred Hitchcock weather that made her jumpy, but she had to admit that she was afraid that yesterday's discovery might be repeated. Out here, away from the other houses, she would have felt hesitant to approach the front door even without the wind and the threatening clouds. She suddenly felt very alone without Derek and sat there for a minute or two, trying to get her courage back up.

She started to get out of the car, still unable to shake the fear no matter how much she told herself to be sensible. Just then, the door of the cottage opened and an elderly woman emerged into the tiny front porch that barely sheltered her from the wind. Seeing Torrance stand up next to the car, she called out, "Can I help you?"

Torrance's sense of dread left her as quickly as it had come. Here was a person who was not only obviously alive, but non-threatening. Torrance walked up the brick garden path.

"Please come in before we both get blown away," the woman said and backed into the house. Torrance followed, shaking her hair back into a semblance of order.

"Thank you," she said to the woman, who was short and frail as well as old. Presumably this was not the young mother whose address this had once been. "I'm looking for Carol Esther Marawik," she went on. "I was given this as her address. Does she still live here?"

The old woman gave Torrance a stricken look. "Oh no," she answered. "I'm so sorry. You've come here for nothing. She did rent this house, but she's moved. To Santa Rosa. How awful for you. How far did you come to see her?"

Torrance tried very hard not to look as happy as she felt at this statement. After all, the woman would never understand that, far from being devastated at not finding Carol Marawik on her first try, Torrance was delighted that Carol not only existed but had apparently moved to some identifiable place. She gave the tiny woman a sweet smile and shook her head slightly. "Don't worry, I only drove down from Eureka. It seemed as easy to come over here as to track her down in any other way. And it worked, didn't it? At least you know where she went. Do you have a new address for her?"

"Unfortunately, the landlord can't be relied upon to pass on any messages whatsoever. Carol knew that, so she talked to me personally and gave me her new address. She was worried about friends who might not get in touch fast enough to get a forwarding address from the Post Office. Young people don't . . . ." A sudden glance at Torrance seemed to remind the woman that, compared to her, Torrance could well be classed as "young." She hesitated and started over. "We old people were brought up to stay in touch by regular letters. That doesn't seem to be the custom anymore." She sighed and looked up at Torrance. "Sometimes I do miss the old ways."

Torrance smiled back and nodded. "Carol was lucky to have you move in. She obviously cares about her old friends, even the ones who've lost the habit of writing."

The old woman moved toward a battered purse lying on a chest of drawers that stood against one wall. She extracted an equally battered-looking address book and opened it to the proper page. "Here," she said, holding it out to Torrance. "Do you want to copy it? Then I won't have to put on my glasses to be sure of the numbers."

Torrance took the little book and copied the Santa Rosa address and telephone number for Carol E. Marawik, which had been entered in a slightly shaky but very legible hand. She returned the book with another smile and a few polite words of thanks. The old woman replaced it in her purse. "You shouldn't go right back out into that weather. Why don't you let me fix us both a nice cup of coffee or tea." She was clearly an isolated old person who saw few people suitable for polite conversation.

Torrance managed to look sad and regretful. She glanced at her watch. "I'm so sorry. I have to catch a plane to San Francisco. It would have been lovely to stay with you for a while. You've been so helpful, I hate to have to run off." Holding out her hand for a goodbye shake, Torrance hoped that the small woman would not remember that Torrance had come here prepared to visit Carol Marawik, and thus couldn't be as short of time as she pretended. She didn't want to hurt the woman's feelings, but a nice long chat over a cup of tea was not something she could hold still for right now. She escaped into her car and headed back toward Eureka. Once again, she needed a telephone.

A few calls and a trip to the airport later, Torrance met Derek for their flight back to San Francisco. They got one of the tiny planes this time, and both looked at the threatening weather with distrust as the plane taxied to the runway. They were buffeted for a while after takeoff, but the further south they flew, the more the weather cleared, and they moved from apprehension to conversation.

Derek was able to relate only more frustration with continued lack of police progress. He was envious that Torrance was successful in tracking down Carol Esther Marawik, not only finding proof that she existed but garnering a current address and telephone number in the process.

"I tried calling her, of course—how could I resist—but there was no answer. I assume she works. I'll try again this evening and keep working on it until I get hold of her. I didn't want to ask the old lady in Fields Landing whether Carol has a baby. As it was, I was very lucky not to be asked who I was and why I was looking for her."

Torrance also told Derek about her request for a computer run on recent infant kidnappings from Justice's Criminal Identification and Information Branch. One of her calls that morning, however, she kept to herself.

With the three suspicious birth certificates in hand, she had again called her old friend Louise Sandowski, the adoptions supervisor. Giving her the three children's names, mothers' names, and birth dates, she asked Louise to run them through the index to the adoptions cases pending with the state. To do this, she had to assure Louise that any information which surfaced would not go beyond the two of them, to be used only to decide whether to follow up the connection with Solomon and Parentbuilders. The state adoptions files were absolutely confidential and although Torrance could legitimately ask Louise to check on a matter which might relate to an adoption scam of some sort, any information she gained could not go beyond their respective offices and the parties involved without a court order. Torrance knew how persuasively Derek would work on her once he knew she had information he didn't have access to, so her call to Louise had to be kept separate from their joint efforts.

When the plane came in for a landing, Torrance had her immediate plans laid out: get the information from C.I.&I. about recent kidnappings; get hold of Carol Esther Marawik; follow up on both; and hope that all of this led somewhere.

For his part, Derek was facing the realization that he was no closer to solving Patrick James's kidnapping than he had been before. Undoubtedly, Marguerite wanted some news. He had nothing to offer her and, worse still, no one to bill for the last three days. Again his mind sifted through the cases he had left on his desk. He knew that the only antidote for his present situation was a little progress on something totally unrelated to missing babies and dead doctors.

17

*T*orrance returned home that evening after a frustrating afternoon at the office trying to concentrate on all the other things her job involved. As she opened the outer door, she had to laugh. Monica had her door open and some music on! Her curiosity was probably killing her. Mischievously, Torrance stuck her head through the door to Monica's rooms and called out, "What's for dinner?"

Monica appeared with incredible swiftness, looking smug. "Cracked crab, fresh French bread, some goodies on the side, and some of that Fume Blanc you like with crab."

Torrance did her absolute best to look disinterested. "I'm sorry, Monica," she started airily, "I don't think I can manage that tonight . . . ." Monica was momentarily taken in, and her face started to fall until she observed the corners of Torrance's mouth begin to twitch. She shook her hand threateningly. "You beast! I fix your favorite food, not to mention keeping those two monsters of yours entertained and fed for the last three days, and look at what you do to me!"

Torrance laughed and picked up her bag. "I have to change and make a phone call, then I'll be down to satisfy your curiosity." She started up the stairs.

"Bah!" Monica called out, "I'm just trying to be nice to you after your trip. There's not a curious bone in my body." That line almost made Torrance fumble unlocking the upstairs door, she was laughing so hard.

After she had responded to Jade's effusive greeting and given Buddha the attention she knew he wanted in spite of his pretended indifference, Torrance was finally able to change out of the clothes she had worn far longer than she had meant to. This brought her back to the awful reality of finding Dr. Moorehead's body. Last night, she had been exhausted and sedated by the large "medicinal" brandy Derek had insisted she finish, but she had still woken up in the middle of the night and had to turn the lights on while she tried to try to chase the image of the bloated face and the memory of the foul odor from her mind. Now she wondered whether the dark-of-night horrors would recur. She shuddered at the thought of more sudden awakenings. Perhaps talking it all over with Monica would help.

Before returning downstairs, she retrieved her note of Carol Marawik's telephone number and called it again. This time there was an answer. Torrance had her lines well thought out. She introduced herself rather vaguely and confirmed that she was indeed speaking to Carol Marawik. Then she mentioned that Dr. Moorehead had died. There were some questions relating to Ms. Marawik's medical records. Could Torrance perhaps see her some time tomorrow and go over them with her? Perhaps at lunch?

Carol Marawik was fortunately willing to set up an appointment without questioning Torrance closely about precisely what she wanted. She gave Torrance the address of the insurance company where she worked and agreed to meet her there at noon. Torrance sighed with relief as she put down the phone. That was easier than it might have been. Now she could mention the birth certificate while sitting face to face with Ms. Marawik and not only see her reaction but make it more difficult for her to terminate the conversation.

"Time for dinner," she said to the two attentive Burmese, and they followed her, tails straight up in the air, as though they understood her precisely. Perhaps they did.

Friday morning found Torrance impatient to get moving. The night before she had gone over with Monica all the ground covered so far, and the two of them had posited, explored, and then reserved or rejected a multitude of rational and irrational theories. Monica has the most Byzantine mind, Torrance thought. What incredible scenarios that woman can come up with! But she knew that Monica's flights of fancy had sharpened her own thinking, and she was eager to move forward as a result. Besides, the discussion with Monica had somehow chased her midnight horrors away, and she had slept well last night.

Since she was planning to drive to Santa Rosa later that morning, she decided not to go to the office first, but to work from her home phone until it was time to leave. Her first call was to Louise Sandowski, whom she knew to be an early worker. The adoptions supervisor was not available, and there was no message. Torrance got up in frustration and paced the room for a while. Finally, she settled back down and attended to other work until it was time to leave.

In Santa Rosa, Torrance asked for Carol Marawik at the insurance company's front desk as she had been instructed to do. The receptionist made a brief phone call, and within moments a young woman broke away from a group of workers leaving the elevator and approached Torrance. She was short and slightly chubby, with shoulder-length brown hair and a dress that did little for her figure. Her face was very young-looking and seemed devoid of make-up. She stepped up somewhat uncertainly. "Ms. Adams?"

Torrance took her in hand quickly and suggested they walk to a nearby restaurant where Torrance had eaten before. By the time they got there, the two were on first name terms at Torrance's insistence. Carol seemed awed at the whole idea of being interviewed in connection with a death, even though Torrance had not told her it was murder, and her wide-eyed interest promised a less difficult interview than most of the previous ones in this case had been.

Once they were seated and had ordered, this proved to be true. Torrance began by explaining that she understood Carol had given birth to a baby in Fields Landing attended by Dr. Moorehead. She didn't state exactly how she knew and it turned out she didn't have to. Carol blushed and looked down at her plate for a moment. "Yes," she said tonelessly. Then she looked up at Torrance, her face appearing even younger than before. "I didn't want anyone to know. I have a good job here, and nobody knows I had a baby. Is it all going to have to come out?"

"Well, I can't be sure until you tell me what it is you don't want to come out; but, no, I don't think there's any reason why the people you work with have to know you had a baby." Torrance tried to sound soothing, since the face across from her looked very close to tears. "I can promise you this. For now, our conversation is confidential. If I think I may have to tell someone who might get back to the people you work with, I'll let you know first and ask you if it's O.K. to pass it on. Will that make you feel better?"

Carol Marawik nodded and sipped at her Pepsi. Just then, their food arrived and provided a welcome diversion. After a few bites Carol looked up, somewhat more composed now. "It's all still very hard for me to talk about. I was so stupid to get pregnant, but I thought he'd marry me." She picked at her food some more, and Torrance gently encouraged her.

"Did you live in Fields Landing at the time, or did you move there after you got pregnant?"

Carol looked up, as if surprised at Torrance's ignorance. "Oh, I moved there to get away. My family's here in Santa Rosa. They helped me out, found me a place to stay. So long as I promised to come back without the baby."

"Was that hard?" Torrance asked gently. The last statement had held the dregs of a lingering bitterness.

Carol nodded. "Yes, at first it was very hard. I didn't want to make that kind of a promise. I thought if I kept the baby I'd have something left of the man. And someone to love." She paused, head down, and then looked up again. "But I know now that it wasn't very realistic to feel that way."

"Did your parents make arrangements for the baby for you?"

"Yes, they did. They sent someone to see me. From an adoption agency."

Torrance could feel her hands getting cold with tension as she heard this. Softly she asked, "Do you remember the name of the agency?"

Carol chewed on a thumbnail. "I think so. At least, I will in a minute." She ate some more of her food, her brow furrowed with thought.

"It won't come to me," she finally said. "It was something real obvious, too." She shook her head in frustration. "I'm sorry. . . . But I do remember the name of the lady who came to see me. It was Shirley Robusson."

As Torrance looked up, her eyes widened and became very green. Those who knew her well would have recognized this as a sign of intense excitement. Shirley Robusson, Torrance thought; Shirley Robusson personally involved in another Moorehead home birth. I'll be damned.

There was no outward sign of how strongly the information had affected her. "Was the agency the Parentbuilders Foundation?" Torrance asked with what seemed like perfect calm.

Carol looked up, surprised. "Oh, yeah, that's the name I couldn't think of. How did you know?"

"Easy," Torrance smiled. "I've met Shirley Robusson. And that's who she works for."

Carol nodded again. "Yeah, that's right. That's who my parents sent to see me. Parentbuilders. They had all these brochures about parents who wanted children real bad. And Mrs. Robusson told me that if I really loved the baby I wouldn't want to raise it illegitimate and on welfare." She glanced up at Torrance, as if to judge her views. "I thought Mrs. Robusson was a little too uptight about morals." When Torrance smiled and nodded her unspoken agreement, Carol continued. "But her bottom line was right. It was better for my baby that I gave him up."

"Can you tell me how it happened that you had Dr. Moorehead attend the baby's birth at your home?"

Carol suddenly remembered the reason Torrance had given for their lunch and gave her an eager look. "Oh yeah, that's why you wanted to see me, wasn't it, Dr. Moorehead. And here I've been telling you all this stuff about myself."

"That's perfectly O.K.," Torrance commented smoothly. "I didn't mind at all listening to you. But I do need to know about Dr. Moorehead."

"My landlady recommended him. I didn't really like him a lot, but he made house calls to a bunch of old people in Fields Landing once a week, so he was convenient. No one else would do that."

"So you saw him before the baby came."

"Yeah. He used to see an old lady down the street, and he'd offer to come in and look at me."

"Was it your idea that your baby should be born at home?"

Carol looked surprised. "Oh no, not me. That wasn't anyone's idea, really. It just happened. Shirley Robusson was there to talk to me, and I wasn't due for another week at least. All of a sudden I went into labor, and Shirley called Dr. Moorehead. I don't know why he came over instead of having her take me to a hospital. It got real bad for me, and he gave me some shots. I can't remember anything after that. At least not until Mrs. Robusson told me she was leaving with the baby and that I'd be fine."

"Did you see the baby before she left with it?"

Carol shook her head energetically. "No. I didn't want to see him. I didn't want to get attached to him. It was bad enough giving him up as it was. If I'd seen him, I'm not sure I could have done it."

"But you do know you had a boy."

"Yes. As Mrs. Robusson was leaving, she said he was a perfect little boy, and he'd make a wonderful family very happy. Then I kind of konked out again." Carol looked at her watch and started to fidget. "I'm sorry, I shouldn't take any more time for lunch." She frowned suddenly and looked straight at Torrance. "I don't really understand what all of this has to do with Dr. Moorehead's death."

"We found some files that we didn't understand," Torrance improvised, "and I needed some background to unscramble them." She signalled for the check, and the two women remained silent as they left the restaurant.

During the brief walk back to the insurance company offices, Torrance asked a final question. "Did you sign a consent to the adoption of your child?"

Carol brightened visibly. "Oh yes. That was around August. I got to meet the people who adopted him. Not that I knew their names or anything. But I did get to see them. They were ever so happy and so nice." She looked at Torrance with an eager expression on her face. "It really made me feel that I'd done the right thing."

Torrance hated to break the mood, but she had to find out. "Who took your consent, Carol?"

"Well, there was someone from the state, I don't remember her name, and the lawyer for the adoptive parents." Again she hesitated, trying to come up with the name she vaguely recalled. Torrance waited. Finally, Carol remembered. "Mr. Solomon. That's who it was, Mr. Solomon. I thought it was an appropriate name. Wasn't it King Solomon who decided who should get the baby?"

Friday morning found Derek impatient also—in his case, impatient to get to work on something a little more productive from his standpoint than the last few days. The previous evening, tired as he was, he poured himself a large Scotch and set to work sorting through the various messages and mail that awaited his return. As expected, there were two calls from Marguerite Albertson-James, which he determined to return later that evening.

First, he wanted to review the new cases he had taken on since the James kidnapping. He selected two that he thought he could knock off quickly before the weekend was over and laid his plans for Friday. Then he called Marguerite with apologies and a half-lie about how he had been working on another case out of town. She was clearly irritated at his lack of progress but, thankfully, didn't say anything openly. There were times when well-bred reticence was a blessing, Derek thought.

He turned his thoughts back to the two cases he hoped to finish off this weekend. One of them was a routine personal liability case—for the defense. Although it would require some checking on files on Friday, Derek knew that the solution of the case would lie in the surveillance of the person who was suing his client. On more than one occasion Derek had surreptitiously filmed people who were supposedly too injured to walk or bend over, doing everything from playing football to sawing wood. This weekend would be ideal for such an assignment, he thought. People were apt to do the craziest things on weekends.

The other case Derek selected had an unusual, and distinctly San Francisco, flair. This one would be fun, he mused. He smiled as he recalled how awkward and uncomfortable the client had been, trying to describe the problem. Derek couldn't blame him—it made one heck of a story. A businessman from Iowa, the client had come into town for a week-long convention, bringing his wife (first mistake, Derek thought). The couple befriended a young man they met at the hotel bar. (Here the businessman's story got a little vague.) After several days of joint partying, the businessman awoke one morning to find both his wife and the young man missing. Gone with the wife were her credit cards and toilet kit, but only one day's worth of clothing—a choice Derek thought wise on her part after inspecting their hotel room and seeing the clothes she had left behind. On the other hand, he noted, the circumstances did not bode well for his client's future credit rating. Derek took his advance fee in cash.

His assignment was both simple and oddly incomplete: find the wife and make sure she wasn't in any danger. He wasn't sure, given the circumstances, if the businessman was really more interested in finding the young man, but it didn't matter. If Derek found the one he would find the other—provided he moved quickly.

Friday morning he swung into action. First, a few phone calls to various contacts lined up credit union, motor vehicle and driver's license checks on both the young man and the litigious accident victim. The next call was to a credit card service bureau. The rest of the morning Derek spent running through court filings and phoning hospitals, to see if the accident victim had a history of similar lawsuits or a suspicious medical history.

By noon, he was ready to track down the young man and the errant wife.

To find someone who's disappeared, he knew, you start by going backward. Find out about the man, his habits and haunts, and sooner or later you will find him.

By evening, Derek had quite a bit to report to the distraught Iowan. To begin with, the wife was in absolutely no danger. The hustler (as the young man obviously was, a fact which Derek had quickly been able to confirm) had a reputation for being both short-sighted and easily bored. He never seemed to get more out of a tryst than some gaudy trinkets, a few additions to his wardrobe, and a week or two of a good time, and then, like the prodigal son, he would suddenly reappear at the door of a certain elderly man with a soft head to match his heart, who lived otherwise alone in the Potrero Hill district.

With the case thus temporarily put to bed (so to speak), Derek could afford to sit back and wait for the phone calls he knew he would get from the credit card companies, as the wife used the cards that Derek had put a watch on.

Saturday found him almost eager to be on surveillance again, fortified against the early start with a thermos of Celebese coffee brewed from his home collection of semi-exotic beans. The accident victim he had to tail lived in the "Avenues," as the area was called, ironically just a few blocks away from the recycled building that housed the Parentbuilders Foundation.

The address proved to be the upstairs flat of an old duplex. It had a wide stair leading down from the door to the street and no other entrance. Knowing how people in these older neighborhoods tend to be close to each other, Derek decided to confuse the curious by parking past the house in question and watching the door through the rear view mirrors. Despite this, he felt oddly exposed. Not for the first time, he wondered whether his insistence on driving a conspicuous classic car represented a subconscious response to his basic hatred of surveillance.

Shortly after nine a.m., he saw the first signs of activity in the upstairs flat. After a few minutes passed with nothing more exciting than the blinds and windows being pulled open, he settled in for the duration.

Inevitably, his thoughts drifted back to the events up north. He still saw no possible connection to his own case, but the mystery was there nonetheless. The half-formed patterns floated in the back of his mind as indelibly as the image of Dr. Moorehead's bloated face.

To pass the time, Derek added the hours between the time Moorehead was seen making a phone call in the local grocery store and when the neighbor saw the sedan drive off, and then he divided that time by various average speeds. The killer could have lived anywhere in a radius from somewhere north of Crescent City south to Marin County—or even San Francisco, if he had a fast car and drove with determination, stopping only at a convenience store for gas and a jug of wine. Half an hour with Moorehead, possibly less, and then a few minutes more to pull the patient files of Jane Robertson and Mary Johnson.

But why? What could be in those files that implicated the killer? And why hadn't the killer taken Carol Marawik's file too, for surely the birth of her baby fit into the pattern. Could it be that somehow her file did not contain the same damning evidence as the other files? Or had the killer in his haste simply overlooked the file or forgotten about the Marawik birth—after all, it was several months earlier than the other two. With a chill, Derek realized that if that was the case, whatever the killer was trying to keep from being discovered was right there in the neatly drawn-up Marawik file.

Painfully, Derek tried to recall everything he had seen in the thin little folder. After some thought, he decided that there was a third possibility which could explain the missing files, but it did not make any more sense out of the situation than the other two.

During this reverie, half of Derek's mind was fixed on his two rear view mirrors, watching for movement on the stairs. The neighborhood was beginning to come to life, and with the increased activity it became progressively more difficult to keep the doorway under surveillance. Passing cars and trucks would momentarily block his view or snare his attention. His anxiety began to rise, just as a slow-moving delivery van ground up the street from around the corner.

With a shock, Derek realized that the van had stopped moving and was double parked right where it blocked his view of the house. Cursing to himself, he jumped out of his car and walked quickly a few doors down to where he could again see the stairs. He was risking exposure doing this, he knew, but he had no choice. The success of an entire day's surveillance depended on not losing contact during anxious minutes like these.

Standing out in the open, though, was clearly not something to do in this neighborhood. Derek noticed that he was beginning to draw the attention of people passing by. One young woman stared curiously and intently at him as she slowly passed by in her car. Derek tried to act nonchalant, pretending to be interested in something down on the corner. Instinct, more than anything else, made him note the model and make of the car as it passed. Habit drew his eye to the bumpersticker as the car stopped to turn right at the end of the block. "Parentbuilders," it said.

Open-mouthed, Derek found himself staring at the disappearing tail lights of a blue 1974 Pontiac Grand Prix.

18

After she returned from Santa Rosa Friday afternoon, Torrance started out facing the usual problems. She sat down at her desk to find messages from Sheriff Oreston, Louise Sandowski, two legislators, and the Chief Assistant Attorney General. After a loud groan, she returned the call from the Chief Assistant first and fidgeted while she answered his question. Then she called Oreston, only to find he was out. So was Louise. Damn, Torrance thought, Friday afternoon, and I can't find out a thing. She decided she needed a cup of coffee, which gave her an excuse to walk up and down the hall. Then she dealt with the legislators.

Finally, just before five, Oreston called back. "I've got that C.I.&I. information you wanted," he drawled at her. "You ready to write?"

Torrance pulled up a pad. "O.K., let me have it."

"I asked them to get me all cases less than a year old in which a kid under six months was snatched. You were right, there aren't very many. They had five. Two were solved and the kid was returned. Do you want to know about those?"

"What were the circumstances?"

"The first was a custody fight. Grandparents grabbed the kid and went out of state because mom is a drug user and lives in sin with a man they don't approve of."

"I don't need any details on that one," Torrance interjected.

"The other was a grab-and-run by a baby sitter. She wanted the kid for herself. Pleaded insanity when they caught her."

"You can spare me that one, too. What are the three unsolved?"

"One you know about, of course," Oreston answered. "The James kid,

Ross, September tenth. That was the most recent. Before that, there was a kid named Thomas Benjamin Bertram, born August fourteenth, taken in L.A., Silverlake area, on August thirtieth." Oreston paused to allow Torrance time to write. When she indicated her readiness, he continued. "Before that, you get Forrest Peace Abengale, male, if you can't tell from the name. Here's the spelling." He went back through the name as Torrance wrote. "Date of birth is May twenty-eighth. He was taken in Garberville, Humboldt County, on June second."

Oreston could hear Torrance's sharp intake of breath. "Mean something?" he asked.

"I'm not sure. It could be just one hell of a coincidence. I interviewed a young woman today who said she gave up her baby for adoption on June second, in Humboldt County. The doctor who attended her was the late Dr. Moorehead, and the adoption was handled by the same people the Bowens dealt with. But I could have sworn the woman really did have a child."

"The other one ring any bells for you?"

"Well, L.A. sure doesn't fit in, but I'm looking for a mother and a child to match a birth certificate for a boy born August twelfth. So a missing kid born August fourteenth is definitely interesting. All I have to do now is get from being interested to understanding what went on."

A sound between a growl and a sigh came down the line from the Yolo County Sheriff. "Well, I'm glad I helped you out, Torrance, but I'm getting a feeling I may not like the bottom line of this. I sure as hell would have preferred not finding the Bowens involved in any trouble."

"I think they were victims, Sheriff," Torrance said with sympathy. "If we find someone's dirty game and stop it, Tyler Havening will see the benefit."

Oreston brightened a little, but not much. He still wished that Michael Bowen hadn't been killed on his turf.

Torrance's productivity, which hadn't been great since her lunch with Carol Marawik anyway, was completely gone after her conversation with Oreston. She pulled out a large sheet of paper and began to work on a complex diagram involving the two sets of three children. Three Moorehead home births. Three kidnappings. Obvious questions, but no obvious answers. Her doodles became more complicated as the clock moved toward six. Although her office door was open, she didn't notice the departure of most of her colleagues.

When the phone rang, she was so deep in thought that she jumped at the sound. She answered "Hello" instead of giving her name, a sure sign of her distraction.

"Torrance?" It was Louise Sandowski on the other end of the line.

"Louise!" Torrance brightened. "I'm sorry, my mind was really elsewhere. What time is it?"

"Just about six. I didn't think there was much of a chance you'd be there this late, but I have some information for you so I thought I'd try."

Torrance sat up straight and pulled over the pad with her earlier telephone notes. "Go ahead," she said simply.

"Your question hit the jackpot. There isn't any adoption file on Russell Robertson, of course, but we know there would have been one if the Bowens had lived. On Corey Johnson, a Petition has been filed. We're still doing the home study. David Marawik has a Petition pending on him also. We've filed the court report recommending in favor of the adoption. It'll go to hearing on October nineteenth. And I'll give you three guesses who's listed as the lawyer on both Petitions."

"I don't think I need three guesses," Torrance said, her excitement mounting. "It's got to be John Solomon."

"Bingo!" Louise answered quietly. She sat back and waited, giving Torrance time to think.

Torrance looked down at her complicated diagram and added Solomon's name to several of the lines she had drawn. "This is going to get nasty, Louise," she finally said. "Maybe you'd better not give me any details about the adoptive parents so I don't slip up on keeping them confidential. I'll probably end up getting a court order for them, though."

"Is this all going to happen before the hearing on the nineteenth?"

Torrance looked at her calendar. "Two weeks from Monday? I think there's a good chance. You're worried about whether you should stop the adoption from being granted?"

"Sure," Louise sounded distressed. "You think these kids aren't who they're supposed to be, don't you? Does that mean someone else is going to want them back?"

Torrance sighed. "I'm very much afraid of that. We're looking at three kidnappings that might fit those three birth certificates. But a lot of things don't make sense yet."

"I think if you're still unsure in two weeks, we'd better have a long talk about whether to postpone the hearing," Louise said sadly. "It'll be awful for the petitioners, but not as bad as going ahead with the adoption and setting it aside later."

Torrance agreed, and after a few more moments of conversation with Louise she hung up and sat back. Poor Louise, she thought. It was terrible for an adoption worker to be forced to tell a good family they had to give back a child for whatever reason. Louise's distress had been obvious from the fact that she had not asked Torrance for further details.

After taking another look at her diagram, Torrance reached for Derek's number and started to dial it. But she hesitated halfway through and replaced the receiver. She decided to give the whole thing some more thought and call him in the morning. Rising, she picked up her diagram, stuck it into a brief case with her other notes, and headed for home.

Saturday morning Torrance woke up to a bedroom already filled with light. She had shut off her alarm clock. What woke her was a moist nose against her cheek and a paw exploring her chin. As she scratched Jade's head, she felt Buddha walking across her legs. "Breakfast late for you guys?" she mumbled and tried to doze for a few more minutes. Of course it didn't work. The cats were thoroughly bored with sleeping.

Torrance got up and fixed breakfast for all three of them. The cats preferred hers, of course, begging for her bacon and paying no attention whatsoever to their bowls.

After breakfast, Torrance got out her notes from the night before and called Derek. His exchange came on the line and offered to take a message. Torrance left her number, suggesting he call after noon, as she planned to be out shopping before then. She had taken one look at her refrigerator and realized that she might not survive much longer if she didn't restock.

In spite of her best efforts at domesticity, Torrance was done with shopping and laundry shortly after lunchtime. With a deep sigh and a glance at her watch, she stepped onto the glassed-in patio and sat down, looking out across The City. She hated waiting for Derek to call back. Finally, she decided to settle down with a book and a glass of wine. She had gone over the facts so many times in her head she was getting confused. Time to get her mind off it entirely until she had someone to talk to.

The Grand Prix slowly began to turn around the corner to the right. For only a second Derek hesitated. Then, without having made any conscious decision, he sprinted back to his car, his eyes glued to the Pontiac. In those split seconds, he formed an instant image—the pattern and shape of the brake lights, the speed and size of the right hand turn signal, the shape and profile of the car from the rear—and most important of all, a fleeting impression, a feeling, for the driving style of the young woman behind the wheel.

The key found the ignition on the first stab and the V-8 roared to life. Derek pulled away from the curb, cut ahead of an oncoming car so quickly that it didn't even have time to honk, and gunned it to the corner. A quick glance at the cross traffic, and Derek was around the corner to the right, his eyes simultaneously scanning the cars for blocks ahead and taking in the pattern of movement around him.

He registered, rather than actually saw, a pattern of light on a car turning right against a red light two blocks away. Weaving crazily through the traffic, Derek hit the light just as it turned green. It was California Street, a main thoroughfare connecting the Avenues to the rest of San Francisco. Operating on instinct, Derek turned right.

He thought he caught sight of the Pontiac, still nearly two blocks ahead, moving ponderously but somehow swiftly at the head of a small knot of cars. The traffic was heavier here on California. Derek cursed as he ducked around vehicles that suddenly seemed to be going more slowly than anyone had a right to on this street—more slowly than the receding knot, pushing the Pontiac ahead of it.

Steadily Derek gained. He slipped through one yellow light, then two, and he was at the rear of the pack. He could barely see the edges of the wide body of the Pontiac through the cars ahead. They were just coming up on Arguello, the boundary line that begins the Avenues. The "Don't Walk" lights were already flashing. The Pontiac started through the intersection. Someone in his lane was turning left. Desperately, Derek switched to the right lane. He had gained three cars on the left lane when a Volvo in front of him suddenly braked. Derek slammed on both his brakes and horn. The light went red as the Volvo turned right onto Arguello, the driver looking back in surprise. An elderly lady who had just struggled across Arguello to the corner looked about in fear, wondering if she had barely escaped being run over.

Helplessly, Derek watched the front half of the knot of traffic disappear down California toward downtown, leaving stragglers behind at each successive intersection.

When the light changed, Derek drove swiftly but smoothly down California to Fillmore, glancing quickly at parked cars and down side streets. The young woman had not seemed to be in a hurry. It was Saturday. Perhaps she was headed for the upscale shopping district around Union and Fillmore. Derek got one block into the traffic snarl that surrounded that intersection when he realized the futility of it all and turned around.

Heading back out to his surveillance spot in the Avenues, Derek finally allowed himself to rationalize about the choice he had made instinctively. I was right, he told himself, despite how it turned out. What was a routine surveillance in a personal injury case compared to a chance for a major break on a kidnapping? At least now he knew that the girl and the car existed, and that they still had reason to be in the neighborhood of Parentbuilders. That alone was worth a lot. Derek had just about convinced himself that the brief chase had all been worthwhile when he glanced at the upstairs flat. His confidence evaporated. The windows and blinds were closed.

Resignedly, he kept on going, stopping at a corner store two blocks away that had a pay phone. He dialed the number of the flat, ready with his best telephone salesman's voice. After twelve rings, he hung up. He bought himself a coke and sipped it slowly as he stood at the curb, his face in the sun.

By the time he was halfway through the Coke, Derek was smiling. If it was not meant for him to get much done today, he wasn't going to fight it. "Well, Mr. Thompson," he said aloud to himself, "when the going gets tough, the tough get going, so. . ."—he looked at his car thoughtfully—"so put your top down; we're going to the beach."

He cruised out Geary to Land's End. As crowded as it sometimes was on weekends, this was still one of his retreats. He loved climbing among the rocks and strolling the clifftops canopied with wind-blasted cypress. He parked his Mustang in a dirt lot above the Cliff House restaurant and bar overlooking the ruins of the old Sutro Public Baths. After re-securing his recalcitrant convertible top, he struck out north on the trails that curved around toward the Golden Gate and Presidio.

After a few minutes of fast walking, Derek had warmed up enough to take off his shirt. The couples and families began to thin, and he saw more and more men, single and in small groups, on the trail. A number of them studied Derek as he walked quickly by. He was used to attracting the stares of both men and women in San Francisco. He generally paid no attention to either. That kind of forwardness always bothered him somehow.

Derek left the trail and climbed down to the sea's edge to a small patch of sand he knew about. This was one of his private places, off the main paths and hidden by a spit of land from the little cove to the west that sheltered a popular nude beach. A trio of huge boulders thrust into the water here. Pounded relentlessly by massive swells, their dark flanks glistened.

He lay back on his elbows in the sun, a light, cool breeze playing across his bare chest. The sand beneath him shuddered with each successive crack of the swells against the boulders. For a long time he lay there thinking about nothing.

After a while, Derek thought of his bronze Buddha, one hand upraised and one hand lightly touching the ground. He thought of Dr. Moorehead's delicate hands, lying useless on his lap; delicate hands that had delivered babies; quavering hands that had barely enough control to make the rough scrawls that had passed for progress notes in his files. Derek thought of what Dr. Moorehead had known that could get him killed, and why any person who was calculating enough to bring a jug of wine to a murder would entrust Dr. Moorehead with that knowledge in the first place. He thought of the kind of person who would kill someone with his bare hands.

Suddenly, he sat upright and opened his eyes, blinking in the brightness. Craning his neck, he could see the broad shoulder of Mt. Tamalpais basking beyond the north tower of the Golden Gate Bridge. In his mind's eye, he retraced the trails behind Buffy Albertson's house, circling up to the knoll where the kidnapping had been planned and. . .from which it had been directed? Derek had seen the bicycle mother, had felt, rather than seen, her drive. In those few minutes he had formed an impression of her that was impossible to reconcile with the kind of person who had so meticulously and boldly planned the theft of young Patrick James.

Staring at the mountain, Derek was suddenly certain: the mind that had planned Patrick's kidnapping was the same one that had coldly plotted the murder of Dr. Moorehead. He knew with every fiber of his instinct that Torrance was right about a link between their cases, but it was not the simple link they had already envisioned and ruled out. He and Torrance were on the trail of the same monster. Find the link, he thought, and we find the monster.

He had to phone Torrance.

Quickly he stood up, brushed the sand from his jeans, and stretched. Taking one last deep breath, he closed his eyes. The Buddha was smiling. Derek turned and climbed quickly up the cliffs back to his car.

As Derek burst into his flat, anxious to call Torrance, he was suddenly worried that her home number might not be listed. He went straight to the room which served as his office and tossed the mail on his desk. His red message light was glowing, indicating that his answering service had tried to reach him. He started to open the telephone book at the A's, suddenly realized how many Adamses there would be, and decided to pick up his messages first. He punched the number for the service.

"Hi, this is Derek Thompson. You've got some messages for me?"

"Just a couple: Frank—no last name—wants to know if you're still alive, and a Ms. Torrance Adams called this morning, saying that it was urgent you call her as soon after lunch as you can. That's all. Here's her number."

Derek copied it down, silently grateful. "Thanks. I'll be in my office but working on some things, so please keep handling my calls. Put them through to the office if it's important."

"Certainly. Have a good evening, Mr. Thompson."

Derek pushed the disconnect button, paused a moment to absorb his surprise at Torrance's call, and punched the number.

"Hello?"

"Torrance? Derek. I just got in and was going to call you, but it looks like you beat me to it. What's up?"

"Derek! Where have you been all day?"

"I went to the beach, but that's a long story. You first."

"I've been working hard on your case, and you run away to the beach?" Torrance's voice rose in good-natured indignation. "That's a fine way to thank me."

"As I said, it's a long story. What do you mean, working on my case?"

"Well, I have something that could be of interest to you, that is, if you're still working on the Patrick James kidnapping."

"Actually, that's why I was at the beach—uh, sort of."

"Uh-huh," Torrance said, unconvinced. She decided it was time to get more businesslike. "I'll let you explain your goldbricking later. I got some information yesterday, and I've been working on it ever since, trying to make some sense out of it all." Torrance paused, unsure of how fast to push. "I think there's more evidence that ties Patrick James to the Bowen baby and Moorehead," she said reluctantly. "Look—I know you doubted the possibility of a connection."

Derek interrupted her. "Hold it, hold it! Forget all that for a moment. You say you got some new information? What is it? Do we have our link?"

"Our link?" Torrance repeated to herself, not sure she had heard Derek properly. His enthusiasm caught her off guard. "Derek, I thought you were taking a dim view of all this."

"Yes, well, the ocean has curative properties." Derek realized he had been standing all this time and finally sat down. He erased the anxious edge from his voice. "I'll come back to that; let's just say I am exceedingly interested in anything you might have come across which might link Patrick's case to the problem you've been working on. . . . Hello?"

"Ouch! Stop that!" Torrance's laughter broke her momentary silence. "I'm sorry, I was playing with the phone cord, and Jade suddenly decided to attack it while my finger was wrapped in it." She laughed again. "Just a minute—there! Now I can talk without being rudely interrupted or mauled."

Derek joined her laughter. The tension evaporated. Quickly, Torrance related the results of the C.I.&I. search, giving Derek the dates, names and places of the three unsolved kidnappings off the chart she had drawn up and reminding him of the dates of the home births attended by Moorehead.

"Fascinating," was all Derek could say.

"This is too much coincidence for me," Torrance went on. "I still don't know how these tie in, but as you would say, it doesn't pass the smell test.

I think we need to find out more about these other two kidnappings."

"Do you think either of these mothers would have footprints—usable ones?" Derek asked eagerly.

"That's certainly one thing we can find out," Torrance answered, still taken aback by Derek's apparent enthusiasm.

"Look, this may sound silly, but why don't we split this up? I have a lot of contacts in L.A., and I know the Silverlake district pretty well. I could go down on Monday and look into the—who was it?"

"Bertram. Thomas Benjamin."

"—the Bertram case. The north coast is your home ground, so you could probably track down any available information on Forrest Abengale much easier than I could. We need to know everything: M.O., time of day, witnesses, suspects—and get footprints if we can. What do you think?"

Torrance shook her head. "I think—that sounds just fine. Derek?"

"Hm?"

"What did you smoke at the beach?"

Derek laughed. "Fair enough. Nothing. I'd like to say I got religion, but that wouldn't exactly fit me. I've had a very interesting day." Derek told Torrance about the day's events and his futile chase of the bicycle mother, ending with his revelation at the beach.

"I thought only women were supposed to operate on intuition," Torrance said finally when Derek was done.

"Yes, well I—um—I have never underestimated the power of women." It wasn't what Derek had started to say, but it would do. "Private eyes need intuition, too," he added lamely.

They spent the next several minutes confirming their plans for Monday. When they hung up, Derek leaned back in his chair, smiling. He knew they were on the trail of the common link between the events of the past several months. He felt it was only a matter of time till he and Torrance unmasked the monster.

Torrance stood up and walked over to her window and looked out at the darkening sky. Buddha rubbed against her ankles. She picked him up and held him, scratching his ears. She hadn't told Derek her greatest suspicions about Parentbuilders and the man she suspected lay behind them. That accusation was almost too dangerous for her to entertain. She wanted Monday to be here. Her chart lay on the phone table, its empty spaces beckoning.

19

Derek's talk about the beach inspired Torrance to get up early on Sunday morning and drive her car across the Golden Gate to the Marin headlands. She parked and took a long walk through the dunes. She felt as though the fresh breeze off the ocean was blowing away some of the brooding and restlessness.

The smell of seaweed as she approached the water's edge reminded her of Eureka, and Eureka reminded her of Derek. A series of pictures ran through her mind. Derek at the Fern Cafe, pushing his black hair out of his eyes and smiling his brilliant smile. Derek at dinner, one eye opening above his glass of Chardonnay, the communication between them instant and intimate. Torrance kicked at what was left of someone's abandoned sand castle and looked out across the waves. Don't start confusing understanding with intimacy, she told herself. We understand each other, yes. But there may be nothing else there. Her mind ran on, seeing Derek at her motel room door—ever so polite—and joking with her as they walked up to Dr. Moorehead's house for the second time. Then the picture of how they found Moorehead suddenly followed, and she forced herself to see the beach in front of her.

After a while, she came up with a plan to get the information she needed about the Garberville kidnapping.

On Monday morning, she called Vince Jones, one of the supervising special agents she knew who was responsible for several ongoing investigations in the north coast area. She told him she needed a copy of the Humboldt County sheriff's file on the kidnapping of Forrest Peace Abengale on June second in Garberville. Jones repeated the name skeptically.

"You're sure you're not putting me on?" he asked.

"I'm telling you the absolute truth, Vince. It came right off the C.I.&I. computer. And I need those records as soon as I can get my hands on them. If they help me put a lot of loose ends together, I may be able to do the sheriff a favor in return."

"Well, I've got a couple of guys up there who could drop in and get the records copied for you, but they can't drive them back down."

"If they can pick them up and take them to the highway patrol office in Garberville, I'll take it from there," Torrance offered.

Jones found this an acceptable deal and promised to have his agents contacted by radio to get the records she wanted. Immediately upon hanging up, Torrance called her contact in the highway patrol commissioner's office. The two did occasional services for each other, and the delivery of urgent packages by way of an informal patrol "courier" system was one that Torrance occasionally requested. It was little trouble to the patrolling officers to hand off a package from beat to beat across the state, and in some of the more remote areas, it was the fastest way to get something moved quickly. Torrance received a promise that the file dropped off in Garberville would be shuttled to the Marin office in Corte Madera. She in turn promised to pick it up there. She arranged to be called once the file had reached Marin, hoping the call would come before the end of the day.

In Los Angeles, the sun seemed far away through the smog. The cars pulsing up the Harbor Freeway were like ghosts on a television set, a diffuse collection of faint shadows. Ahead, distances faded into a horizonless haze. Objects lost their edges in such a light.

Derek eased his rented car over to the right lanes and began to watch the exit signs. Years ago, when he lived in Los Angeles, he would have remembered the distances between various exits and known the patterns of traffic in the merging and diverging lanes. He would have stayed in the left lane until precisely the last moment when he could slip swiftly, almost unnoticed, to the far right lane and his desired exit. He no longer had what to him was the highest skill a Los Angeleno could develop—the one skill which set a Los Angeles native off from the denizens of any other urban area—an instinctual feel for navigating the intricate web of freeways.

"Just like a damn tourist," Derek told himself as he saw a sign declaring that the Sunset Boulevard exit was still a distant three-quarters of a mile away. It was an unfair accusation, and Derek knew it. He couldn't get lost in Los Angeles if he tried, and still he proudly referred to the freeways by their names instead of their numbers. It was merely the edge of his skill that was gone. Nothing in Los Angeles was keeping its edges today.

Derek pulled off at the exit ramp and turned left onto Sunset, heading west, only to find himself dumped into the middle of a block-by-block crawl of heavy traffic. He settled back for the duration and thought about the report on the Bertram kidnapping he had picked up earlier that morning after interminable delays at the downtown headquarters office of the Los Angeles Police Department.

It was unusual in a number of respects. Thomas Benjamin Bertram, age two weeks, was missing from his mother's home in the Silverlake district of Los Angeles. The prime suspect was the baby sitter, a young Mexican woman, who had also disappeared on the day of the kidnapping and not been seen since. She had been heard from though. According to a follow-up report written the day after the story headlined the local papers, a woman identifying herself as Pacita Benvenides, the baby sitter, telephoned the police and in broken English denied that she had taken "Tomasito" or knew where he was. She claimed that she had left him out in the garden in his crib when she went inside for "just a few minutes" to talk with her boyfriend who had just happened to stop by to visit her and when she went back outside the baby was gone. Frightened that she would get into trouble for letting her boyfriend come over and fearing that she would be blamed for stealing the child, she ran away. And she was right, wasn't she? Now the papers were saying she took the baby. She called to say that it was a lie and someone else must have taken him.

The call was traced to a pay phone in a supermarket in East Los Angeles, the heart of the Chicano district. Pacita never returned home, according to her aunt and uncle who answered the door, who also denied all knowledge of Pacita's boyfriend. The East L.A. district officers put the word out on the street that they were looking for a young Latina and her boyfriend who had an Anglo baby, and that they considered this a high priority case.

Derek knew the message that had been delivered: either something breaks on this case fast, or business in East L.A. starts suffering, starting with the local rackets and moving up the line to more legitimate and bigger stuff. In the weeks following, the intense pressure had produced only three things: a young Chicano who was fingered as Pacita's boyfriend was grilled with no result; the "definitive" word on the street came back that Pacita was an illegal and that she would never be seen in Southern California again; and a delegation of Hispanic leaders descended on the Mayor's office to protest the harassment of their community by the police department on the groundless and racist assumption of guilt by association.

The last report filed only a few days ago stated that the Immigration and Naturalization Service had files on half a dozen women named Pacita

Benvenides, ranging in age from three to forty-eight, including a young woman who had been deported as an illegal alien two years earlier when she was sixteen years old. The officer noted laconically that this might mean that they would be seeing Ms. Benvenides again in two years' time.

Derek turned off Sunset and headed up the hill into the Silverlake district. As he saw it, there were only two ways that the L.A.P.D.'s theory on the Bertram kidnapping could be right: either this Pacita Benvenides was a very disturbed young woman who took Thomas for herself, or she had done it for pay. If the former, they would have picked up both Pacita and the kid by now. Nuts don't run very far, and nuts don't phone the police with a long alibi.

On the other hand, he mused, it didn't make much sense as a contract job, either. The baby sitter was sure to be suspected. Why would an illegal alien, especially one who had entered the country twice, risk exposure and a certain jail sentence followed by deportation on what could only be a one-shot deal? The more he thought of it, the more Derek felt that there was something missing, a piece that would make it all clear. He drove up to Silverlake through the haze.

He found the Bertrams' house without too much difficulty and parked just up the street from it. The house was nestled on the downhill side of Upper Lake Drive, one of several narrow little streets that coiled up the sides of the hills which held in the Silverlake Reservoir. Derek had phoned ahead on Sunday, so he knew that Nancy Bertram, the mother, was expecting him. Still, he stood outside the car for a few minutes and looked around.

Like much of Los Angeles, the Silverlake district was a hodgepodge of life-styles and incomes. Upper Lake Drive itself was for the most part graced with large ranch-style homes, with a few shingled or redwood "rustic cabins," dating from the twenties and thirties sprinkled in, all solidly upper middle-income. A few yards up the Drive, however, was one of the narrow stairway streets the district was famous for—streets that were so steep they were nothing more than paved steps. The houses that lined the stairway paths were typically little more than glorified wood and glass shacks. The people who lived in them, Derek knew, were a mix of aging hippies and artists, retirees, gay couples, and various other assorted Hollywood types.

Derek walked down the street. Like many of the houses in the area, the Bertrams' house was largely hidden from the street by overgrown shrubbery. A metal chain link gate with a mailbox in it pierced the bushes. Derek opened the gate and went through, noting that it had only a simple latch.

The gate opened to a steep path of stone steps. These led down to a garden and a narrow strip of neatly-trimmed lawn, setting off a gracious, late-fifties ranch house. The effect was like stepping into a different world. Derek paused and looked around in surprise. The little yard was completely isolated from the street above. Only the brown knob of the top of the hill was visible in the circle of sky above the garden.

The front door opened almost before Derek rang the bell. The woman was in her early thirties, pretty, but with skin and hair that had seen too much sun. She wore a stylish blouse and a grey skirt that was clearly the lower half of a suit. Nancy Bertram worked in a Wilshire Boulevard office during the day and had agreed to meet Derek at her home during her lunch hour. Her stockbroker husband had decided to leave this business to her, obviously pessimistic about whatever assistance or information a private eye from San Francisco could provide.

"Hi. You must be Mr. Thompson." Anxiety showed through her cool professionalism.

"Derek Thompson, please. And you're Nancy Bertram. I really appreciate your being able to meet with me on such short notice," Derek replied.

"Yes, well, won't you come in?" She held open the door. "I must admit your request was somewhat unusual, and after all these weeks with no word. . . ." Her voice trailed off. "Would you like something to drink?" she said, more forcefully.

"I'll join you if you're having something," Derek answered.

She headed for the kitchen. "I'm afraid that I'm just finishing a diet shake. That's my lunch. But you're welcome to something stronger, if you'd like. Beer, perhaps?" she called over her shoulder.

"Any soft drink will do," Derek called back. He heard the refrigerator door open and the sound of bottles and cans rattling. Derek took the opportunity to inspect the interior. The front hall opened directly to a living room which ran the full depth of the house. The kitchen and dining room were on the left, and a door apparently led off to the bedroom wing on the right, but it was the living room itself which commanded attention. The entire back wall was glass and showed a spectacular view of the reservoir below.

"I have Coke, diet Pepsi, diet orange, and some natural fruit sodas," Nancy's voice called from the kitchen.

"Coke is fine, thanks," said Derek, as he stepped up to the glass wall. The hill dropped off sharply. He was looking nearly thirty feet straight down onto the back yard of a house that belonged to Nancy Bertram's neighbor. The hillside to the right and left was thick with brush.

"Lovely view, isn't it?" said Nancy, coming around the corner from the kitchen, holding two glasses. She handed Derek his Coke. In her other hand, she swirled a glass of thick pink liquid, partially drunk. She took a sip. "Not many houses around here have a view like this. Ben and I were very lucky. We bought it five years ago right after Ben got his present job while houses in this area were still affordable. It was only two and a quarter, if you can believe it!"

Derek nodded agreeably, thinking that from his viewpoint houses like this had not been affordable for nearly twenty years. "It's a beautiful place. I've always liked the Silverlake district; it reminds me of some of the neighborhoods in San Francisco."

"That's right, I guess you have a lot of hills there, too," Nancy replied. "I haven't been to San Francisco since I was six with my parents." With that, she dismissed both the topic and the city.

"I'll have to get back to my office before long. I don't really know what you had in mind coming down here and all. I've got the footprints, like you asked." She pointed in the direction of the dining room. A large brown manila envelope lay on the table. She stared at it a while, then sighed. "I've kept them on hand ever since Tommy disappeared."

"I really appreciate this," Derek interjected soothingly. "As I promised, I'll have them back to you no later than next Monday. I've read the police reports and have just a couple of questions. Then I'll be on my way. As I told you over the phone, there's only a slight chance that your son's disappearance will tie in to the kidnapping case I'm working on, but for both our sakes, I think it is worth looking into."

This triggered something in Nancy Bertram. "We're glad to be of whatever assistance we can, Mr. Thompson, especially if there's a chance it could lead to finding Tommy or at least catching the person who did this, but I think I have to make it clear we can't afford to hire a private investigator to look into every possible theory that pops up. The police have already spent hundreds of hours checking all kinds of leads. . . ."

Derek held up his hand, "Don't worry, Ms. Bertram. You're not paying for my time, and I wouldn't dream of trying to bill you for it. My client is up north."

Nancy relaxed visibly. "Well, then," she said, moving to take a seat on the sofa, "why don't we get started?"

Derek followed her and took the chair opposite her. "As I said, I have only a few questions. Like the police, I'm interested in how Pacita came to you in the first place, and how long she was with you before the kidnapping. But I'm also interested in what you and your husband did on a daily basis from Tommy's birth until the day he was missing. In particular, I'd like to concentrate on your activities the week before he disappeared."

"The week before?" she repeated, trying to remember. "The place I work kept calling with questions, so I started going down there in the mornings. Actually, it was good for me to get out of the house for a while every day."

After twenty minutes, Derek felt that he had all the information he could get. As he suspected, the Benvenides girl had come to the Bertrams innocently enough and with good references. More important, prior to her baby sitting, she had been the Bertrams' maid before Nancy got pregnant. As for Nancy and Ben's habits in the two weeks before the kidnapping, they had both quickly settled into a routine after the initial week's excitement. Pacita's duties were expanded to include taking care of Tommy. She was there every morning and any other time the Bertrams were gone.

Nancy maintained her control all through the questioning until she came to the point in the story when she returned from work to find an empty house. The terror, disbelief and panic were visible in her face. Derek tried somewhat ineffectively to calm her and finally let her relive it until she was drained.

Finally, she regained her composure. Embarrassed, she began to apologize. Derek assured her that no apologies were necessary. "There's another young mother in Marin who has been through the same ordeal," he said soothingly. "I intend to do everything I can to get to the bottom of this. If there's a link between your two tragedies, I'll find it." She looked a little hopeful.

He thanked Nancy again for her cooperation and picked up the envelope with Thomas Benjamin's footprints. He glanced inside to confirm the envelope's contents. He was hardly an expert, but they appeared to look every bit as clear as Patrick James's prints. Maybe this will lead to something, he thought.

Nancy showed him to the door, picking up her purse and suit jacket. She had to return to the office. Derek stepped out onto the front porch, and Nancy locked the door behind them. Automatically he looked up. He found himself looking straight at the bare hilltop.

He turned to Nancy. "Is this the only yard?" he asked.

"Just what you see," she replied. "Actually, we're quite fortunate to have this much land on the hill. None of the other houses on Upper Lake have yards like this until you get over toward the Thoresons, near the bottom. But then, they don't have the view we have either."

Derek wasn't listening. He quickly paced the length of the garden and lawn as Nancy Bertram watched. No matter where he stood, the brow of the hill followed him.

"Then this must be where the crib was when Thomas was taken," he interrupted.

"If I can believe anything that girl said, it is. When I came home, the crib was here." Nancy indicated a point below the kitchen window. She turned toward Derek, anger in her eyes. "Honestly, I don't know why the police don't just arrest that Mexican boy and keep him in jail until he talks!"

Derek was taken aback. "Uh, you mean Pacita's boyfriend?"

"If that's what you want to call him, that's who I mean," Nancy replied, firmly.

"Why? I thought the police did question him."

"He was in on it from the beginning. He's nothing but another liar. I know for a fact that he used to visit Pacita every day. I'm certain they went straight back to our bedroom—our bed, mind you—and played around. That's why she washed the sheets every day. He's probably just waiting for things to calm down so he can bring Pacita and Tommy out of hiding."

"Wait a minute," Derek interjected. "Why wasn't any of this in the police reports?"

Nancy made a sour face. "They're not interested any more. I just found out myself two weeks ago. Mrs. Rankin, next door, told me that that Mexican fellow used to park in front of her house every morning at ten, like clockwork, and would leave just before I returned at noon. Can you imagine? That girl was entertaining a strange man in my house every day. I'm surprised that Tommy was the only thing missing," she added with bitter humor.

"But he *was* the only thing missing, wasn't he?" Derek asked. Nancy nodded ruefully. Derek continued, "That's why I'm beginning to think that your case has more in common with mine than you or I might realize yet." Nancy stared at Derek in surprise, and again a look of hope flashed across her face. Derek bid her goodbye at the gate. She continued to stare after him as he got into his car, and then turned to walk slowly down the hill to where she had parked her own vehicle, a clean but older model BMW.

20

A dispatcher from the Marin highway patrol substation called Torrance at 4:40 p.m. to tell her that a package for her had been dropped off by an officer who had been patrolling 101 north out of Corte Madera. Torrance said she would leave immediately to pick it up. She had brought her car to work in anticipation of the trip.

By the time Torrance got her Porsche out of the lot and onto Van Ness Avenue going toward the Golden Gate Bridge, the rush of Marin suburbanites trying to get out of San Francisco for the day was well under way. Traffic crawled and tempers flared, especially at the aggressive drivers who insisted on trying to cut in and out even though no one was going anywhere fast. A stalled car on the bridge made it worse than usual, and the speeding up after passing the disabled car was momentary. Torrance thanked God that she was able to get off at Paradise Drive. The trip had already taken her close to an hour and her nerves, unused to rush hour traffic, were wearing thin.

The highway patrol office was just off the freeway, and it took Torrance no time at all to pick up the file that had been left for her. She asked that thanks be passed on to all involved in the relay and left the office almost in a run with her treasure clutched under her arm. The dispatcher, watching her eagerness, was convinced that the efforts made to deliver the file were worth the trouble.

The run back to the city was a lot better in spite of Torrance's impatience. If it hadn't been for her desire to be near the phone in case Derek called when he got back from L.A., she would have read the file right there in the highway patrol parking lot.

Like most of San Francisco's Victorians, Torrance's house had a garage added after it was built. But, since it was an afterthought, the garage was less than convenient. It was almost impossible to get the Porsche into it without scraping some part of its body on the sidewalk, and once you were in, you had to close and lock the door from the driveway, since there was no inside connection to the house. Torrance found this trying, but then she remembered the traffic to Marin and gave the house a little pat as she came up to the front door.

Monica had been warned that Torrance would be running in and out, and her door was closed. Upstairs, the cats were impatient. They were sitting right inside the door and meowed as Torrance walked in. It was not clear whether this was in appreciation of her appearance or as a complaint that it had taken her so long to get home.

Torrance put the file down on the kitchen table and looked at the clock. Half past six. No wonder she was hungry. She opened the refrigerator— freshly stocked, thank God!—and found some cream cheese, ham, and half a bottle of wine left over from Saturday afternoon. She added some pita bread and a few leaves torn off a head of lettuce and carried the whole thing up to her favorite thinking spot, the enclosed patio off the bedroom. The Garberville file, of course, went under her arm, and the cats followed her single file up the stairs. No need to starve before reading the file, she thought, but she didn't have to change out of her suit. She sat down in a chair where she could see the light fading over The City, arranged her food where she could reach it, and opened the envelope.

The file consisted of investigating officers' narratives, a victim's statement, and a few other documents Torrance didn't immediately recognize. She started with the narrative, wincing as she usually did at the stilted jargon common to police reports.

Just as she was about to find out what happened to V in the general vicinity of W1 and W2, the phone rang. It was Derek, impatient. "I've been trying to reach you ever since I got off the plane. I thought I'd get back early enough to catch you at the office, but you left before five."

"You make it sound like I went home early, but you know I didn't if you've been calling here."

"You're right. So where have you been?"

"Derek, I hope this relentless cross-examination is a sign that you have something exciting to tell me, rather than an indication that your personality is disintegrating."

She could hear Derek take a deep breath and then laugh. "O.K., sorry. Here I am positively bursting with news and I couldn't reach the only person I can talk to about this case who wouldn't think I'm insane."

"Don't count on it. But to put your mind at rest about where I've been, I was battling the world's worst traffic in order to get the file on the Forrest Peace Abengale kidnapping. It's right here in my hand. So the question is, where are you?"

"I'm back in my flat, across from Buena Vista Park."

"Well, that isn't half the earth away from here. Do you want to come over and trade discoveries?"

Derek hesitated briefly and then agreed. He let Torrance give him directions and promised to be there within the half hour.

As soon as she had hung up the phone, Torrance gathered up her file and food and moved downstairs to the living room. It wouldn't do to walk Derek through her bedroom to the patio. Then she plunged back into the documents, absently munching at a sandwich. "V" (the victim of the alleged crime, although that was really poor little Forrest, wasn't it?) was a young woman from Chicago named Tanita Abengale. After attending college in California she had dropped out of her upper-middle-class background. (The child's name was beginning to make sense to Torrance now.) How Tanita had happened to move in with a carver of redwood burl furniture and curios in Garberville was unclear, but she had done so a year before the kidnapping of her child—or the *alleged* kidnapping, as the report put it.

The child had been born on May 28. The investigating deputy had obtained a copy of the birth certificate which showed that the wood carver, Gordon Reynolds, was named as the boy's father. Forrest was born in a hospital, but the file did not indicate that anyone had checked on his footprints.

On June second, Tanita Abengale put the baby which she was nursing into a carry-basket and took it to Gordon's shop. Evidently this surprised the investigating deputy. She herself didn't find it odd, since the couple's living quarters were upstairs in the same little house, and the shop on the first floor had a sprawling porch. On a nice June day, Tanita's actions were understandable.

What she did, apparently, was sit on the porch next to the baby, waiting for customers and presumably guarding the stock while Gordon worked inside. When a pair of customers came along, she showed them the merchandise. In doing so, she left the sleeping baby in its basket next to the chair. She walked around to the side of the house with the couple who seemed likely to buy if they found the right item. She said she didn't leave the baby out of her sight for more than ten minutes. The customers confirmed this. They'd seen the basket with the baby. When the trio walked back to the front of the house, the basket was gone. No one could say whether a car had stopped. The little shop was situated to take advantage of the flow of tourist traffic, and a car could easily have come and gone unnoticed.

Torrance was just reading through the part of the report that explained the investigators' early dropping of the case when the doorbell rang. She trotted downstairs and let Derek in.

"Was that your guardian watching me through the front windows?" he asked while he looked around the hall with interest.

Torrance laughed. "I don't know how well Monica guards me, but I can see her being very curious about any men who come to see me after hours."

She preceded Derek up the stairs and opened the second-floor door. He tried not to stare too obviously, but he did observe the detailed restoration work that had been done. To the left, a wall had been pierced to join what had once been a narrow hallway to an expansive living room with windows at the back of the house. As Torrance led Derek through the broad entry, he saw two sable-colored cats observe him gravely from a position of safety at the foot of the steps leading to the third floor. He knew enough about cats to let them approach him at their own speed.

Torrance noted Derek's look of interest when he saw her sandwich, and she quickly got him to admit he hadn't eaten. She offered to get more of the same, and he accepted. While she poured more wine, he stuffed half a pita and talked while he worked.

"Well, do you want it all from the beginning or should I give you the best part first?"

"The best part first and *then* from the beginning."

"O.K." For effect, he took a bite of his creation and a sip of wine while Torrance obediently mimed impatience. "I have here"—he patted an accordion file next to him—"the very good-looking footprints of one Thomas Benjamin Bertram, kidnapped on August thirtieth by a person or persons who operated exactly like the person or persons who took Patrick Albertson-James on September tenth."

This announcement, as he had expected, brought a flood of questions from Torrance, and by the time Derek told her all about his trip, the food was gone and Jade was friends with Derek. Even Buddha, shy of strangers, was curled up on a sofa across the room.

Finally, Torrance pointed to the Garberville file and said, "My turn now."

She repeated the part she had already read to Derek, then found the next entry, and they went through it together. It appeared that Tanita had been having increasingly bitter fights with Gordon before the birth of the child. Her preoccupation with the baby, once it was born, seemed to have improved things, but after the kidnapping the relationship fell apart again. Gordon kicked Tanita out. Tanita moved on. No one knew with whom or where to. No one really cared. Gordon made it clear he didn't really want the child. So the overworked cops put the file in the permanent unsolved category. Case closed.

Torrance put the papers down and poured out the rest of the wine. Derek scratched Jade's chin. "It's wrong," he said.

Torrance nodded. "You mean this one couldn't have been planned."

"Exactly. The kid was brand new, only five days old. This was probably the first time he was left alone. He must have been snatched on the spur of the moment."

"You do see this as a genuine kidnapping though?"

"Yes, don't you?"

Torrance nodded again. "Yes, there were witnesses there. Obviously, the father didn't run off with the baby, and if the mother had wanted him to herself she could just have left."

"It's too close in time and place to Carol Marawik's delivery for us to ignore it, but it sure doesn't feel like the other two kidnappings." He reached for his file and pulled out a set of footprints in a separate envelope. "Meanwhile, we need to get these prints for the Bertram kid checked out. How fast can you get a comparison with the Bowen baby?"

Torrance did a quick calculation, "Wednesday afternoon."

"Wednesday!" Derek groaned. "Can't you do anything tomorrow?"

"Not unless I want to drive them to Sacramento myself, which my office would seriously frown on. I can put them on tomorrow's courier. That means they arrive in Sacramento Wednesday morning and get delivered to the print examiner Wednesday afternoon."

"Could I run them directly to the examiner?"

"You really think these are likely to be Michael Bowen's prints?"

"If they're not, we're out of leads, aren't we?"

"I think so. The Abengale child would have been too old to be Michael, and there are no other unsolved kidnappings. But why are you in such a hurry on my part of the case?"

"Well, I told you, I believe the two kidnappings are linked. If we know where the one stolen child went, we may be able to track the other one. It's the best I've got on my end, too."

Torrance could see his point. "You want to drive up first thing tomorrow?"

When Derek nodded, she got up and invited him to follow her into the kitchen. While he admired the room, Torrance dug into her purse, which she had dropped on the kitchen table much earlier, and headed for the telephone with her address book and credit card. She dialed a number and credit card code. After a swift response on the other end, she identified herself and asked that Tim McDonald be contacted at home, if possible, and asked to call her.

"Impressive," Derek commented. "May I ask who that was?"

"Justice command center. They're on duty twenty-four hours a day, and they can get hold of just about anybody who works for the A.G." She gave Derek a wry smile. "Sometimes I'm the person they get hold of at some ungodly hour."

Derek realized that it must be late and looked at his watch. It was almost ten. Just as he started to comment on how quickly time had passed, the phone rang. Torrance answered. It was Tim McDonald, the baby footprint specialist, returning her call.

When Torrance asked him whether he would be available the following morning to check out another possible match for the Bowen baby footprints, he gave an immediate O.K. He shrugged off apologies for the late call and sounded interested in this new possibility. Torrance thanked him and, prompted by Derek, told him to expect Derek at around ten o'clock.

"Well, there you are," Torrance told Derek after the call was completed. "All you have to do is show up at Justice headquarters tomorrow morning and ask for Tim."

"You get the most amazing service," Derek said admiringly as they returned to the living room. "It's quite something for an unimportant private eye to watch."

Torrance turned to him and gave him a level look. "Hogwash," she said. "You have your sources and I have mine. They're just different."

Derek conceded her point with a slight bow and a raised eyebrow. She was right, of course, even if she didn't know quite how different some of his sources were. "Well, I'd better get some sleep if I'm going to leave for Sacramento at dawn."

Torrance walked downstairs with him and let him out the front door after he promised to call her the moment the prints had been compared. She returned to the living room to clean up the food and shut off the lights. It suddenly seemed very empty. For a moment she sat down next to Buddha and stroked his fur. Jade came over and sat at her feet, looking up as though trying to understand her mood. "You guys are nice," Torrance told them. "But you're not in the same class as Derek."

Tuesday morning found Torrance less wistful. She caught an early bus to the office and rummaged through her form file until she found a Petition and Order for disclosure of adoption records. With a few changes, she could use these to seek official access to the identities of the persons who were seeking to adopt the two other children whose birth certificates had shown home births attended by Dr. Moorehead. First, however, she needed a client.

After several telephone calls, Torrance finally had a conference call set up with Louise Sandowski, the Chief of Adoptions for the Department of Social Services, and that department's Chief Deputy Director. She gave them all a succinct briefing on the basic facts—three possibly suspicious birth certificates, three possibly related kidnappings, three adoption files with John Solomon as the attorney for the Petitioners; Parentbuilders involved in at least two of the three adoptions, as well as linked to the kidnapping of Patrick James; the ominous death of Dr. Moorehead. "I think your department needs to worry about the integrity of the process when it comes to these adoptions," she concluded. "If the footprints of the child kidnapped in Los Angeles match the child who died in the I-80 crash with the Bowens, we should get an immediate court order allowing your department to cooperate with law enforcement by making a limited disclosure of the parties to the other two adoptions."

Torrance's recommendation brought about the flurry of debate she had expected. While Louise Sandowski was on her side and argued vigorously in favor of a rapid investigation and resolution of the questions Torrance had raised, the Chief Deputy was skeptical, and the Adoptions Chief kept reiterating his position that adoption records should be disclosed only under the most compelling circumstances.

Torrance let everyone talk for a while, then she decided to bring things under control. "O.K., folks, let me remind you how this conversation started out. I suggested we get a court order if it turns out that the child placed with the Bowens was kidnapped from its home in Los Angeles. If that's the case, then the Russell John Robertson birth certificate was a fiction. Everything you were told about the placement of that child may have been a fiction. Aren't those sufficiently extraordinary circumstances to require you to look into two similar situations before those other two adoptions are finalized?"

The logic of her argument was difficult to contradict, and after some more discussion the consensus was that a court order should be sought if the prints turned out to be those of Michael Bowen. It was clear to Torrance that the Chief Deputy agreed to this only because he was absolutely certain that the required contingency would not occur, and that the whole conversation was nothing but a waste of his time. But she could also tell that the Adoptions Chief was worried, and that Louise Sandowski was afraid for the families who had innocently taken these children into their hearts.

For Derek, Tuesday began when he woke a full thirty minutes before his alarm was set to go off, having spent a restless night. He quickly showered and dressed and sat in the pre-dawn light by the window leading to the deck, sipping coffee and munching on a toasted bagel with Swiss cheese. He glanced indifferently at the morning paper and put it aside. His hands kept returning to the manila envelope containing Thomas Bertram's footprints, rearranging it on the table beside him or simply patting it, as if losing contact with it might somehow cause it to disappear or alter its contents.

Finally Derek could stand it no longer. He left his coffee and, wrapping the remains of his bagel in a napkin to finish on the way, grabbed the envelope and left.

Derek's preoccupation was such that he hardly noticed the miles between San Francisco and Sacramento slip by. He had a dim recollection of passing hundreds of cars waiting patiently behind the toll booths to cross the Bay Bridge into The City and a fleeting sense of relief that he lived in San Francisco and was going in the opposite direction from the morning commute. Then the cars thinned out past Vallejo and he sped on through the open farm land of the valley. It was still only 9:30 in the morning when he crossed the bridge over the river into Sacramento.

Following Torrance's directions, Derek had little difficulty finding the headquarters building of the Department of Justice's Law Enforcement Division out on Broadway. It was a massive, sprawling four-story complex, painted an odd shade of red ocher like old public buildings in Spain or Italy, but almost totally devoid of windows or ornamentation to break up the blankness of the walls. He parked in a visitor space beside the building and went in the front door.

Derek's initial reaction was that he had walked into the observation and holding room of the San Francisco County Jail by mistake. It was a glassed-in enclosure, monitored by cameras and a laconic uniformed agent sitting at a desk behind the glass. Derek asked for Tim McDonald, and after being transferred from one number to another the guard finally reached him. Following a brief exchange, the guard hung up the phone and wordlessly slipped a card under the glass for Derek to fill out.

In a few minutes, Derek had a temporary badge pinned to his lapel and was ushered by a receptionist past the electronic doors back to the fingerprint division of C.I.&I. As Derek approached the counter of the fingerprint division, a short, plump dark-haired man with thick horn-rimmed glasses too large for his face detached himself from his desk and came over, hand outstretched.

"Derek Thompson, is it? I'm Tim McDonald. Ms. Adams told me to expect you." His eyes were bright behind the thick lenses. They struck Derek as having an intensity common to people who were into esoteric pursuits like designing computer architecture or deciphering ancient Sumerian languages. Tim McDonald's voice hovered on the edge of a squeak. "I understand you have something for me to look at," he added, eyeing the manila envelope in Derek's hands.

"Yes, these are the footprints," Derek replied, handing over the envelope at once, all social niceties forgotten. "They belong to Thomas Bertram, who was kidnapped from his parents' house down in L.A. in September. I just brought them up last night. . . ." Derek paused.

McDonald totally ignored Derek. He opened the envelope, carefully extracted its contents, and turned his back on Derek as he started toward his desk, deep in concentration. Suddenly he stopped.

"Jeesus Christ," he said softly.

"Something the matter?"

McDonald turned back toward Derek. "Look at this! See that loop there?" His fingers quickly traced a pattern on the right footprint. "I'd know that pattern anywhere. I can almost guarantee you we've got a match here."

Derek frowned. "Just like that? You can tell?"

McDonald bustled over to his desk and pulled out a second set of footprints and slid them into a viewing screen. "Yes and no." McDonald looked up, his eyes huge behind their lenses. "It'll take me about half an hour to do all the comparisons before I can say that these two sets of prints belong to the same person." He turned back to the viewing screen. "But after you've done this for a while, certain things stick in your mind. That loop on the Bowen baby's right foot is very distinctive; I noticed it right off. Now, if you'll excuse me for a few minutes, I have some work to do." With that, McDonald slid into his chair and was gone to the world.

The next half hour seemed interminable to Derek. He tried amusing himself by overhearing snatches of conversation around him and trying to parlay them into clues on a major case of statewide importance. Unfortunately, much of the conversation consisted of the typical coffee break inanities of clerical staff.

Finally Tim McDonald stood up from his desk and looked around, blinking. He saw Derek sitting by the counter and came over.

"Mr. Thompson? I can state, based on over a dozen points of comparison, that Thomas Bertram and the baby boy killed in the Bowens' car are one and the same. Under normal circumstances, congratulations might be in order for solving a difficult case. In this situation, I'm not sure what to say."

Derek took a deep breath. "Unfortunately, I'm afraid this case is far from solved. I have the feeling it's just getting started. Thanks for your prompt service." McDonald shrugged off the compliment. "Now then," Derek continued, "do you suppose I could use your telephone? It's long distance, but it's to an Assistant Attorney General we both know."

Tim McDonald smiled. "Absolutely. Here, call on the lease-line." He began pushing buttons and then handed the receiver to Derek. "Now just dial the last four digits of her number. Oh, and can you ask her if she'd like me to write up my formal report for Sheriff Oreston?"

The phone was ringing, so Derek simply nodded. After the second ring, Torrance's familiar voice came on the line. She sounded anxious.

"Torrance? Derek. Hang on tight. It looks like you have a positive I.D. on the Bowens' baby and we all have a real mess on our hands."

There was a long pause at the other end of the line, followed by a long exhalation of breath. "My God," Torrance said. "So the prints were clear enough for a positive identification?"

"McDonald says yes."

"Well, that makes my case a criminal case too." Torrance paused. "I'm going to have to report this to the criminal division and go for a court order allowing me access to the adoption records of the two other babies that Moorehead supposedly delivered. I presume you're going to head on back into The City?"

"Yeah, I guess I'm done here, unless there's something you want me to bring back."

"I can't think of anything."

"Torrance, who gets to tell Nancy Bertram?"

"Oh, God, I hadn't thought of that." There was a long pause. "Actually, I think it would be best if she gets the word officially from law enforcement officers. The word should come down to the L.A.P.D. from Sheriff Oreston, once he's convinced that he has a positive I.D."

"Thanks for not saying I should do it. But that reminds me. Tim McDonald wants to know if he should make his formal report to the Sheriff."

"Absolutely. Then Oreston can take it from there. But I'd like a copy."

"O.K., I'll tell him. Then I'm headed back to The City, I guess. It sounds like you've got your work cut out for you."

"I'm afraid so. I'm not looking forward to this. Oh—and Derek?"

"Yes?"

"Thanks. I know this really wasn't your case."

"At this point, you'll never convince me of that."

"No," Torrance replied thoughtfully, "nor me, either. I'd better get to work; I'll call you this evening and let you know what happened."

Derek rang off. He thanked McDonald again for his help and passed on Torrance's message. Stepping outside the building, Derek found that the day had turned into a typical Indian Summer day. He put down the top on his Mustang and cruised at sixty miles per hour all the way back to the Bay

Area, letting the wind buffet him as he sifted through what he and Torrance knew.

As he left Davis behind, what he had to do next was clear. He allowed himself to hope that Torrance's efforts to open up the adoption records would succeed in locating Patrick James. But for Derek, that was no longer enough. Someone had to pay for what Marguerite and Nancy had been put through. And the only clue which could tie the whole thing together was a young woman in a blue 1974 Pontiac Grand Prix.

21

*I*t was a good thing that Torrance had spent much of the morning planning her course of action if Derek turned out to have discovered the true identity of Michael Bowen. Derek's phone call left her so excited and eager to do everything at once that only the carefully reasoned priorities she established earlier kept her from rushing off in the wrong direction.

First, she spent half an hour drawing up her papers for a disclosure order. She gave these to her secretary to type and asked that an appointment be made for the late afternoon with the judge who handled adoptions cases. Louise Sandowski also had to be informed of the court time and asked to meet Torrance at her office beforehand to accompany her to that appointment.

Having set this in motion, she called Sheriff Oreston. The Sheriff was out—Torrance was glad, since she didn't want to tell the same story more often than she considered reasonable—and she left a message for him to contact Tim McDonald about the Bowen baby's prints.

Next, Torrance made the call she wanted least to make, to tell Assemblyman Tyler Havening that the baby his sister was driving home had been kidnapped from a couple in Los Angeles. Havening's composure had improved greatly in the two weeks since Torrance had last spoken with him. Still, the news of the link established by the footprints shook him considerably. It took him a while before he absorbed Torrance's assurances that his sister and brother-in-law undoubtedly had no idea of the child's true identity.

When Torrance told him about the possibly connected cases and indicated her desire to move as quickly as she could to check out the legitimacy of those adoptive placements as well as to uncover the guilty persons, Havening became decisive and firm. He wanted those creeps caught, and he wanted them caught quickly. If it took another call from him to Zeke Wilson to make sure Torrance had adequate time and resources to pursue this, he'd be glad to do it. Torrance assured him that the Attorney General had already given her a free hand but promised to call if she had the slightest difficulties getting cooperation from everyone. She also promised to keep Havening informed.

Before ending the call, Havening asked Torrance when the identification would hit the press. Torrance couldn't make any promises. Soon too many people would know about the matching prints, and there would be almost no way of preventing a leak.

"I'm not in favor of letting the information out now," Torrance said. "We're undoubtedly after someone who's smart and careful. The longer we go without him or her knowing what we have, the better off we are."

"Well, the press sure isn't going to hear it from me," Havening replied. "At least not until I can say we've got all the facts and they prove my sister was an innocent victim."

"That's what we're on our way to doing," Torrance promised. "I'll keep in touch."

Her next chore was to inform her office's Criminal Division of the total picture she and Derek had found. It was now clear that she was involved on the fringes—if not in the middle—of a criminal investigation, and it wouldn't do to have only a civil lawyer as the liaison with law enforcement. Torrance walked a few doors down the hall and entered the office of Darrell Schoenig, the Assistant Attorney General in charge of criminal matters for the San Francisco office.

Darrell was on the phone, apparently with someone in a D.A.'s office. He motioned Torrance to a chair, grimaced at the receiver, and shrugged his shoulders. Torrance nodded sympathetically. If there was anything she was familiar with, it was the phone call you couldn't quite get out of.

Finally, Schoenig hung up and looked interested. "I was wondering when you'd come in. I hear you discovered a murder victim. Heavy duty stuff for a person who claims not to be interested in criminal law."

Torrance's eyebrows rose. "You have quite a grapevine. Where did you hear about the body?"

"It was disappointingly straightforward. Your secretary told my secretary."

"Ah! Well it isn't exactly the body I've come to see you about, although it undoubtedly ties in. Let me give it to you from the beginning."

Torrance started her story with the I-80 crash and her inability to identify the dead child. Next, she explained how Derek and the kidnapping he was investigating had come to her attention. "The link was Parentbuilders," she said. "It made us both wonder whether there was a bigger picture we weren't seeing."

She went on to relate the trip she and Derek had made to Eureka, Fernbridge, and Ferndale, and the finding of the body. Then she explained about the two other kidnappings and her plan to get access to adoptions records on the two children whose birth certificates she questioned.

Darrell Schoenig listened to Torrance with interest, asking a question here and there. Then he shook his head. "I'm beginning to get confused about who's who in this." He looked at his watch and continued, "Were you planning to eat any lunch? It's twelve-thirty. We could continue this in the cafeteria."

Torrance agreed, and she and Darrell resumed their conversation over sandwiches. Torrance had brought along her chart on which the various players were lined up and cross-referenced. Darrell went through all of the facts with her again and nodded. "A real mess from the law enforcement standpoint. At least five jurisdictions involved already and probably more to come." He scrutinized Torrance's diagram for a while and pointed to a note next to the square representing the Patrick James kidnapping. "What do you mean by 'Jeannie may be able to identify'?"

"That's Derek's witness. I don't remember her full name. She was the first person on the scene after the baby was taken, and she probably saw the person who did it. We think that person is a young woman who's linked to Parentbuilders. Jeannie may be able to identify her once we get some pictures."

Darrell nodded again and picked up the debris of his lunch. "Let's go back to my office while I think a minute."

Once the two were seated again, Darrell took another look at Torrance's chart, scratched his chin at some length, and then looked up at Torrance.

"Who is this you've got written in here?" he asked, his finger moving over the places where Solomon's name appeared on the chart.

"That's the lawyer who is handling the two pending adoptions and was handling the Bowen adoption. If you're asking me who would benefit if there's something funny going on, he certainly is the most obvious one."

"But you haven't got the slightest evidence that he knew this Bowen child was not Russell Robertson, right? And on the other cases you've got no evidence so far that there's anything wrong at all."

Torrance got up and stood in front of Schoenig's desk with her arms crossed. "Darrell, my dear, that's why I've brought you into this whole mess. Getting evidence is supposed to be a law enforcement job. Since not a single one of the many cops involved in this knows even half the facts, I thought you could get someone to help them all out." She smiled a slightly sharklike smile. "I wouldn't want anyone to accuse me of withholding what little evidence I do have."

Darrell sighed and looked pained. "Yeah, I'll pass it along. Are you going to give me those adoption records when you get them?"

"Yes. I've got an appointment with the judge at three-thirty, so you should get them today. I'll see you then."

Torrance gave Darrell a little wave and left his office. She wasn't altogether sure she'd convinced him there was more than a single stolen child who had somehow been fed into the legitimate adoption market.

At four o'clock, Torrance and Louise Sandowski were seated in Judge Rifkin's chambers. The judge, a short, plump woman wearing half-moon glasses with strands of gray hair escaping from a knot at the nape of her neck, was still reading through the papers that had been presented to her. She knew Torrance well and had a great deal of respect for her yet she found the allegations of the Petition hard to believe.

She looked up at Louise Sandowski. "You signed the supporting declaration, Ms. Sandowski. Do you truly believe that there is a multiple kidnapping scheme involved here?"

Louise fidgeted. "Your Honor, I'm not sure that's the only possible answer. But what I *am* sure of is that we have to find out quickly before these adoption petitioners go any further—before these children continue to bond with families they might not be able to stay with. That's why our Department agreed to come to you with this Petition."

Torrance raised one hand from her lap in a slight gesture that drew Judge Rifkin's attention. "We're asking you to balance the possible harm here, Judge. The request for disclosure is only to persons directly involved in the investigation of the three kidnappings and Dr. Moorehead's murder. If it turns out that the two other children we're concerned with were legitimately placed, the investigation will have done the two families involved a minimum of harm. On the other hand, if we find that one or both are in fact kidnapped children, any delay at all would cause great harm. Both the adopting parents and the parents from whom the children were kidnapped would suffer a great deal if it took an inordinate amount of time to discover the truth."

Judge Rifkin asked some further questions and listened to the answers. Torrance's calm and persuasive style finally won out, and the judge picked up her pen. "I'm not utterly convinced you're drawing the right conclusions, Ms. Adams," she said, looking at Torrance over her glasses. "But I agree with the balancing of the equities as you've presented them. I'll give you your order, but I'll require you or your client to give the two families notice of its issuance as soon as possible. I don't want them to hear about it from the police."

Torrance thought this condition over for a moment and decided she had no objection. Whether the families heard about the order from her or from law enforcement, the risk existed that they would alert Solomon or Parentbuilders. It couldn't be avoided. "I'll be happy to comply with that, your honor," she said. Judge Rifkin handed her the signed order, and Torrance thanked her politely and left, Louise close behind.

Once they were out in the hall, Louise shook her head. "I don't know how you managed to go through all that without ever mentioning Solomon's name."

"I couldn't," Torrance answered. "He's in Judge Rifkin's courtroom all the time. She would have thought we were both crazy if I told her that Solomon is the other link between those cases."

"When you mentioned Shirley Robusson, I was afraid the judge might know about the connection between her and Solomon and have the same reaction."

Torrance looked confused. "You mean you thought she might know that Solomon uses Parentbuilders as an intermediary?"

"Oh no," Louise answered, "I was afraid she would know that Shirley Robusson is Solomon's sister."

Torrance came to an absolute dead halt to the great chagrin of three other attorneys who had been walking down the corridor behind her. "What?" she virtually shouted at Louise.

Louise took Torrance by the arm and pulled her out of the stream of traffic toward the wall. "John Solomon and Shirley Robusson are brother and sister. Didn't you know that?"

"I had no idea. Why on earth didn't you tell me this sooner?"

"I thought you knew. I thought that's why you were so suspicious of Solomon."

Torrance acknowledged the irony with a dry laugh. "Just goes to show how jumping to the right conclusions can get in your way. I suppose you've been so supportive of my arguments because you were sure that anything Shirley was doing brother John had to be in on."

"No, not really. I'm still not convinced he's directly involved. Shirley might be referring cases to him, and he might believe what she tells him."

Torrance shook her head. "I can't buy that. Shirley would want some of the money he's making. After all, donations to her Foundation must be smaller and harder to walk off with than his legal fees. Besides, he referred the Bowens to Parentbuilders, not the other way around. "

"I still want to think that there's some possibility that neither of them is actually stealing these kids. I mean, I don't like either of them, and I don't like the unlicensed baby brokering they do, but kidnapping? That's a lot worse than I'd have thought them capable of."

"They're the ones who are making the money, Louise. If someone else is doing the stealing, what would be their incentive?"

Louise had no answer. She stood there, turning the facts over in her mind until Torrance put a hand on her shoulder. "Come on, let's go to my office and look at these files you've been ordered to give me." Each wrapped in her own thoughts, they left City Hall and walked back across Civic Center Plaza to the State Building.

The files were much what Torrance expected—not too much use to her except for disclosing the identities of the adoptive petitioners and confirming the fact that Solomon had filed the two adoption petitions. There weren't any surprises, no previously secret facts that would suddenly make all the pieces fit together. Torrance sighed and told herself not to be greedy. She made three copies of each file and returned the originals to Louise.

"I see the petitioners are in Folsom and Merced. It'll be a tight squeeze for time, but we'll have to try to notify both of them tomorrow. I'd like to talk to them myself. Do you want to go with me or should I take the assigned workers?"

Louise thought for a moment. "I don't know whether they're available. Can I call you first thing in the morning and let you know?"

Torrance agreed, and Louise left after receiving thanks for her help in court. By then it was almost five. Torrance decided to take one copy of the file to Darrell Schoenig before doing anything else. But his chair was empty and there was no indication where he was. Torrance left the papers prominently displayed on his desk with a note advising him of the Judge's requirement that Torrance notify the adopting families of the court order. She was about to add a statement about the relationship between Shirley Robusson and John Solomon, when her secretary appeared in the door to Darrell's office and told her that Sheriff Oreston was on her line. Torrance added a quick "See me—there's more" to the note and rushed down the hall to her phone. She knew that she would have to do another thorough retelling of the whole case before she tried to reach Derek.

Wednesday morning, Torrance picked up Louise Sandowski from her office in Berkeley before heading for Folsom. Louise had to go along because the workers involved in the two adoptions cases were not available on such short notice. Torrance had managed to reach both families the night before and talked them into meeting with her and an adoption worker. She had let them know it was a serious matter related to the adoption but had insisted that the subject could only be discussed face to face.

The first family they were to visit had one child whose birth certificate said he was David Richard Marawik. David was now called Joseph Hewitt, Jr., and his parents-to-be were Joseph and Ellie Hewitt who lived in an expensive neighborhood bordering Folsom Lake. Torrance was conscious of the fact that as she drove up Interstate 80 toward Sacramento she was following the same route travelled by the Bowens when they were taking home a child who was supposed to be Russell John Robertson, born in Fernbridge, but who was really Thomas Bertram, kidnapped in Los Angeles. She was glad that she was not the one to tell the Bertrams what happened to their child. From what Derek said, she gathered that Mrs. Bertram was quite sure the child was still alive and held some hope of getting him back.

As Torrance drove, she thought about her conversation with Derek the evening before. She had started out with the most interesting new fact to her mind, the fact that Solomon and Robusson were brother and sister. She and Derek agreed this could be very important. Then she explained the court order to him and told him that she had carefully worded it to allow him access to the adopting parents' names, so long as he used them only in connection with his investigation of the James kidnapping. She offered to leave one copy of the adoption files at her office for him to pick up with the understanding that he would not directly contact either of the two couples without first clearing it with her. Derek for the first time told her some of his personal thoughts about the cases. He spoke of the "monster," the coldly calculating planner who, Derek was sure, was behind the kidnappings in Ross and Silverlake, and behind the murder of Dr. Moorehead. But for the moment, he continued, he would put his speculations aside and do some basic investigating—trying to identify the "bicycle mother" Jeannie Walker had seen. Torrance wished him luck, and they promised to talk again the next day.

Torrance abandoned her thoughts of Derek as she approached the scene of the pile-up in which the Bowens had died. She pointed it out to Louise, and they looked around with interest. There was almost no evidence that this had been the crash site. Really, the only signs at all were the fire-blackened field and freeway shoulder crossed by the tracks of various vehicles. But those could have been caused by nothing more than the fire itself and efforts to put it out. By March when the winter rains would cause a lush new growth of grass over the burnt areas, nothing at all would remain.

Following Louise's directions, Torrance took Highway 50 out of Sacramento, then left it to take Folsom Boulevard into Folsom itself. After passing through the tiny downtown area, she crossed the bridge over the American River and headed up Auburn-Folsom Road, where she soon passed Folsom Dam with Folsom Prison lying on the far side. After a few more miles Louise told Torrance to turn right again on one of the streets leading up into the hilly area fronting the lake where houses commanding a water view were very expensive indeed.

The handsome redwood-and-glass custom home was by no means among the largest in the neighborhood. It was built into the slope of the hill that faced away from the lake. Torrance parked her Porsche at the curb and checked her watch. She was only a few minutes late for the noon appointment she had set up. She and Louise walked up to the front door and rang the bell set next to a large modern stained-glass panel depicting a brilliant blue clematis climbing a trellis.

Joseph Hewitt answered the door and asked them in. Torrance knew from their conversation the night before that he was spending the morning at home because of her visit. The adoption case file indicated that he was a well-paid executive involved in finance and real estate development. The file also indicated that the Hewitts had repeatedly asked that the child's birth name and mother's identity be kept a secret from them. While they had met the mother, they had not exchanged names.

The living room was half a floor up in the free-form house and looked out at the carefully landscaped hillside which gave it a sense of isolation from nearby houses. Ellie Hewitt rose from a sofa, obviously tense, and shook hands with Torrance and Louise. A four-month-old child was dozing on his stomach in a playpen nearby. Torrance suddenly understood why Louise had been so unhappy all along. This was going to be awful.

After the polite introductions were out of the way, Torrance handed Joe Hewitt a copy of Judge Rifkin's order. "This is why we're here, Mr. Hewitt," she said. "The Judge allowed the Department of Social Services to turn over your identity to law enforcement personnel investigating three kidnappings, but she ordered that we explain it to you first before any investigators approach you. So I'll tell you as much as I can."

At Torrance's words, Ellie Hewitt turned absolutely white. Her husband saw her reaction and moved from his chair to the sofa to sit next to her and put an arm around her. Holding her close, he looked up at Torrance wordlessly. She suspected he didn't trust his voice, and she wasn't sure she could trust her own.

Quietly, she told the couple that a baby who had been kidnapped in Los Angeles had been placed for adoption with a Sacramento family. Two other kidnapped babies might possibly have been similarly placed. There were certain similarities in the three adoption cases which had led the judge to believe they needed to be investigated. Theirs was one of them.

"Joey?" Ellie Hewitt asked in a dead voice. "You're saying that Joey might have been kidnapped? That someone wants him back?"

Joe Hewitt looked at the play pen where Joey was beginning to stir. He turned toward Torrance. "That can't be right," he said. "We met his mother. Are you saying the woman was a complete fake?"

Torrance shook her head. "No. I talked to her, and I was convinced she really had a baby. But we can't be absolutely sure that the baby she had was the baby you got. After all, she never saw it, and you didn't get it directly from her."

Joe Hewitt frowned. "You suspect the Parentbuilders Foundation gave us the wrong child?"

Torrance shook her head again. Her suspicions were not germane to this conversation. "I don't know what to suspect. The whole reason for the court order is that we need to find out what did happen. That's up to law enforcement. Our job in coming to see you is only to warn you that questions will be asked, and that there is some possibility that Joey is not who you think he is."

Joey began to cry as though in protest at her words. Ellie, a little color returning to her cheeks as her mind focused on him, got up and picked him out of the play pen. She checked his diaper and looked at her husband. "I'll have to change him."

Torrance looked at Louise who took her cue well. She rose and walked over to Ellie. "I'll go with you," she offered in a quiet voice and followed Ellie out of the room.

Joe Hewitt stood up also and walked over to the large window overlooking the hillside. As he stood there looking out, Torrance spoke again.

"There is one very important fact you should be aware of. The mother of the kidnapped child who is the same age as Joey disappeared after the kidnapping, and the father doesn't seem to want the child back. I don't want to suggest you have nothing to worry about, because that's not realistic, but there is a good chance that even if Joey is the kidnapped child, you could keep him. You'd probably get the father's consent, and if the mother can't be found, her rights could be terminated for abandonment."

Joe Hewitt turned around and returned to his seat. He seemed less shocked and was beginning to think ahead. "How are you going to establish whether Joey is the child we thought he was or this kidnapped baby?"

"I need to have his footprints taken. There are footprints of the kidnapped child, and I've asked for them to be made available for comparison, but

I don't know yet how good they are. Unfortunately, there are no footprints of the child you were supposed to get. That complicates things. We may have to go to blood tests. And if the missing mother can't be found, those could be inconclusive too."

Joe Hewitt thought about this for a moment. "What happens if we never find out for sure who Joey is?"

"There shouldn't be any question about your keeping him if no one can prove he belongs to someone else."

Hewitt sighed. "I appreciate your telling me all this. It doesn't sound totally black. What happens next? Is someone from the police going to come and interview us?"

"I imagine they will. I'm not involved in that end. What I would like to do though is send up a print examiner as soon as possible to get Joey's footprints for comparison. Is that O.K. with you?"

Hewitt nodded vigorously. "Oh yes. I want this over with as quickly as possible."

"All right," Torrance answered. "I'll call from here before I leave and arrange it. There's just one more request I have of you. It would help if you talked about this to no one except people working on the case. I know John Solomon is your attorney for the adoption and you have every right to consult with him, but it would help if you could wait a while before telling him anything about what I've said to you today."

When Joe Hewitt started to answer, Torrance held up a hand. "No, don't tell me yes or no. I want you to think about it and be clear in your own mind what you need to do. It wouldn't be fair for me to ask you for a commitment. I just wanted to let you know the considerations."

Hewitt nodded, and Torrance stood up and asked for permission to use the telephone. While she did so, Ellie Hewitt and Louise returned. Both looked emotionally drained, but they were smiling a little as they returned a now happy Joey to his play pen.

Almost three hours later, Torrance got off the freeway in Merced. Crossing through town, she followed Louise's instructions once more until she arrived at a large brick ranch-style home in the Bear Creek area. She had come to see George and Marcia Evandale, the prospective adoptive parents of Corey Daniel Johnson, whose existence was supported by nothing more than a birth certificate and Dr. Moorehead's vague statement about how many babies he had delivered.

George Evandale was a bank vice president, and his wife had been the manager of a florist's shop until the child was released to them. The case worker's interview notes were cautious. This was a couple who had expressed great desperation for a child, and there was some suggestion that they depended on the arrival of the child to hold their marriage together. Torrance knew that most social workers feared this attitude. A shaky marriage was rarely improved by a child's arrival, and the child was then often blamed for having failed to meet those unrealistic expectations.

As Torrance parked her car and got out in front of the Evandale home, she felt tense. This was the child that could be Patrick Albertson-James—the child Derek was looking for. Unlike the Hewitts who were not necessarily at risk of losing their child, the Evandales had no chance of keeping Patrick if that's who their baby was.

The doorbell was answered by a greying, heavyset man in a business suit. While he escorted Torrance and Louise into the living room—a traditional room with a brick fireplace and glass doors overlooking a patio and swimming pool—he reiterated his criticism of the night before, asserting that he thought this could have been done by telephone without requiring a meeting when he had other things to do.

Marcia Evandale, a small woman who looked stylish and well groomed but ill at ease, rose and came forward to greet them. There was no child to be seen. George Evandale finally abandoned his complaints, and they sat down after introductions were completed.

"Well," Evandale started out, "what's this problem you claim you have with our adoption? I was going to have our lawyer present but, with the kind of notice you gave me, that wasn't possible."

Torrance wondered whether this meant he had already talked to Solomon, or only that he had thought about it. She went through the same routine—handing over a copy of the order, explaining the circumstances. Marcia Evandale shrank into her chair and looked terrified. George turned red and sat up very straight. Finally, he interrupted.

"Do you have the slightest bit of evidence that our child is not who his birth certificate says he is?"

Torrance, sitting very straight herself, looked at him and replied firmly, "At this point it's circumstantial evidence, but there is evidence to suggest that, yes."

"The mere fact that you say you have evidence to suggest it means you don't have evidence to prove it. So you have no right to come in here and distress my wife with your speculations."

Torrance pointed to the order Evandale had thrown down on the coffee table. "As I told you, the judge who signed that piece of paper ordered me to tell you about it because she wanted to protect you from having a police officer show up on your doorstep without warning. I've driven here from

San Francisco to comply with that. The idea was to avoid distress to your wife, not to cause it."

Evandale didn't seem to hear her. "You've come here to tell a woman who can't have her own children that when she finally finds a baby to adopt you're trying to prove that it's someone else's."

Marcia Evandale receded further into her chair, and Torrance could hear Louise Sandowski's sharp intake of breath. She knew what Louise would think of a man who blamed his wife in public for their joint misfortune. "I'm not trying to prove anything, Mr. Evandale." she said. "My function here is only to deliver the order and to warn you that an investigation will be done. I know the news I've given you is devastating. But my whole purpose in coming here and in bringing along Ms. Sandowski is to help you to understand the problem before you're confronted with the investigation itself. I can't turn back the clock and undo the evidence that exists already. All I can do is to try to help you get ready for the possibility that the end result will be one that none of us could have wished for."

"Well, you've done that. Now perhaps you could leave our house and allow me some privacy to try to undo the damage you've done to my wife."

At this statement, Marcia Evandale looked embarassed and leaned forward a bit. "George," she said softly, "Miss Adams didn't have any choice about coming. The Judge ordered her to do it. And I appreciate the warning."

George gave her a sharp look but didn't rebuke her. Torrance, much as she wished she could simply leave, had one more thing to do. "Mr. Evandale, we have a clear set of footprints belonging to a kidnapped child that's roughly the same age as the child in your home."

"Justin," Marcia Evandale suddenly interrupted in a pleading voice, "he's called Justin."

Torrance looked at her and tried hard to smile. "Justin," she repeated. "So we need a set of Justin's footprints for comparison."

George Evandale erupted from his chair and stood in front of Torrance, leaning over her, his face uncomfortably close to hers. He did not raise his voice, but the low, cold way in which he spoke seemed more threatening than a shout. "No way. No way are you going anywhere near that child. If you so much as try it, I'll have my attorney get a court order to force you to stay away."

Torrance suddenly realized the child they were discussing was conspicuously absent. Had he been hidden somewhere to keep anyone from checking on his identity? But she hadn't told the Evandales anything specific about why she wanted to see them. They hadn't had any cause to hide the child so far. With a great deal of self-control she managed to hold her position in spite of George Evandale's closeness. "Mr. Evandale, the quickest way to make this all go away is to have Justin's footprints not match the footprints of the kidnapped child. That would leave you out of it completely and take away any obstacle to your adoption case."

Evandale finally backed away and stood up straight. His voice though was still threatening. "And if they do match?" he said.

The answer was obvious, and Torrance hesitated. Suddenly, Marcia Evandale spoke up. "George, I don't want to wait to find out. I want to know now who Justin is. Please. Let them do the prints. Maybe then it will be all over and we'll be left alone."

The Evandales began to argue while Torrance sat by helplessly. Her marriage had never deteriorated into this sort of unpleasantness, and she hated to watch it. She felt sorry for Marcia Evandale, who seemed to be a nice woman trying her best to deal with a less than cooperative husband. Louise likewise sat by. There wasn't anything else they could do.

Finally, the argument ended when George Evandale lost his temper completely. "I have gone to a lot of trouble to get you the baby you wanted," he shouted. "I'm not going to let you throw it away out of stupidity." He turned to Torrance and looked at her challengingly, apparently unembarassed by the scene she had witnessed. "The answer is 'no,' do you understand?" With those words, he stalked out of the room and slammed the door.

Marcia Evandale turned toward Torrance and Louise. "I'm sorry," she said. "You mustn't think badly of George. He's acting this way because he really cares about Justin. He just doesn't know how to let his feelings show. He substitutes anger for his unhappiness."

Torrance doubted that Mrs. Evandale's perception of her husband was more than wishful thinking, but she didn't think that this was the time to disagree. She tried to lighten the atmosphere. This allowed her to find out that Justin had been left with a baby sitter because of their visit. Finally, Torrance and Louise thanked Marcia Evandale and left, concerned that she might not be able to cope with the situation.

It was after five now, and a long trip back to the Bay Area lay ahead of them. Torrance was glad of Louise's company. In spite of the progress she had made that day, she was tired, and it would help to have someone to talk to on the way back. She was worried about George Evandale telling all to Solomon. There would have been no point in asking him not to. Just mentioning it might have spurred him on. Torrance hoped that his anger at them and at his wife had temporarily driven thoughts of his lawyer out of his mind. As she headed north on Route 99, she started to go over everything with Louise.

22

*D*erek returned to outer Clement Street shortly after eight-thirty on Wednesday morning, made a quick scan of the cars parked in the blocks surrounding the Parentbuilders offices, and settled into a parking space half a block away from the old Victorian. He had watched the office uneventfully the previous afternoon until the older woman who was obviously Shirley Robusson locked the front door shortly after five and left in her white Cadillac. Now he waited for someone to arrive to open up the office at nine.

He was not disappointed. At eight-fifty-five, Shirley Robusson's Cadillac crossed Clement on a side street looking for a parking place, and within a couple of minutes she rounded the corner on foot, unlocked the front door, and went in.

At nine-thirty a couple in their mid-thirties entered, looking anxious. Derek took some photographs for identification purposes just to be safe, even though they appeared to be legitimate clients. They didn't leave until nearly a quarter of twelve, the woman carrying a folder containing what appeared to be various papers and brochures, the contents of which they appeared to be discussing animatedly. Shortly afterward Shirley Robusson locked the office for lunch. After confirming that she was eating alone, Derek took a desperately needed break, thinking all the while how unfair it was that private eyes in the movies never seemed to have bladders.

He found Shirley at the cafe again and just after twelve-thirty tailed her back to Parentbuilders. To his surprise, two young women were waiting at the front door, chatting easily to each other. They greeted Mrs. Robusson as if already acquainted. Shirley admitted them before Derek could race back to his car to pull out his camera. Grimly, he settled down for the duration. He vowed they would not leave without his getting a good I.D.

About an hour later, one of the young women emerged from the front door, carrying what appeared to be several bookkeeping ledgers. Alert, Derek snapped several photographs before she finished descending the front stairs. He casually emerged from his car as she jaywalked across Clement and headed toward the corner. "Great," he thought to himself. "Now I can demonstrate the simple private eye's trick of watching two things at once, just like I did the last time I was in this neighborhood."

The young woman reached the corner and turned up the side street. Derek hurried to the intersection. She was walking slowly, digging into her purse as she went. Derek noted with relief that there were no large Pontiacs in sight.

Worriedly, he glanced at Parentbuilders, then back at the young woman. She stopped beside a battered silver Toyota, unlocked the passenger side, and put the ledgers on the seat. Derek turned his attention to the door of the Victorian, scanned the street in front of it briefly, and looked back at the young woman when he heard her car start up. Quickly, he started to walk up the side street to where he could see the license plate of the Toyota as it pulled away. The Toyota continued pulling out and made a full U in the middle of the block. He pretended to be interested in a storefront as the young woman drove past him, looking around just in time to note her license plate number.

Anxiously he waited until the Toyota turned at the intersection, and then he sprinted back to the corner. The door to Parentbuilders looked as quiet as before. Feigning calmness, Derek returned to his car, sat back, and let out a big sigh. Just as he was starting to feel pleased with himself he realized that he had forgotten to write down the Toyota's license plate number. "That would have been cute," he said to himself as he scribbled down the number in his notebook along with the young woman's description. Satisfied, he closed the notebook and settled back again.

At three o'clock the door to Parentbuilders was suddenly pulled open from inside. It stood there, a dark empty hole. Derek grabbed his camera and waited. Suddenly the second young woman emerged, her hand flickering between her face and her hair. She glanced anxiously in both directions on Clement just as Shirley Robusson burst out behind her. Shirley pulled the door closed and locked it and, grabbing her younger companion by the elbow, steered her down the steps. As if in response to a question, the young woman pointed vaguely past the Victorian. With Shirley still holding the girl firmly by the elbow, the two hurried up Clement and turned left.

Derek had reeled off six closeups. "Derek, my boy, I think this may be it," he said to himself. He started his car, pulled out of his parking space, slowly eased up to the intersection, and stopped where he could look down the block to the left. The women were walking rapidly down the sidewalk, oblivious to everything around them. They reached the far corner and turned left again. Quickly checking the traffic, Derek made a left turn across Clement, gunned it to the next intersection, and stopped.

A third of the way down the block, Shirley Robusson was just getting into the passenger side of a large blue sedan. The young woman got behind the wheel, started the car, and pulled out. Derek knew it was the Pontiac before he could clearly see it.

They crossed directly in front of him, Robusson apparently giving directions with her outstretched finger. He could read the license plate number clearly. "Now I have you, you son of a bitch," Derek addressed the passing sedan as he jotted down the number in his book. "Let's see if you can lose me now." He turned right to follow the two women.

The Pontiac wound its way back toward Pacific Heights, Derek staying not quite a block behind. At first, the woman who had to be the bicycle mother drove so slowly that Derek was afraid he would wind up getting burnt. On several occasions he found himself stopped directly behind the two women at an intersection, contemplating how to make a '66 Mustang convertible momentarily disappear. After a few blocks, however, he realized that Shirley and the bicycle mother were totally preoccupied. The bicycle mother's eyes went to her rear view mirror purely out of habit; they were vacant and unregistering. Slowly Derek began to relax.

The women turned into one of the finer residential streets of Pacific Heights. Seeing the Pontiac's brake lights come on partway down the block, Derek hung back and waited. Shirley Robusson got out of the car, crossed directly to the garage door of a beautifully restored two-story late Victorian, and opened it. Slowly, with Shirley giving advice, the Pontiac inched into the garage. The two women stood briefly together in front of the house, then Shirley closed and locked the garage, and escorted the bicycle mother through the front door.

A few minutes after they disappeared inside, Derek cruised by the house to note the address. He parked a block away to wait.

After about twenty minutes, a Yellow Cab appeared in front of the house and stopped. The driver walked up to the front door just as Shirley Robusson opened it. She locked the door behind her, followed the driver back to his cab, and left.

"Curiouser and curiouser," Derek mumbled. He decided to stay right where he was.

Shortly after five p.m., his decision was rewarded when Shirley Robusson returned in her Cadillac. She parked it in front of the house and went in, and that was it. At nine, Derek decided that nothing more was going to happen. Wearily, he called off the surveillance.

Before returning home Derek had one last piece of business. He dropped the exposed film off at a little photo studio on Mission Street near twenty-fourth, sealing it in a brown envelope and including a brief note. Carlos Alvarez, the proprietor of Alva-Photo, always began his day at six a.m. Over the years, he and Derek had developed the kind of mutual professional confidence that required few words. Derek knew that if at all possible, Carlos would have eight by ten glossies of all the faces Derek had snapped ready by mid-morning. Besides, Carlos always found Derek's jobs to be a welcome challenge and relief from babies and weddings.

That done, Derek circled back to his flat. Fixing himself a Scotch, he collapsed gratefully in a chair looking out past the deck on the lights of the city. Tomorrow first thing, he thought to himself, he would call his contact at the S.F.P.D. and get a make on the Pontiac—and the Toyota too, just in case. Then it would be time to visit Jeannie Walker again.

Derek downed his Scotch and microwaved a dinner, being too emotionally drained for anything else. Just before he went to bed, he checked his phone directories and confirmed what he already knew: the house in Pacific Heights belonged to Shirley Robusson. Derek crawled into bed and promptly lost consciousness.

Although Torrance arrived home late from Merced that night, she took pity on Monica's burning desire for a status report. She needed time to unwind from the drive, and a conversation with Monica would help. Torrance hoped it would allow her to get some of her thoughts in better order, so she asked Monica upstairs for some vintage port and a chat.

What Torrance particularly wanted to talk about was how Carol Marawik's baby and the Forrest Peace Abengale kidnapping could fit into the picture that was beginning to emerge. She was curled up in a corner of the sofa, absent-mindedly running a hand through her hair.

"How likely is it that there are three kidnapped babies and three babies who were placed for adoption, and they have nothing to do with each other?"

Monica's snort of derision was enough of an answer, but she also gave Torrance a look of disbelief as she said, "About as likely as you and I just happening to be the kidnappers."

Torrance nodded abstractedly. The two sets of babies matched so closely in sex and age that it seemed impossible to believe they became involved in her case coincidentally, without any relationship.

"So, do you think that there were never more than three babies altogether?" she asked. "Each is kidnapped and placed for adoption, and that's it?"

Monica contemplated her port while she thought. "Why not," she finally said. "It's the simplest way of looking at it. Why should we try to make it more complicated?"

Torrance squirmed and moved her legs, prompting a look of disapproval from Jade, who had been leaning against them. "It makes a lot of sense for the two babies who don't seem to have any reality prior to the adoptive placement. We can find no mother, not even a place where the mother lived. But I can't believe David Marawik never existed. I talked to his mother. I saw where she lived. I believe in him."

"And the day he was born, there happened to be a kidnapping less than seventy miles away," Monica pointed out. "Do you think that's just a coincidence?"

Torrance shook her head, got up, and paced for a while. She and Monica continued to toss facts and speculations back and forth, but they came up with no new insights.

Finally, Torrance firmly announced that it was past her bedtime. Monica, full of new facts and eager for new theories, found it difficult to leave—after all, Torrance thought, Monica didn't have to get up at dawn—but Monica sympathized with Torrance's need for sleep and withdrew.

Before shutting off her light and going to sleep, Torrance took a long look at her alarm clock. Deciding there was a limit to her masochism, as well as to her devotion to duty, she reset the alarm for an hour later than her usual six o'clock.

Torrance's late arrival at the office Thursday raised no eyebrows. She was more compulsive about being early than anyone else in the office, and even late, she still arrived ahead of most of the people.

She knew before she arrived that her desk would be cluttered with mail and messages from the day before, but the reality exceeded her expectations. Well, she told herself, time to forget about babies for a while and pay attention to the rest of my job. She delved into the letters, memos, and phone slips and stuck to her resolution to keep her mind on them until Derek called her at ten.

Derek was bubbling. Torrance could tell he had something after no more than three words were out of his mouth. When he told her that he had the probable identity and current location of the "bicycle mother," her mood quickly matched his.

"Shirley Robusson's house!" she exclaimed. "That's interesting. So what are you going to do next?"

"I've been waiting for prints of the pictures I took of her. I'm on my way to pick them up now, and then I'm off to meet Jeannie to see whether she can identify the woman."

"If you checked on her car registration, you must know her name by now, right?"

"Tina Patterson. She lives in an apartment in the Sunset district. The other thing I plan to do this afternoon is to snoop around her place to see if she's shown up again. I'm considering whether to have a little talk with her. Right now I think I'll hold off on that for a while."

"That sounds right to me, too. You know, it seems funny to have a name instead of just 'bicycle mother.' We've talked about her that way for so long, now suddenly I have to think of her as Tina Patterson."

"You're right, it still seems strange to me, too. Well, I've got to run. I'll try to get back to you later today if I have anything more."

"Yes, please do, even if you have to call me late at home. Can I wish you luck, or do detectives feel the same way actors do?"

"I don't usually, but just to be safe, why don't you just tell me to break a leg?"

"O.K., Derek. Break a leg. And make sure you let me know when you're through doing it."

"I promise. 'Bye."

Torrance hung up the phone and leaned back in her chair. Derek was getting all the good breaks in this case. She wished she was in a position to run around and investigate things personally. Then she recalled Dr. Moorehead's purple bloated face, and her less active participation suddenly seemed fine. Besides, she had discovered the involvement of Solomon and the relationship between him and Shirley Robusson.

Suddenly, Torrance remembered that she had not yet told Darrell Schoenig about that relationship. She got up and walked down the hall to his office.

Darrell was reviewing an appellate brief and seemed glad at the interruption. Torrance reminded him of her incomplete note and told him that the additional fact she had found out was that John Solomon was Shirley Robusson's brother.

"It seems to me law enforcement would want to know that before they interview him. After all, he isn't going to say anything indiscreet about Parentbuilders if it's going to get his sister in trouble."

Schoenig nodded. "You're right, it probably would affect their strategy. I know who's on the case for the S.F.P.D., so why don't you just sit here a minute while I give him a call. He may have some questions for you."

Torrance stayed put while Darrell made the call and proceeded through a maze of transfers to the officer he was trying to reach. Finally, his face brightened. "Ted, I've got a piece of information you may be interested in. Our civil attorney who brought me this case was talking to an adoption worker who sprung it on her that Shirley Robusson at Parentbuilders is that attorney John Solomon's sister. She thought you would want to know that when you interviewed him. I've got her right here if you have any questions. Sure. Here she is." Darrell held the receiver out. "Captain Ted Arriera. He wants to talk to you."

After the polite introductions were over, Captain Arriera asked Torrance what difference it made that Solomon and Robusson were related.

"I can't say yet," Torrance answered, "but I thought it would certainly make a difference in how much information one will give you about the other. In particular, I thought you people should take it into account when you interview Solomon."

"Actually, I interviewed him yesterday afternoon," Arriera responded. "And I don't think this information would have made any difference. He was pretty straight with me. Told me how he works with Parentbuilders because he doesn't want to get involved in helping these couples find babies. He just likes to do the legal work."

"Did he tell you that Shirley is his sister?"

"No, he didn't, but I don't suppose there was any reason for him to. I pushed him pretty hard, big-shot lawyer or no, so I guess he didn't feel like volunteering anything."

"Excuse my curiosity, but what do you mean by pushing him hard?"

Arriera laughed. "No rubber hoses, if that's what you're worried about. I just made him think we know a lot more than we do. I told him we had a witness who thought she could place someone from Parentbuilders at the scene of the Ross kidnapping."

"What was his reaction?"

"Not much. He looked morally outraged and lawyer-like. I didn't get the impression it worried him."

"I hope you're right," Torrance answered. "If he *was* worried by it, he might start destroying records before you can get a search warrant."

"Ms. Adams, trying to get search warrants for lawyers' offices makes a man get old before his time. Anything else you want to know?"

"No, thanks, unless your investigation's come up with something new already."

"No, we're still doing background. I'll let Schoenig know if anything breaks."

After Torrance hung up the phone, she looked at Darrell. "Is it really that difficult to get at a lawyer's records when he's the one who's the suspect?"

"Pretty much, yeah. Judges hate to order any legal files to be opened, no matter what the lawyer did. They'd rather we caught the guy some other way."

Torrance thought about that for a while. "I suppose that should make me feel a little better about how much Arriera told Solomon. If we can't get his records anyway, I guess it doesn't make too much difference if he destroys them."

"You shouldn't second-guess the S.F.P.D., Torrance, unless you want to start working in the criminal division."

"No thanks!" Torrance had a horrified expression on her face, but gave Darrell a smile before she left his office.

On the way down the hall, however, she started worrying again about what Ted Arriera had said. Solomon off his guard had been difficult to deal with. But Solomon warned, she thought, would be a very tricky adversary.

After hanging up the phone with Torrance, Derek drove down to Alva-Photo to see what Carlos had for him. Carlos brightened when he saw Derek enter his shop. "Ah, Derek! You are getting better, I think." Carlos spoke English with a soft Mexican accent. Derek imagined that his Spanish was impeccable, however. "Perhaps one day you are going to be a real photographer; then maybe we can go into business together, huh?"

"Hi, Carlos. Only if you handle all the kids." Derek crossed the room. The two shook hands warmly.

"I'll take the kids, if you take all the weddings! I swear, Derek, mothers at weddings, they will kill me. But wait here, let's see what you left me this morning." Carlos went into the back room and returned shortly carrying a number of eight by ten glossies, which he carefully laid out on the counter.

"Be careful, some of them are still damp," Carlos warned. "I cropped them as closely as I could to have only one subject in each picture, like you wanted. This young lady was more difficult." Carlos pointed to the pictures of Tina Patterson. "The old lady, she is like the mother of the bride—always at her daughter's side. Winds up in every picture." Carlos beamed wickedly. "So here, I airbrushed her out!"

"They're perfect. Carlos, you have outdone yourself." Derek kept looking from one photo to the other. Carlos shrugged.

"Your focus was a little short in these," he indicated several photos he had laid to one side, "so I spent more time on the ones you see here."

"Again, perfect. You'll bill me?" Derek scooped up the photographs.

"It's already on account. Good luck, *amigo*."

"*Hasta luego*, Carlos. I'll tell you how this all comes out."

Derek felt like a little kid at Christmas as he jumped back into his car. He cut over the top of Twin Peaks to head out north to Jeannie Walker's house.

Jeannie greeted Derek nervously at her door. She had been surprised when Derek called her the night before. Agitation seemed to be her natural state.

"Mr. Thompson, come in. I can't believe this is happening."

Derek was admitted to her living room. "I'll only take a few minutes of your time. What can't you believe?"

"I mean, it all seems so long ago, it's like it was just a bad dream—you know, that horrible kidnapping, and that poor woman screaming and all, and you coming around and everything. I just got to the point where I didn't think of it every morning when I took Christopher to day care and went out running." Jeannie motioned Derek to sit. "And then all of a sudden you call out of the blue, and this morning. . .it's like the whole thing were picking up right where it left off. I just can't believe this is all happening still."

Derek smiled soothingly. "Well actually, quite a bit has been happening in the meantime. Luckily, I haven't had to involve you. But I think we're getting close to solving this kidnapping and, hopefully, getting little Patrick James back safe and sound. And if I'm right, we'll be putting a particularly bad person behind bars before we're done. But in order to do that, right now I need your help."

Jeannie sat forward, earnestly chewing her lower lip. "I'll do what I can. Sorry. I'm just a little nervous, that's all."

"I don't blame you. No apologies necessary. Now then, do you remember telling me about the bicycle mother?"

Jeannie nodded in assent.

"I haven't told you anything about my speculations on this case before now. I just asked you to try to identify for me all the people you could remember seeing out on Mt. Tam the week before the kidnapping." Jeannie's head bobbed in agreement, her teeth still working on her lip. "Well, I'm beginning to think that the bicycle mother is a very important person in this whole affair, and I'd like to see if you can pick her out in a group of photographs."

Jeannie was incredulous. "You suspect that young mother of having something to do with this? But she's my age! She has a baby of her own!"

"I didn't say that she necessarily did the kidnapping," Derek said quickly. "On the other hand, I think she knows who planned the whole thing, and I'd like to talk to her." Jeannie settled back, warily. "Do you think you could recognize her if you saw her again?"

Jeannie's nervousness resurfaced. "I—I don't know. I think so. I mean,

I've always had such a good memory for faces and all, but I'm just not sure."

Derek started to open the manila envelope he brought with him. "Well, why don't we just give it a try? I'm going to show you photographs of four women. Just look at them and tell me if you recognize any of them, and if you think any of them is the bicycle mother."

Jeannie nodded, and Derek carefully laid out one photo each of Shirley Robusson, the bookkeeper (as he labeled the first young woman from the day before), the prospective client, and Tina Patterson. Jeannie wrinkled her nose at Shirley's photograph.

"Oh, not this one. She's way too old."

"Just testing you. Ever see her before?"

Jeannie looked back at the photo again. "No. She doesn't look familiar." Jeannie looked up, worried. "Should she?"

Derek laughed. "No, not necessarily. I'm just sort of giving you a line-up here. How about the others?"

One by one, Jeannie studied and discarded the photographs of the bookkeeper and the client. Her eyebrows knitted as she looked at the last photo in the pile. Derek tried to keep from betraying any emotion.

"That's her!" Jeannie suddenly said, her voice quiet with conviction. "I don't believe this, but that's definitely her." Jeannie put her thumbs on the edges of Tina Patterson's face, covering up her hair. "See? She was wearing a headband, to pull her hair back out of her face. . . . Oh, I'm sorry. Of course you've never seen her before." Jeannie looked up at Derek, slightly embarrassed.

"You're absolutely sure that's her?" he asked. Jeannie nodded, staring at the photograph.

"Well, I must say, you've been a big help. I don't know where all this is going to wind up, but what you've done today is very important. If you don't mind, I'd like to know where I can get hold of you for the next several days. You weren't planning on taking any trips out of town, were you?"

Jeannie shook her head. "No. We don't have any plans."

"Good. I may need you to talk to the police about your identification." Derek started to put away the photographs, as Jeannie, still shaking her head, mumbled to herself.

Derek looked up sharply at her. "What did you just say?"

"I was telling myself that I still can't believe this is all happening again."

Derek looked puzzled. "That's the second time you've said that. What do you mean by 'all happening again'? What's happening again besides me coming by?"

"Like I said. First you call out of nowhere, and then this morning I suddenly see that executive again. . . ."

Derek cut her off. "Which executive? Where?"

Jeannie looked startled. "Why, the one I told you about who we never found. You know, the one with the little pack and the fancy headphones and stuff?"

"Where did you see this guy?"

"Just this morning, out jogging. I passed him on the trail. I nearly tripped over myself, I was so surprised to see him again."

"What was he doing? Did he say anything to you?"

"No. He just sort of nodded at me, the way people do." Jeannie shrugged. "He seemed to be walking along, getting some exercise. I passed him kind of quickly. Do you think it's important?"

"I have no idea," Derek replied. "But, like you, I pay attention to coincidences." Derek got up to go. "If you see him again, give me a call immediately. Do you still have my card?"

"Sure. Right here." Jeannie started for the phone table.

"Just so long as you have it," Derek stopped her. "Again, stay where I can get in touch with you for the next few days. You've been a tremendous help, and I think my client is going to be very grateful to you before this is all over."

Jeannie blushed as she showed Derek to the door. When the door closed behind him, Derek allowed himself a little hop of excitement, clicking his heels together. Then he practically ran to his car. "Marguerite," he said to himself, "we are on our way." The car roared to life, and Derek spun a U-turn and headed for Marguerite James's condo.

She was more pale and drawn than he remembered. The weeks of uncertainty had taken their toll. Derek swore to himself that she would smile again and soon if he had anything to do with it. Then he thought of Nancy Bertram, and the horrible news she must have received by now. Quickly Derek shut those thoughts out of his mind. His mission now was to give Marguerite hope. He started to tell her how things looked to him, and why he thought it meant Patrick was safe.

Marguerite had heard part of Derek's theories before. What was new, Derek explained, was that with one possible perpetrator identified and with a court order for various adoption records, there was a chance that he could get a major break in this case soon. Marguerite looked both skeptical and expectant, as if she no longer dared to hope. Finally, Derek finished bringing her up to date. He sat back and looked at her.

"This is all very rough on you still, isn't it?" he said softly.

Marguerite's composure melted, and she held her face in her hands. "I just don't know how much longer I can take this," she sobbed.

For a long time, Derek and Marguerite simply sat there, Derek's hand on her shoulder. Finally, she sat up, wiping her face with a Kleenex. "Ronald calls every day. He feels guilty, as if none of this would have happened if he hadn't left me." A look of pain flashed across her face.

"And what about you? Do you still feel the way you did about his leaving?" Derek asked.

"I'm not sure. I guess that if he really is—that way—there's nothing he can do about it. It's better than living a lie, I suppose," she added bravely.

"And it's better for you to think like that than to sit around and hate him. Have you been talking to someone who's helped you understand?"

Marguerite gave out something between a sigh and a half-laugh. "I have a friend in The City. She's an absolute saint, and it's such a relief to be able to talk to someone about all this."

"That's good. I think you needed that. It's beginning to look as if maybe you and Ron can part as friends," he added hopefully.

"Yes. Maybe," Marguerite said wistfully. "It's still over between us I guess, but at least we can talk to each other now. If this tragedy has led to anything good, I guess it has done that."

"If I have anything to say about it, that won't be the only good that comes out of this. I intend to get Patrick back. And I'm finally allowing myself to hope that this is all going to work out right. So you'll have to be brave a little longer, O.K.?"

Derek stood up. "I have to go now. There's some business I have to get to in The City. I'll let you know the minute there are more definitive developments." He motioned for Marguerite to stay seated. "I'll let myself out. Keep the faith; I think it's almost over." He left Marguerite on her couch, staring hopefully after him.

An hour later found Derek in the Sunset district neighborhood where, according to the Department of Motor Vehicles, Tina Patterson lived. She apparently had an unlisted phone number like many single women.

Derek drove by and circled the block. There was no sign of a Pontiac, and the apartment building, a fourplex, had no garage. He parked and went up to the door. The mailbox for unit number four, upstairs, simply said "Patterson." The name on unit one read "S. Khoury, Manager." Derek rang the bell. The door was promptly opened by a plump, dark woman in her late fifties or early sixties, her graying hair escaping in strands from a bun pulled together on the back of her head.

"Yes, can I help you?" She eyed Derek suspiciously. He couldn't exactly place her accent, but it sounded Middle-Eastern.

Derek tried to look sheepish. "Excuse me. I'm sorry to disturb you. I'm looking for a young woman who rides her bicycle around here—a very attractive woman, a few years younger than me. Her name is Tina. I met her while jogging around the park." Mrs. Khoury's suspicion was turning into skepticism. Derek leaned forward conspiratorially. "This is really embarrassing. You see, she gave me her address and phone number and I lost the match book I wrote them down on. I promised her I would call. If I don't phone her, she's going to think I'm some kind of flake. I thought I remembered the address, but now I'm not sure if she lives here or on the next block. Do you know of anyone who fits her description?" Derek proceeded to describe Tina Patterson in terms appropriate to a smitten man. Mrs. Khoury was decidedly melting. Finally, she smiled and nodded her head. "Ya, ya. I know this girl, Tina, I think. Perhaps she lives upstairs, no?"

Derek looked relieved. "Upstairs! That's fantastic!" Suddenly he looked worried. "She's not in right now, is she? Maybe she overheard us?"

"No worry. Her car's not here. I haven't seen her since she went to work yesterday." Mrs. Khoury's hand suddenly flew to her mouth, as she realized the implication of what she had just said. Derek pretended he hadn't heard.

"We've just talked a few times," he went on. "And yet, she's so different. Not like most of the girls you meet. Do you know what I mean?"

Mrs. Khoury nodded happily.

"But I have a problem. I can't just come over unannounced. She gave me her phone number. She obviously expects me to call. You wouldn't happen to have it, would you?" Mrs. Khoury was completely caught up by Derek's predicament. She bustled inside to retrieve Tina's number.

"Here. She lives in number four, upstairs. Her last name is Patterson." She handed Derek a piece of paper. Derek thanked her profusely.

"One last thing," he suddenly interjected as he started to leave. "I thought for sure I saw her the other day riding her bicycle with some kind of baby carrier on it. She didn't tell me that she had a baby. Was she baby-sitting for someone?"

"Tina?" Mrs. Khoury looked incredulous. "No, not Tina. She has no baby. I never see a little one here."

"Well, perhaps it was someone who looked like her from a distance." Derek smiled and thanked Mrs. Khoury again.

She beamed. "Don't worry," she said. "I don't tell her a thing about you come by. You phone her. She won't think you are some kind of flake, O.K.?"

Derek beamed back. "O.K.!" He ran off in the direction of his car as Mrs. Khoury watched him, her hands clasped in front of her and her head tilted to one side as if in a reverie.

Derek was in his own reverie as he got behind the wheel. He started the car. "Dinner—then I'd better call Torrance."

Torrance went home, still not having heard from Derek. Monica was silhouetted against the front windows, but Torrance didn't want company just now. She went up the stairs, gave Jade and Buddha a semi-distracted greeting and changed into jeans and a sweater. She poured herself a glass of sherry and sat down in the covered patio with her feet on the table.

As she sat there sipping her sherry, she thought back over her conversation with Captain Arriera. The idea that Solomon now knew what they were looking for and had been warned that it had something to do with Parentbuilders made her nervous. Until the interview with Arriera, Solomon (and by extension Shirley Robusson) had presumably not suspected that any connection had been discovered between Parentbuilders and the Patrick James kidnapping. Torrance sighed. She didn't really know much about criminal investigation, but she had cross-examined many witnesses in civil trials. It always seemed to her that you got the best results by not warning witnesses about the traps you might be able to spring on them.

Finally, she stopped worrying and went down to the kitchen to fix herself some pasta for dinner. Pasta was the working woman's salvation, she thought. You could keep a lot of different kinds around for a long time, it didn't take long to cook, and you could toss anything from last night's leftovers to a can of clams on top of it for variety. After rooting around in the refrigerator, she decided on leftover chicken, some mushrooms which needed to be used up, and a generous helping of snipped parsley. With a little butter, pepper and onion powder the result was, she thought, quite nice. The cats, however, were disappointed that there was not enough chicken for them.

Torrance put the remains of her dinner away and moved into the study when the telephone finally rang.

"Hi, it's Derek. Am I disturbing your evening?"

"You just interrupted a very important session of staring at a book without reading it. Mainly, I was hoping you'd call. Did you get to talk to Jeannie?"

"Yes, I did. And she identified Tina Patterson as the bicycle mother without any doubt. But the most interesting part was that she saw the second executive today."

"I'm sorry, I'm not following that. Who's the second executive?"

Derek reminded her of the terms Jeannie used for all the people she met when she ran, and of how he had seen only one of the two "executive types" she had seen the day of the kidnapping. "The other one never showed up again. Until this morning."

"Am I supposed to make something of that, Derek? I mean, it's a weird coincidence, but how does it fit?"

"It's not concrete yet, but neither were a lot of the things you believed in earlier, remember?"

"Touché. But since you seem to be the one with the intuition right now, explain it to me a step at a time."

"Well, you have to start out with what I saw yesterday. It looked as if Shirley Robusson was taking Tina Patterson and hauling her off to Shirley's house. After all, if they were just going there in a friendly fashion, why all this stuff about taking Tina's car, going back in a taxi, and then picking up the Caddy? Then Shirley sticks the Pontiac in her garage, right? The Pontiac that someone might have seen at the scene of the kidnapping. She leaves her Caddy out in the street. Does that strike you as normal behavior for that woman?"

"Now that you put it that way, no, it doesn't."

"Well, it doesn't to me, either. It looks to me like someone is getting scared. Maybe one of the parents you talked to got in touch with Parentbuilders and warned them about inquiries. The wagons may be circling the camp."

"I have something to tell you about that. But I still don't understand how you think the reappearance of Jeannie's second executive fits into the pattern."

"I'm guessing he's scared too. Maybe he's looking for something, checking the place over to make sure that there isn't any trace of what happened."

"So you think he was involved in the kidnapping itself?"

"Well, let me put it this way. I don't think Tina Patterson planned it and carried it out. She doesn't strike me as either smart enough or determined enough. So, yes, I do think another person was involved, and the second executive seems to be the only person we haven't accounted for. And now that he's reappeared, I sure would like to know who he is."

"Derek, do you have a description of this man?"

"Not much of one. He seems to be more nondescript than anything else. Middle age, middle size, middle height, middle everything. Jeannie is very observant and gave me some very vivid descriptions, so I assume this guy just blends in real well. Why are you asking?" Derek heard Torrance sigh and hesitate. "Come on," he said, "you're thinking something. Tell me what it is."

"I don't like what I'm thinking, Derek. That's why I'm having a hard time saying it. But here goes. Do you think Jeannie's second executive could possibly be John Solomon?"

"I was about to ask you whether *you* thought that. I've been working my way up to seeing Solomon as the brains of this whole operation, but I don't know enough about him yet. I can't say whether he would be likely to be right there at the scene, for example. But for a start, does he fit the description?"

"I guess so, such as it is. He doesn't have any features that would really stand out to someone." Torrance paused for a moment, then went on animatedly. "We could resolve all this if we could show Jeannie a picture of him, couldn't we?"

"Sure, it would help a lot. I was going to try to get one tomorrow."

"Well, if you'll hold on a minute, I may be able to help you."

Derek held the phone in amazement while Torrance ran to one of the bookshelves in the study and pulled out a large volume similar to a photograph album. She returned to the phone and explained while she leafed through the book's pages.

"I keep a scrapbook of my press clippings, you see, and I had a case about two years ago that he got involved in after I was already out of it. So we never actually met, but I think I saved a clipping with his picture on it. . . . Yes, here it is. It's a good picture too. He's sitting smiling behind his desk. The paper must have sent a photographer to his office. Now that I've been there, I recognize the setting. So do you want to borrow this to show to Jeannie?"

"I'd love to. It'll save me a lot of time. If Solomon was up on Tamalpais yesterday, though, it definitely has to mean he's been warned."

"Oh, I started to tell you about that, but then I got sidetracked. I found out for sure today that he definitely has been warned. I was mad as hell about it, but I was told not to second-guess the people who know all about criminals."

"Excuse the rudeness, Torrance, but what the hell are you talking about?"

"I had a conversation today with Captain Ted Arriera of the S.F.P.D., who told me that he, quote, pushed Solomon pretty hard, unquote, by telling him that there was a witness who could place someone from Parentbuilders at the scene of the Patrick James kidnapping."

"He did what?"

"Just what I said. He told Solomon that a witness saw someone from Parentbuilders at the Patrick James kidnapping."

"Where the hell did he get that idea?"

"My notes that I turned over to the criminal division indicated that there was a witness who might—and I stress might—be able to identify the perpetrator. I guess Arriera decided to play cute with Solomon and pretend he had a lot more than that just to see if he could shake him up. Solomon apparently wasn't shaken. Of course, I figure he won't shake easily even . . . ."

"Wait a minute," Derek interjected. "When did this guy talk to Solomon?"

"Yesterday afternoon some time. My guess is that the only thing that maneuver accomplished was to warn Solomon about the line the investigation is taking."

"It may have done a lot more than that."

"Well, I figured it would make Solomon and Shirley get together and get rid of any incriminating documents they might have had around. But Arriera didn't seem to think that mattered. His attitude was that those records would not have been opened to a search warrant in any case, so what was the big deal if they got zapped."

"I'm not thinking records, Torrance. Go back to what we were talking about. Shirley Robusson is out hiding Tina and the Grand Prix in her house. So now I worry. Is it because they've heard from Solomon about a witness? Do they think there's a witness out there who saw Tina or her car at the scene of the kidnapping? At the same time, the second executive—and I'll assume for the moment that he is Solomon—suddenly reappears wandering around on Mt. Tam at the time that Jeannie goes out running. Before, I thought he might just be trying to make sure his tracks were covered. Now that I know he's worried about a witness, I start to think it may be the witness he's looking for."

"Now wait a minute, Derek. You're suggesting Solomon is out looking for Jeannie to...to do her some harm? Solomon? He's an eminently respectable lawyer. I can see him making money off babies with questionable origins. I can see him shredding documents and erasing tapes. But wiping out a witness?"

"Didn't you agree that he could have been involved in the kidnapping itself as a sort of mastermind? Aren't you the one who asked me if the second executive looked like Solomon?"

Torrance's voice suddenly sounded very subdued. "Somehow kidnapping doesn't seem quite as bad as...."

"Murder?"

"Is that what you think he has in mind?"

Derek could hear Torrance's distress at the thought. He paused and then answered gently, "I think we have to take the possibility very seriously."

23

*T*he alarm woke Derek out of the kind of deep sleep which comes in the early morning after a night of restless dreams. The memory of the dreams faded during his groggy attempts to find and turn off the alarm. All that was left was leaden fatigue and a vague, unsettling sense of unease.

The memory of what he had to do today flooded into Derek's consciousness. He leaped out of bed and stood undecided for a moment. He looked at the telephone and more longingly at the bathroom and shower. He glanced at the clock. "Plenty of time to call Jeannie after I shower," he calculated. "If I call her now, she'll just be starting breakfast and helping everybody get ready to leave." He headed for the bathroom.

He showered quickly and started to shave, still troubled. The mirror in the shower steamed up quickly. In irritation, he stupidly flicked water on it with his left hand while his razor was still moving across his neck. He felt the sting of shaving soap in an open cut and cursed loudly at himself for carelessness. Turning the water colder, he stood under it for a few minutes longer, hoping the cold water would slow the bleeding.

Finally, he gave up and turned off the water. After towelling himself dry, he completed his morning routine in front of the sink. Just as he was about to finish combing his hair, the cut on his neck started to bleed again. With another curse he took a small square of toilet paper and stood in front of the mirror, chin up, pressing directly against the recalcitrant nick. He pressed hard for a few minutes and changed the paper carefully so as not to reopen the cut.

Suddenly, Derek realized the time. He ran back to the bedside phone and quickly punched Jeannie's number. On the sixth ring a man's voice answered with a questioning "Hello?"

"Is Jeannie Walker there? This is Derek Thompson."

"Oh hi, Mr. Thompson. This is Don, Jeannie's husband. Jeannie's talked a lot about you, but we've never met."

"No, I guess we haven't. Perhaps we'll be able to correct that soon. Is Jeannie there? It's important that I talk to her before she leaves for her morning run."

Don hesitated. "Gee, is it very important?"

Derek fought back a strong surge of irritation and impatience. "Yes, it's important. Is she still there?" he added worriedly.

"Well, no," Don answered reluctantly. "That's why I asked. You didn't miss her by more than a few minutes."

Inwardly, Derek groaned. "A few minutes?" He looked at the clock. "I thought she wouldn't be leaving for her run for at least another half hour."

"Oh no, she's rarely that late, especially on a Friday," Don replied.

"Why a Friday?"

"Fridays Jeannie usually does her hill climbs. She always likes to get started a little early on hill days." Don spoke mechanically, as if this speech had been delivered many times. "Oh yeah, and today she was going to meet a bunch of the girls for lunch, so she especially wanted to get an early start—and an early finish."

The feeling of unease that had been with Derek all morning grew stronger. He thought quickly. "Where will she be running today? At the same place—Lagunitas?"

"Yeah, as far as I know. She never runs anywhere else. She knows the area real well and all the people so she feels safe running there. Is there anything wrong?"

"I don't know. . .I'm not sure. I just wanted to go out with her this morning. Jeannie thought she saw someone yesterday on her run who may have been involved in the case I'm working on. I want to be there on the chance she runs into him again."

Don didn't answer immediately. "I was just leaving for work when you called, and I'm afraid I'm a little late. In fact, you're lucky I heard the phone and came back in the house. Is this important enough that you think I should try to catch her at the park before she takes off?"

Derek weighed the options and realized that he really didn't have anything solid that suggested that Jeannie was in any danger. A thought occurred to him. "Who's taking Christopher to day care?"

"Jeannie's got him."

"Good. Look, I can be at the parking lot at the end of Lagunitas in thirty minutes. I don't have any reason to believe Jeannie's in any kind of danger, so I don't want you to get all worried or not go in to work or anything but can you do me a quick favor? See if you can catch Jeannie at the day care center by phone. Tell her I'll meet her at the parking area. Tell her to wait there for me. O.K.?"

"You got it," Don replied.

"Great. Thanks. I hope I get a chance to meet you soon."

Derek hung up and quickly punched Torrance's home number. She answered on the first ring.

"Torrance? Derek. There's been a slight hitch. I couldn't catch Jeannie at home, so I'll have to meet you directly at the Lagunitas Road parking area as soon as you can get there." He quickly explained what had happened.

"I'm on my way out the door," Torrance replied. "'Bye." She hung up.

With a shock Derek realized that he was still wearing nothing but a damp towel. He quickly pulled on running shorts and a tank top, grabbed his shoes and a pair of sweats and started for the door. With another curse at himself for not thinking straight, he checked himself and ran back into the bedroom to retrieve his wallet and keys. He flew down the stairs to the street.

Derek took every side street he knew to be uncrowded at this hour and raced north across the Golden Gate Bridge toward Marin. He glanced repeatedly at his watch. His only hope of catching Jeannie was Don's reaching her at the day care center. Worriedly, he turned his thoughts to Torrance. How would they ever connect if they missed each other at the parking area? He pushed the thought out of his mind as he turned off the freeway at Sir Francis Drake and headed up toward Mt. Tam.

Derek's heart sank as he pulled to a stop at the end of Lagunitas. Jeannie's car was there, as were a number of others, but there was no sign of Jeannie or of Torrance's Porsche. "This morning is not going well," Derek said to himself in a bitter understatement. He pulled in next to Jeannie's car and started to lace on his shoes. Just as he was standing up and pulling on his sweatshirt, he heard a deep-throated roar behind him. Torrance's Porsche came into view and pulled up right behind Derek's Mustang. Torrance jumped out, dressed in slacks and a blouse, but with socks and running shoes on her feet.

"Boy, am I glad to see you," Derek greeted her.

"I'm just glad no one caught me driving the way I did to get here," Torrance replied. "I take it we missed Jeannie." She looked around. "Do you recognize any of the other cars here?"

Derek noticed them for the first time. "To tell you the truth, I hadn't even looked at them yet. The little green one here is Jeannie's. Those two I've seen up here a number of times," Derek continued, pointing. His gaze stopped at a large black Mercedes four-door sedan parked under the trees at the lower end of the parking lot. "I've never seen that one before," he said quietly.

Torrance looked at Derek. "That's the first thing I noticed. Not too many people drive their Mercedes sedans to go jogging. Even in Marin."

"Yeah," Derek replied absent-mindedly, still staring at the incongruous black vehicle. His eyes and Torrance's met, both conscious of the same unspoken thought.

Once again, it was Torrance who broke the spell. "I think we'd better try to find Jeannie."

Derek turned to stare in dismay at the wooded slopes rising toward Mt. Tam in front of them. "Yes," he said again, deep in thought. "But how?" He looked back at Torrance. "Don said that Jeannie was going to do hills today. When I ran with her those few times we mostly stuck to the trails near the scene of the kidnapping, but she pointed out a couple of trails she used for hill work. . . . Damn! If I can only remember where they are!" Derek started toward the trail head and suddenly stopped. "Should we try splitting up or should we go together?"

Torrance was slightly irritated. "Derek—I've never met Jeannie, remember? And I don't know the area. We'd better stick together, and I think we'd better hurry. I have a bad feeling about this."

"Then let's go. I think I'll recognize the trails she pointed out better once we're moving. The first part is the same anyway."

"Hold it," Torrance interjected. "I think someone's coming!"

They could distinctly hear the pad of feet approaching hard and fast. This was no easy jogging pace but a flat-out run. Through a break in the trees, Derek and Torrance caught a fleeting glimpse of a young, slender woman with light brown hair, legs and arms churning desperately.

"Jeannie?" Derek said aloud. "I wonder what. . . ." Just then the young woman burst into full view. Derek started toward her and then stopped, confused. Torrance looked over at Derek expectantly. The young woman's grim face broke into a smile as she coasted to a stop in the parking area. She let out a big sigh as she caught her breath and began walking in small circles, hands on her hips. Derek went over to her.

"Hi. Sorry to bother you, but can we talk to you a minute? It's kind of important." Torrance's hopes fell at Derek's words. This was not Jeannie, after all.

The girl looked at Derek and Torrance. "Sure, if you don't mind me walking on while you talk—I don't dare stop now," she answered between breaths.

Derek continued. "We're looking for a woman just about your age and build—maybe a little taller—and with hair a bit lighter than yours. She's a regular. She jogs here practically every day. Have you seen anyone that looks like her today? Her name's Jeannie."

The woman's face, which had clouded with suspicion at the beginning of Derek's speech, visibly relaxed at the mention of Jeannie's name. "I think I know who you're talking about. That's her car there," she pointed in the direction of the green compact.

"That's her! Have you seen her today? It's very important we make connections."

"You'd have better luck waiting here by her car," the woman replied.

"Unfortunately, we can't afford to do that," Torrance interjected.

The woman looked at her, surprised. "No—what I mean is, I already passed her on my way out. She should be circling back to her car by now."

"Damn! About how long ago was that?"

"Maybe twenty minutes. She was jogging. I passed her going in the opposite direction."

"Where? Can you remember?"

"One of the upper trails. It was just before I passed that weirdo."

"What weirdo?" Torrance asked sharply.

"Some older guy wearing brand-new running sweats. He was just standing by the side of the trail doing calisthenics, way up there. I decided he was a weirdo because of the way he looked at me. It was creepy—he gave me this real intense stare like he thought he knew me or something—you know?"

Torrance shuddered. Derek jumped in. "This guy—have you ever seen him before?"

"Not that I can recall. But he sure seemed to be checking me out."

"Look, this is very important," Derek said. "Where did you see this guy? Try to remember."

The girl shrugged her shoulders. "I couldn't really say for sure. Somewhere along one of the upper trails that run behind the Country Club. You start up the Allen Trail off the lake, but then you cut back to the left to come down canyon. There's a couple of branches, and they're not marked. I think it's the second or third left—I don't know." She twisted her mouth in a helpless smile. "I could show you easily enough, but I'm lousy at giving directions, you know?"

"So are a lot of people," Torrance said, hiding her irritation. "One last thing. Would Jeannie be likely to come back the way she went out, past the spot where you saw that guy?"

"Sure. That's what most people do. There's some loops past there that circle back to the main trail, and it has a nice mix of ups and downs."

"Thanks." Torrance turned to Derek, fear in her eyes. "Twenty minutes. Jeannie should have turned around and been on her way back by now—right past that man."

Derek was lost in thought, staring up at the steeply rising hillside. Suddenly he snapped back into awareness. "Let's go. I think I know where to find him, and if I'm right, we don't have a minute to lose. I just hope we're in time!" His last words were shouted over his shoulder as he was already starting up the trail. Torrance ran quickly to catch up. She looked questioningly at him. Derek's face was set, preoccupied with running and deep in thought. She turned her attention back to the trail and the placement of her feet.

Derek pointed ahead and left. Wordlessly, the two of them veered quickly at a signpost that marked the Allen Trail. The path climbed steeply. They both slowed against their will. Derek was laboring, his breath coming in huge gulps.

All at once, Torrance felt the artery in the right side of her neck begin to throb painfully. Her head began to spin dizzily. She stumbled and gasped as she fell headlong. Derek glanced back and saw her fall. He stopped awkwardly and ran back to where Torrance was painfully pulling herself to her feet. He helped her up, his own face twisted with pain and drenched with sweat.

"Are you all right?" he gasped.

Torrance nodded wordlessly. A part of her mind registered dismay as she saw that her slacks were covered with dirt. Unconsciously, she began to brush herself off.

"We should be near the turnoff soon," Derek said between breaths. "You think you can make it?"

"Yes. Sorry. Let's go." Torrance waved him on. She stumbled forward after him. The throbbing returned, joined now by a dull ache in her left knee. Desperately, Torrance tried to block out the pain. Tears and sweat blurred her vision. She felt as though she was running up a narrow dark tunnel.

"Here! This way!" Derek shouted. She blinked her eyes clear and saw him standing on a trail that cut off to follow the contour of the mountain. "I hope to God this is right," he panted. "You still with me?"

Torrance nodded and started forward. Derek turned and ran, faster now that the trail was more level, racing against time, afraid that he had chosen the wrong cutoff. He knew they would not have time to find the right trail if his memory was faulty. He picked up the pace even more, his heart pounding.

The trail slipped swiftly by, and still Derek wasn't sure. He had been on so many paths when he was running with Jeannie. Nothing looked familiar. His heart began to sink, even as he ran desperately on.

Suddenly, he saw it: the little track that he had passed by so many times before he noticed it—a stony little path that plunged down off the main trail to disappear behind a thicket of low-hanging branches. He gasped triumphantly and leaped down the path. Torrance skidded to a stop, hesitated a moment in surprise, and then ran down the hill after him.

Derek forced his way through the brush, heedless of the branches scraping at his legs and face. Suddenly he broke through to the edge of the cliff, stopped, and spun to his right. For only a second he stared at the figures on the knoll, and in that moment, his hopes fell.

A man in his mid-forties in a new sweatsuit stood bending over with his legs spread apart on the top of the knoll. His face was turned toward Derek, his mouth hanging stupidly open, a look of surprise and panic frozen on his features. But it was the lifeless bundle hanging suspended from the man's arms that held Derek's attention.

"Jeannie!" Derek roared and charged. The man loosed his grip. Jeannie's head fell heavily to the ground just as Derek crashed into the older man knocking him backward.

The two men fell together at the edge of the knoll, Derek on top. The only sound was their labored breathing as they wrestled. Their struggles began to dislodge a steady rain of dirt and stones from the top of the knoll.

Torrance heard Derek's cry and the sound of the two bodies hitting the dirt-topped knoll as she began to fight her way through the brush standing up. Almost without thinking, she ducked down and crawled through the brush on her hands and knees. She skittered through almost unimpeded, slid to a halt just before the cliff, and looked to her right, following the sound.

"Jeannie!" she cried and quickly got to her feet. The two men were still wrestling at the very edge of the knoll. Not five feet from them lay the limp, apparently lifeless body of a young woman, her face blue and contorted, a dark streak around her neck. Torrance ran quickly to her. A dark cotton rope of the type used for drawstrings was pulled tightly around her throat. Desperately, Torrance clawed at the rope and its half-formed knot. She pulled it free just as a heavy blow caught her on the shoulder and sent her sprawling to the edge.

Torrance looked up in fear and surprise. The two men were still rolling on the ground. As she watched, the legs of the man on the bottom thrashed wildly, coming closer with each blow to landing on the body of the young woman. One such vicious kick had nearly thrown Torrance over the side. Trying to avoid the flailing legs, Torrance crawled back, grabbed the woman's arms and backed up, pulling her to safety.

Derek realized from the second the two of them crashed to the ground that the man was stronger than he appeared. Wordlessly, they both struggled for an advantage. The man suddenly arched up his knees, trying to thrust Derek over the top of his head and off the cliff. Derek kicked at the man's lower leg, flattening the arch. He wrapped his right leg around the man's left leg, grabbed both of the man's wrists, and began to pin him down.

The man on the bottom began to thrash wildly, kicking violently with his right leg. All at once his left leg was also free, and the knee came crashing up into Derek's crotch. Derek gasped and froze, fighting to retain consciousness.

In that instant, the man's hands found Derek's throat. The strength of their grip and the speed with which the fingers found their way to the carotid arteries was frightening. The hands were like two great spiders, closing about Derek's throat. Derek's ears began to buzz.

Derek reached around with his left hand and grabbed the man's left wrist. Planting his right knee, Derek arched his back and pushed away. The man's left arm straightened. With his last strength, Derek thought to bring the heel of his right hand around in an arc to land just above the man's left elbow. Somewhere in his consciousness, he realized that his hand was not responding.

All at once there was a dull thud by Derek's ear, followed immediately by a loud crack. Splinters of wood flew up into Derek's face. The man grunted. Miraculously, the grip on Derek's throat loosened.

Gratefully, Derek gulped for air and brought the heel of his right hand around to the man's elbow. The elbow gave a small pop, and the left hand flew off to one side. Before the man could recover, Derek snapped his right knee upward into the man's groin. His throat was now completely free. With all the strength he could muster, Derek smashed the heel of his right hand against the tender spot behind the man's left ear, and suddenly the man was still.

Derek fell back on his haunches panting and rolled over to look around him. Torrance was standing to one side, frowning at the splintered end of the hefty branch she had used to whack the man over the ear. She looked down at Derek.

"It broke," she said disgustedly and tossed the end over the side.

"That's O.K., it did the job. I owe you one." Derek managed a tired smile. Just then a slight movement caught Derek's attention. The man's breath was coming irregularly and painfully.

Quickly, he patted down the man's front side and rolled him over to repeat the job. From a sweatshirt pocket, Derek extracted a set of keys and a wallet. He twisted the man's arms behind him and crossed the wrists. The man grunted as Derek pulled on his left arm. He was returning to consciousness. Derek looked around wildly. He saw that Torrance was bending over Jeannie's limp body.

"Quick! Do you have anything I can use to tie him up?"

Torrance glanced around. Grimly, she grabbed the cotton rope she had pulled off of Jeannie's neck. "Try this," she said, tossing it to Derek. "It would serve him right." Derek rapidly bound the man's wrists and then to be safe tied his shoelaces together. Suddenly he was aware of a soft coughing and gagging behind him and Torrance's soothing voice pouring out a steady stream of encouragement. He turned around in surprise. "She's alive?" he asked. Jeannie lay with her head cradled in Torrance's lap. Already the color of her face was beginning to turn pink. Her eyes were still closed, but her chest was taking short gulps of air between coughs. Torrance looked up at Derek, tears welling up in her eyes.

"Just barely, but yes, she's alive. She was unconscious for the longest time—whether it was because of near-strangulation or this nasty bump on her head, I can't tell." Torrance gently patted Jeannie's hair as she spoke. She lightly touched a spot on the side of Jeannie's head and Jeannie groaned, coughed, and slowly opened her eyes.

"Hi," Torrance greeted her. "Just lie there for a minute. Everything's all right now." Jeannie blinked, disbelieving, and then turned her head slowly as Derek came up to them.

"Hi, Jeannie. You just had a close call, but it's all over now."

"How did you . . .?" Jeannie started. Her voice sounded awful.

"No questions for now. Just rest a bit. Jeannie, I'd like you to meet a very good friend of mine. You owe our being here as much to her as to me. This is Torrance Adams."

"Hi," Jeannie said weakly, looking up.

Torrance smiled. "I'm afraid Derek exaggerates a great deal. You just rest a little longer, and then we'll think about getting you off this mountain, O.K.?"

Just then the man began to moan. He struggled briefly under Derek's watchful eye and then gave up. Derek sat down on his haunches and turned his attention to the contents of the man's sweatshirt pocket. As expected, the keys were to a Mercedes. Derek put those aside and opened the man's expensive leather wallet. He whistled softly.

"Torrance," he asked, "have you had a chance to look at this guy?"

Torrance looked up. "No. I barely looked at him while you were fighting, and then I was busy with Jeannie."

Derek stood up as Torrance was talking and walked over to where the man still lay on his belly, wrists tied behind his back. He rolled him to one side with his foot. "Take a look. I think you two may be old friends."

Torrance got up. Her face clouded with anger when she saw the man's face. "Solomon!"

At the sound of his name John Solomon's head jerked up and his eyes met Torrance's. Confusion and panic played across his face. "You! What are you doing here?"

"I'm afraid you're the one who's going to have to answer all the questions," Torrance replied angrily. "You're going to face charges of attempted murder, kidnapping, and about a dozen violations of other laws, including illegal baby-selling."

"And the murder of Dr. Moorehead," Derek added grimly. Torrance and Solomon looked up at Derek in surprise. He was standing with Solomon's wallet open, looking into one of the pockets.

"How. . .?" Torrance started to ask. Carefully, Derek extracted two business cards from Solomon's wallet, holding them by the edges.

"You certainly have an interesting collection of business cards, Mr. Solomon," he said. "What I find especially intriguing is that you have both Torrance's and my cards right next to each other. Now Torrance's, I'm sure, you could have gotten when you first met her, but there's only one place where you could have gotten mine, or mine and Torrance's together—the side table in Dr. Moorehead's front room!"

"That's crazy!" Solomon spat. "You'll never prove. . . ."

"Try us," Derek said. "You used gloves in Moorehead's office, but one will get you five you never thought to wipe off these cards when you picked them up. All we need to do is to find Moorehead's prints on one of these and you're dead meat—and Torrance knows just the folks who can do it, too."

Solomon's face turned purple, but he didn't answer. Derek replaced the cards carefully and turned toward Torrance. "What do you think? Is Jeannie in any shape to make it back down the hill?"

Jeannie answered for herself. "I'm O.K. I think the sooner we get down, the better I'll feel—and the sooner I can get away from that man."

"Is he the second executive you told Derek about?" Torrance asked.

Jeannie nodded as she got up shakily, and Torrance gave Derek a triumphant smile.

The four of them made an odd little parade back down the trail, Solomon and Derek bringing up the rear. Derek had untied Solomon's shoelaces to let him walk but had left them loose and flopping so that he would lose his shoes with any sudden move. Solomon stumbled along after the two women, losing his balance more than once and landing hard on his butt. Derek always helped him to his feet but made no move to catch him when he fell.

Finally, they limped into the parking area, dirty and banged up, to the astonishment of the various hikers and fishermen. After a quick consultation, Torrance agreed to drive down to the Lagunitas Country Club to use the phone there. Several jurisdictions of police had to be notified, in addition to her own office, and she could start that ball rolling with only one or two calls. Solomon, meanwhile, was unceremoniously tied to the bumper of Derek's car with some rope supplied by an eager fisherman, to await the arrival of Detective Morelli of the Ross P.D.

Within a few minutes, the parking area at the end of Lagunitas was crowded with official cars, an ambulance for Jeannie (despite her protests), and a tow truck for Solomon's Mercedes. Morelli listened open-mouthed as Derek briefly described the morning's events and the details of the kidnapping of Patrick James.

Morelli shook his head. "I don't believe you, Thompson. You come waltzin' in here and bust one of the most prominent attorneys in San Francisco for practically everything this side of mother-raping, and now I imagine you expect to dump the whole mess right in my lap, right?"

Derek smiled innocently. "Hey, give me a break, Morelli. I'm not leaving you to face this all alone. Look at all the help I brought you: the Attorney General's Office, the police departments of at least five different jurisdictions from Eureka to L.A., adoptions agencies in three different counties. . . ."

"Shit," Morelli cut him off. "I'll let Dickson take your statements—my head hurts. Don't do me any more favors, huh?"

"Sure. I'll buy you lunch the next time I have some stolen silver to buy back." Morelli glowered and walked off to talk to Sergeant Dickson. Derek looked over at Torrance and smiled.

She looked worried. "Derek, I've been thinking," she said quietly as she came up to stand next to him. "There's still two players missing in all this—"

"Robusson and Tina Patterson. They'll be picked up soon enough."

"One of them will be picked up soon enough," Torrance corrected him. "Shirley Robusson will be at Parentbuilders by now. But it's not her I'm worried about. When was the last time you saw Tina Patterson?"

Derek thought. "Wednesday afternoon. She and her car disappeared into Shirley Robusson's place in Pacific Heights."

"And she hasn't been seen since. Derek, we're dealing with a man who killed one witness and just tried to kill another. I'm scared."

"Jesus," Derek whispered softly. "You may be right. How long do you think it would take the S.F.P.D. to get a search warrant for Robusson's house?"

"Too long, if Tina's in any danger."

"I agree. I think we'd better get out of here. Let's take your car—mine's blocked in."

They ran quickly to her Porsche. Dickson and Morelli looked up and yelled at them to stop as the engine roared to life.

"Urgent business for the Attorney General," Derek shouted as Torrance backed the Porsche into a tight U. "We'll have statements for you later!" The car leaped out of the parking area. Derek looked back to see Morelli and Dickson standing together, Dickson with his mouth hanging open while Morelli's round face was a dark purple cloud. Then they were lost to view.

Torrance guided the little car swiftly around the curves. After the first turn Derek fastened his seat belt, noting that somehow Torrance had already fastened hers. They sped through town to Highway 101 south across the Golden Gate to San Francisco.

Derek's directions got them quickly to the quiet street in Pacific Heights where Shirley Robusson lived. Torrance parked directly in front of Shirley's house and they both got out. There was no sign of any movement at the house.

Derek ran up to the still-closed garage door and tried the handle. It was locked. Vainly, he tried to see into the darkened garage through a crack at the side of the door.

"What now?" Torrance asked.

"Well, we could always try the doorbell," Derek replied, heading in that direction. Torrance frowned and followed him. Derek leaped up onto the porch and leaned on the doorbell long and hard, bringing forth a steady ringing from inside. Then the two of them listened. Not a sound came from the big house. They tried again with the same result. Derek looked at Torrance.

"I think you'd better turn your head—I don't want any witnesses to a breaking and entering."

"Derek, you can't break that door down," Torrance protested. "It's too heavy and—" She was cut off by the crack of splintering wood as Derek landed a swift kick just to the side of the deadbolt. The door moved slightly. With two more hard kicks, the door frame suddenly gave way and the door flew open, rebounding against the doorstop. Pieces of trim and frame shot into the front hall.

"—and besides, it's illegal," Torrance stared transfixed at the open door quivering on its hinges.

"They'll have to sue me," Derek replied, stepping into the house. "Any evidence we come across I found, O.K.? I don't want anything thrown out for illegal search and seizure. As a private citizen, I can get away with all kinds of things, but I'm not so sure about you."

Torrance followed Derek into the house and began inspecting the rooms to her right as Derek turned left. "I'm not sure either—but I'm not a peace officer, so I may be O.K. too."

"Well, let's just not take any chances," Derek replied. He found a door under the side of the staircase leading upstairs and pulled it open. "Here's the garage!" he said, fumbling for the light. He found the switch and took a few steps down. "And here's the Pontiac still."

"That means that Tina is probably still here, somewhere," Torrance replied. "I'll check the upstairs."

"I'm right behind you."

Swiftly, the two of them searched all the upstairs rooms in vain. Derek found the trap door to the attic and stuck his head through. It was dark and quiet. Judging by the dust and old insulation that cascaded onto his head when he lifted the trap, it appeared not to have been opened for years. Coughing and brushing himself off, he returned to the top of the stairs.

"Let's try downstairs some more," Torrance said. "That garage doesn't take up all the space under the house. Maybe there's a cellar or furnace room or something." They retraced their steps downstairs, more carefully this time. Torrance went into the kitchen. She opened the door into the pantry and was about to close it again when something caught her eye.

"Derek! I think I've found something!" she called out. Derek quickly joined her. There, against the side wall of the pantry between the shelves was a narrow door with a bolt pulled across it. Torrance started to open it, hesitated, and stepped back. The memory of Moorehead's office flooded into her mind's eye. "Maybe you'd better try it," she said quietly.

Derek shot her a quick glance, took a deep breath, and slid the bolt. A gust of cool air greeted them. The door opened to a dark, narrow stairway leading down into blackness. Derek felt in vain for a light switch. "Do you see a switch behind you?" he asked.

"No. . .wait! Here's one." Torrance reached between some shelves. A single bare bulb came to life at the top of the stairs. Derek started down. He caught a glimpse of racks of wine bottles against a wall. He took two more steps down when he caught a sudden movement out of the corner of his eye and ducked.

His reflexes saved him. A heavy wine bottle came down hard against his right shoulder, just barely missing his head. It flew out of his attacker's hand and broke with a loud crash on the cement floor. At the same time, he heard a scream of anguish.

Derek turned quickly, in time to grab the small fist that was coming at him. He struggled briefly with his assailant and finally saw her face.

"Tina! Tina, stop it! We're friends." Gradually, her struggles slowed and then ceased. "It's over, Tina. You're safe now."

196

Tina Patterson's tear-streaked face looked up in surprise at Derek, and then at Torrance, standing behind him. She began to sob quietly. "Shirley Robusson locked me in here. She tricked me—she said we had to hide my car. Then she sent me for some wine and locked me in. I don't know how long I've been here; no one could hear me screaming. I thought you were someone coming to kill me," she wailed.

Torrance pushed past Derek and put her arm around Tina's shoulder. "Let's go upstairs," she said quietly.

24

*T*wo weeks later, Torrance was sitting across from Derek at Monica's dining table, which was littered with the remains of assorted shellfish, French bread, and several empty bottles of wine. Monica had convened this as a celebratory dinner, although her real motive was to get the whole story from Derek and Torrance. They, in turn, were happy to oblige.

"You should have seen Derek when Tina tried to knock him unconscious with a bottle of Cabernet Sauvignon," Torrance laughed, reaching for another crab claw.

Derek raised his glass of Chardonnay. "I'm glad you told me to bring a white wine. I'm not sure I can look at the red stuff yet without ducking!"

Monica was an excellent audience, wide-eyed and hanging on every detail. Whenever she had to remove dishes or fetch another course, she made them swear not to talk while she was gone, leaving the two of them communicating with gestures, meaningful glances, and occasional uncontrollable laughter until Monica returned.

Over the last of the crab and crayfish, they reached Tina's confession of the kidnapping of Patrick Albertson-James, as an assistant to John Solomon. "Once she realized what the whole story was, she didn't want to have any part of it any more," Torrance said. "She thought she was doing a lot of good for childless couples and not hurting anyone."

"How could she think that?" Monica protested. "It's a little difficult to believe you're not hurting the person whose baby you've kidnapped!"

"I think she really convinced herself that Patrick was just a toy for Marguerite. She didn't know any of the circumstances, just that the baby was being taken care of by Marguerite's mother. In reality, Marguerite desperately needed her job to keep some self-respect after her husband left her." Torrance glanced at Derek, who nodded. "If Marguerite had stayed home with Patrick, she might not have been able to handle it. But all that Tina knew was what Shirley told her—that here was this supposedly rich young woman who couldn't be bothered to care for her own child."

"Did Tina know what happened to Patrick afterwards?"

This time Derek answered. "Yes, she did, which was lucky for us. She knew he had been given the Corey Johnson birth certificate and placed for adoption with the Evandales in Merced. Because of that, we were able to go right to court and get an order requiring the Evandales to give him back to Marguerite."

Monica looked thoughtful. "I'm sure that was wonderful for Marguerite, but what about those poor people who lost the child? It must have been just awful for them."

Torrance and Derek both nodded. "It was very bad for Mrs. Evandale," Torrance said. "She's a nice woman and she wanted a child very badly. I'm not sure her husband really cared, except maybe about how upset his wife was."

Monica demanded another moment of silence for table-clearing purposes (help in her kitchen was not something she tolerated). Then she moved her guests to the sitting area at the front of the large room while she put on coffee. When she returned, she sat down and folded her hands in her lap.

"Let me see if I understand this now. Tina Patterson and John Solomon kidnapped Patrick. Tina turned him over to Shirley. Shirley took him to the couple in Merced and said he was Corey Johnson. Right so far?"

"You're doing fine," Derek commented.

"Where did Tina think this Corey Johnson birth certificate came from?"

"She knew it came from a doctor up north who provided it for Solomon. Shirley Robusson told her there was no such child—the doctor had just made up the birth."

"Was that true?"

"Yes, we're convinced now that Corey Johnson and Russell Robertson— the baby that the Bowens were supposed to have—never existed. That's why I never found their files in Dr. Moorehead's office. For the longest time, I tried to imagine what was in those files that would have been incriminating to Moorehead's killer—that would explain why he took them," Derek went on. "It wasn't until much later that it occurred to me that the real importance of the missing files might be that they never existed in the first place."

Monica nodded enthusiastically. "Was Tina ever given any reason why this doctor was willing to make up fictitious babies for Parentbuilders?"

"She was told he cared a lot about helping childless couples," Torrance explained.

"And she bought that?"

Torrance smiled at Monica's patent disbelief. "She's very young and very idealistic. Besides, she was paid well. I don't think she thought too hard about any of it until Shirley locked her up."

"O.K., so *she* bought this story about Dr. Moorehead's magnanimity, but I don't. Why did Dr. Moorehead really do it? Do we know?"

"Yes, we do," Torrance went on, "but only because Shirley Robusson told the police. Otherwise we never would have found any evidence of what happened. You remember Carol Marawik? She was the mother of the very first baby that Dr. Moorehead certified he delivered at home." Monica nodded. "Well, Carol Marawik really did have a baby. That's why the facts about her end of the case never seemed to fit the pattern. She went into labor while Shirley was with her, and Shirley called Dr. Moorehead who was Carol's doctor. Instead of sending Carol to Eureka in an ambulance and meeting her at the hospital, Moorehead went out to where she was staying. He had a good reason—he was drunk, and he didn't want to be seen at the hospital. Well, Carol had a lot of trouble with the birth, and he gave her a shot to knock her out. Then the baby was born dead.

"Shirley was determined to do something, but she didn't know what. She had promised this baby to a very nice couple and she just couldn't accept having to tell them she'd failed. So she told Moorehead to keep Carol sedated, and she drove down Highway 101 looking for some way out. What she says is that she was hoping to buy a baby from one of the hippies living in that area. That may or may not be true. What she did was to snatch a baby off the porch of a woodworker's shop in Garberville. She says she knew when she saw the baby alone like that it was God's way of telling her that he was meant to go to a better home." Torrance shook her head. "Somebody who thinks like that is capable of pretty much anything. Anyway, she grabbed the child, who was named Forrest Peace Abengale, and she took him back to Carol Marawik's house. There, she passed him off to Carol as her baby, told Moorehead to play along, and left for San Francisco with a perfectly legitimate-seeming child in her car."

"According to Shirley, Moorehead was desperate to cover up the Marawik baby's death," Derek added. "We figure that's how they got him to play along. And you remember that very neat file for Carol's delivery when all his other files were a mess? He wanted proof that everything went O.K., so he created a decent medical record for once."

As Monica nodded, Torrance went on. "Once Shirley told her brother what happened, he realized that all you needed to provide papers for a kidnapped baby was a record of a home birth. With a hospital birth, it's very difficult to invent a nonexistent child, but with a home birth, it's easy so long as you have a doctor who's willing to lie."

"And Moorehead was willing to lie in return for not being turned in for what happened with Carol Marawik," Monica added.

"You've got it," Derek chimed in. "It probably seemed that making up nonexistent babies wasn't too bad. Besides, he was getting paid for it."

"Did he know what those birth certificates were being used for?"

"We doubt he knew it outright, but he must have been closing his eyes to some pretty strong suspicions."

Monica thought about this for a moment, then she suddenly jumped out of her chair. "I almost forgot. Coffee and dessert."

"Omigod!" Derek groaned. "Dessert? I couldn't possibly manage another bite after the way I've stuffed myself already!"

Monica gave him a hurt look. "Just the tiniest bit of white chocolate mousse?"

Torrance chuckled as Derek made faces and squirmed in his chair but finally gave in. "You'd better be telling the truth about those tiny portions," she warned Monica, "or we'll have to spend the night sitting here, because we won't be able to get up."

Monica dramatically crossed her heart and left for the kitchen. She reappeared with coffee and reasonably small portions of a white mousse decorated with dark chocolate curls. Like the rest of the meal, it turned out to be delicious.

Monica didn't wait to finish eating before asking her next question. "I understand what happened to the other two kidnapped children. The one from Silverlake died in the car crash, so he can't be given back. Patrick went back to Marguerite. But what about that baby from Garberville—what was his name?"

"Forrest Peace Abengale."

"I like that name," Monica said with a broad smile and then became serious again. "What happens to him now?"

"That's one of the most interesting parts," Torrance answered. "He was actually born in a hospital, so we got his birth footprints to compare them to Joey Hewitt's. He's the baby with the very nice couple in Folsom who thought they were getting Carol Marawik's child. You remember, they actually talked to Carol, and she was so pleased that they were the ones who had her baby. Well, it turned out the footprints weren't good enough for a comparison. So, even though Shirley said it's the same baby, there isn't any conclusive proof. You see, no one knows where Forrest's mother is, so we can't use blood tests to prove his identity. But, assuming he is little Forrest, his father is willing to sign papers allowing the couple in Folsom to adopt him."

"It seems to me the whole thing worked out pretty well for little Forrest," Derek commented. "I think he'll have a much better life than he would have had with his real parents. They were pretty weird."

Monica looked pained. "Watch what you say around here. Some perfectly good people are considered weird by those who don't understand them."

Derek held up his hands in mock surrender. "You're right. And I, of all people, should know better."

Monica gave him a level look. "Yes, I imagine you've had some problems yourself, especially in your line of work."

Derek didn't respond at once. He looked at Monica and Torrance uncertainly.

"After all," Monica continued, "I don't imagine that the cop types you deal with are the most understanding and tolerant of people, especially where someone like you is concerned."

Torrance at first was appalled at Monica's comment. Then she noted Derek's expression and smiled. "Monica's a very blunt person, but I hope you can assume you're among friends here."

Derek gave her his crooked grin. "Monica's very perceptive, and yes, I do think I'm among friends. It's just that when I first met you, it was in a context where you were a part of the law enforcement establishment. Monica's right. Even in San Francisco, people don't have a lot of tolerance for a gay private investigator. So I generally keep my private life to myself."

"You don't have to worry about me," Torrance said calmly, "or about Monica."

Derek nodded and sipped the rest of his coffee. A feeling of relief suddenly rushed over him. He realized that a tiny knot of residual tension had just dissolved. He *was* among friends, and pretenses were no longer necessary.

He pushed his hair out of his eyes and gave Monica his most brilliant smile. "So—anything else you want to know?"

Monica thought for a minute, then nodded. "I'm still unclear about what you got Solomon for. You caught him trying to do in Jeannie, so that charge ought to stick. And I assume Tina's testimony is enough to get him for the Patrick James kidnapping. But what about the kidnapping in Silverlake? Can you tie him to that?"

Derek shrugged his shoulders. "I'm not sure. Shirley won't say a word that will incriminate him, and all we've got otherwise is some loose circumstantial evidence. We know the kid was kidnapped and Solomon ended up offering him to the Bowens, but it may be impossible to prove he was actually involved—or Shirley for that matter. Of course, someone had to have done it, and we may be able to pin it on them yet. Personally, I'm sure Solomon was there."

"I am too," Torrance added.

"You don't have to convince *me*," Monica said to Torrance. "I told you all along he did it." While Torrance and Derek were still laughing, Monica went on. "And the murder of Dr. Moorehead? I know you're sure he did it because he had the business cards that disappeared off Moorehead's table, but will that be enough to make it stick?"

"It's looking pretty good," Torrance answered. "He didn't use a gasoline credit card on his way up there, but they found the place where he stopped for gas and some wine for Moorehead. Being from the city, he wasn't sufficiently aware that someone at a small place in the country would probably remember him. A stranger in a black Mercedes who drops by while business is slow is bound to be considered interesting."

"That's good," Monica said with relish. "And he'll lose his license to practice law too."

"You sure are out to get the man," Derek laughed. "And you're right. He turned into a monster. I'm out to get him too. Shirley and Tina had some ideals, however misguided and blind to the realities they were. But I'm convinced John Solomon did it all solely for the money. That makes it worse in my mind."

Derek suddenly yawned and Torrance looked at her watch. "Past all of our usual bedtimes, I think," she commented.

They saw him to the door. Derek walked to his car while Torrance and Monica watched from the front window.

"You like him a lot," Monica diagnosed.

"Yeah," Torrance answered laconically.

"And you didn't know he was gay."

"I wondered because of some things he said."

"But you hoped you were wrong."

"Yeah."

Monica put her arm around Torrance's shoulder, and the two returned inside. As Torrance began to walk up the stairs, she turned around and smiled. "It's O.K.," she said, "I think he'll be great as a friend."